CU00867202

Never

SHAY LYNAM

This edition published by Indie World Publishing & Author
Services via CreateSpace
Text © Shay Lynam 2014
ISBN: 978-0692288429
ISBN-10: 0692288422

Indie World Publishing & Author Services
www.indieworldpub.com

Cover Art by: Kellie Dennis at Book Cover by Design
www.bookcoverbydesign.co.uk

To learn more about Shay Lynam, visit her website at
www.facebook.com/shaylynam

To Mike

Two trees, one oak, one birch, grew entwined above her grave. On the bad days, he came out and sat in their shadows until his grief was lost in the dancing patterns of light. The silence was pervasive enough that for a moment all he heard was his own heartbeat thundering in the dark. The stars at last were close enough to touch and he held them in his hands, tiny sparks that burned with everlasting fire and slowly thawed him from the dark.

He looked up from his handful of stars at the name on the grave marker.

Wendy Moira Angela Darling.

Being immortal, he decided as he blew the stars out of his hands again and watched them float back into the sky, was only fun for the first two lifetimes.

Chapter One

The bus came to a jarring halt with a *whoosh* of its hydraulic brakes and I lurched forward in my seat bumping my head against the one in front of me. No matter how many times I rode to and from ballet practice during the week, I never seemed to be able to anticipate the sudden stops or the sudden goes of the city bus. Maybe I'd be more prepared to brace myself if I paid attention. I couldn't help it though. The loud, rock music pumping out of my headphones and into my head drowned out the sounds of Los Angeles like nothing else. This city is too loud.

Marty sat next to me, drumming her fingers on her knee to the beat in her own ears, unfazed by the jerky motions. I glanced down at her pink and black striped leg as it hit the invisible pedal to an imaginary bass drum with the beat. Even over my own music I could hear the double kick and screeching of metal coming from Marty's headphones.

The bus lurched again causing me to bump my head once more against the cushioned seat in front of me. Ugh, I could not wait to get my own car. Even though I still didn't have my license, having my own car would at least get me one step closer, right? I mean what parent would make their seventeen-year-old daughter ride the bus everywhere? Mine would. Even if I had to save every penny I earned working at the movie theater, I'd find a way to get my own wheels. I needed to get out of my boring house in my boring suburb as soon as possible. Maybe it wasn't even the fact that my neighborhood was boring, except for Marty living just a block away, but rather it was the fact that if we ever wanted to do anything exciting, I had to rely on the city's mode of transportation. In other words, this stupid bus that gurgled along like a cranky old turtle.

"Did you get your English paper finished?" Marty yelled over the music blasting in her ears. A few annoyed passengers turned their heads to glare at the loud girl.

I couldn't help but smile a bit at my friend's lack of self-awareness. Marty's person screamed eccentric from her bright pink and black striped leggings and purple leg warmers to her blue mini skirt and tight green ninja turtles t-shirt that was on the verge of being inappropriate – in a good way of course. Everything about her was outspoken, from her big mouth to her garish wardrobe.

I shook my head "No," I sighed and rested my forehead against the foggy window. "Do you think

Mrs. Jesson would let it slide if I said I was still grieving?"

"Probably not," Marty replied twisting an orange polished finger around one of her bright yellow extensions. "It's already been over a month, Wynn. You're going to have to do some work eventually."

I nodded glumly in reply and watched through the fogged glass as passersby shielded themselves with their coats, umbrellas, briefcases, or whatever, from the drizzle. The gray clouds looked so dark and heavy it wouldn't have surprised me if they just broke all of a sudden and rain blasted everything like water from a fire hose.

It wasn't supposed to rain in Southern California. We got maybe three inches a year and only in the middle of winter. But there we were toward the end of March and the dreary weather had been non-stop since the end of February. Weird how it had started around the time Great Gran died. Like the earth was mourning the loss of another good person. Our whole family had taken it pretty hard, especially with Great Gran being the last one in that generation of the Darling/Harper family.

It was weird when her illness had really set in. She'd always been known to have a warm, fun loving attitude and a genuinely young soul. But slowly, almost unnoticeably, Great Gran started forgetting the little things. Pretty soon the little things turned into big things and before long, all she did was sit in her chair at the nursing home silently, watching with fear and suspicion filled eyes. After a while I didn't even want to go visit her. We'd always been close and I couldn't deal with seeing her turn into a stranger. Though I guess it was scary for her to see all of us turn into strangers too.

Another lurch of the bus and Marty was on her feet waiting for a gap in the line of people trying to shuffle their way off. I got up clumsily, getting myself tangled in the cord of my headphones.

Finally, I just ripped the cord out of my iPod, cutting off my music, and stuffed it into the pocket of my leather jacket. Marty was already almost to the front. After slinging my backpack with my ballet gear over my shoulder, I stepped in between a grumbling man in business attire and a woman in sweats and a dirty t-shirt.

What a perfect depiction of LA we were. The man with his expensive gray suit, dry clean only, the woman in her grungy sweats and Bugs Bunny t-shirt and then the short, pale, goth girl with the black mini dress, purple tights and high-tops sandwiched in between them. Oh the clashing smells I could describe. The pleasant aroma of cologne was made so much less pleasant by the stench of body odor and cigarettes wafting into my nostrils from behind me. I needed off this bus.

The slow shuffle to the front took an eternity and I found myself gasping for clean air by the time my feet hit the sidewalk. Marty was waiting a bit down the block with one hand stuffed into her purple and black checkered jacket. The other hand was clutching the two sides of her hood around her face in a piteous attempt to keep the wind and rain out. I let a gust blow the hood of my own jacket off my head and pelt me with tiny water droplets as I made my way toward my best friend. We still had a few streets to go before we would be warm in my house.

With Marty whimpering beside me, I quietly relished in the way the wind danced around my legs giving me goose bumps. Frigid air made its way up my sleeves and raised the hair on my arms making my skin tingle. I liked this weather more so than the sun beating down on my sensitive skin making me go from glowworm to lobster in nothing flat.

My leg muscles were starting to tighten and ache after having taken a break from ballet while everything happened with Great Gran's funeral. This had been my first time back. After much persuading and pleading from Marty, I'd finally agreed to start going again even though a month before I had told myself I was done for good.

It had been weird when I'd walked out of the changing room and into the middle of class. Madame had given me her always charming smile and a nod to take my place at the bar for stretches while Marty had let out a squeal and bounced up and down excitedly from where she was standing on the floor, her blue tutu flopping like a puppy's ears.

Even having been in ballet since I was seven, my body griped and complained from having just one month off. Luckily, I was still able to do a perfect split. That would have been outright embarrassing. Especially with Annabel Miller standing right behind me at the bar. Ever since fifth grade when she told the entire class I'd gotten my period, we hadn't really seen eye to eye.

By the time my house was in sight, the weather was starting to wear on me and the thought of hot chocolate and a shower seemed wonderful. Marty and I picked up the pace and jogged to the front steps.

My mom had apparently read my mind because two steaming cups of hot chocolate sat on the counter in the kitchen when we walked through the door. I only got one sip in before she appeared in the doorway with a smile on her face. I'm sure she was just as relieved to see that I had gone back to ballet as I was to see that she was slowly beginning to wear more than just sweats and baggy t-shirts.

She'd especially taken Great Gran's death hard. Great Gran had been like a mother to my mom, especially after my parents had gotten married and grandma died of lung cancer. My grandfather died a long time ago when my mom was still little and she didn't have any grandparents of her own. Then my father died when I was too little to remember and Great Gran had taken her under her wing and really helped her out. I felt so bad for my mom. There was just too much death in this family for her to handle.

"How was practice?" Mom asked folding her arms and leaning against the doorframe.

I took another sip and relished in the feeling of the hot liquid warming my insides. "Pretty good," I finally answered with a satisfied sigh.

Marty took a big gulp, contorting her face as it burned her mouth. "Yeah, and she only fell on her butt a few times."

I elbowed her in the ribs and furrowed my eyebrows. "I did not."

The corners of my mom's eyes crinkled as she smiled wider in amusement. "Glad to hear," she said and absentmindedly brushed a piece of my black hair off my shoulder. Great Gran and I had the same light brown hair. Then I dyed mine right after her death. I caught a small glimpse of sadness in my mom's eyes as if she were thinking about it.

"I'm really glad I'm back again," I said trying to get the sadness to go away.

Again the lines appeared in the corners of her eyes, though not as deeply. "I am too," she said.

When Marty and I got to my room, she put her mug on the dresser and flopped down onto my bed, burying her head in a red fuzzy pillow. I went straight to my iPod dock and plugged in my iPod, filling the room with loud rock, music from one of my favorite bands.

"Do you have to work tomorrow night?" Marty asked as she started to pluck red fuzzies off my pillow.

"Every Friday night," I told her pulling the pillow away before she picked the whole thing apart. "Every Friday night for the past six months."

"Except for last month," Marty added carefully.

I tossed the pillow onto the end of my bed. "Right," I sighed.

I'd gotten a job at Royal Cinemas back in November to support my half of Marty's and my social life. Friday had become my favorite day of the week ever since the two of us had discovered a chain of underground clubs on the outskirts of LA. They were all the same with their loud, obscure bands playing their tantric music. So many different types of people; a lot of high school kids but also adults – some still in their work clothes – came and just packed the small rooms making it hard to breathe. That was one of my favorite parts. Along with the lights and the band, the feel of everyone squished together like we were one organism dancing to the music made it easy to forget everything outside. So many people would pair up or dance all over each other but I liked to close my eyes and pretend I was alone and then I would just follow whatever my body wanted to do. It says jump, I would jump. It says shake, I would shake.

"So you went to ballet today, does that mean you're going to start going to school again so I don't have to keep bringing your assignments like your dang mailman?"

I picked up my red pillow and threw it at her face. "Try being a little more subtle," I said with a chuckle then my smile fell. "I guess I have to face everyone eventually, don't I?"

Marty shrugged sympathetically "Not to mention homecoming is Saturday night and you can't expect me to go by myself."

I'd barely left my room all month let alone the house. It had taken a lot of nagging from Marty just to start going to ballet again. I'm glad I did it but could I really continue on as if nothing had happened? As if I hadn't just lost one of the most important people in my life? What would Great Gran have said to me? "Buck up, Wynnie. Life is a grand adventure but only if you actually live it."

Chapter Two

I spent the entire bus ride to school trying to figure out why the heck I decided to go back on a Friday. Why didn't I just wait until Monday? New week, new start. The two go hand in hand, right? Though it was amusing seeing Marty bounce up and down on the seat next to me. I guess she was excited to have me back. I know I'd be bored out of my mind if she'd decided to barricade herself in her room for a month. But then again, I didn't really have anyone else. Marty was the kind of person that was hard not to like. I, on the other hand, was less known for my personality and more for my Neverland obsessed great grandmother. I'd made it all the way to high school without one word about her crazy stories getting out. I could thank Annabel for breaking the streak.

Cheesy, glittery posters for homecoming littered the walls of the main hallway and every other locker was decorated with a bright blue flyer. I picked at the corner of the one on my own locker with a black fingernail as Marty jabbered on about what she was going to wear to the dance. She mentioned something about purple fishnet and a turquoise and green corseted back but I couldn't take my eyes off the giant gold star painted in glitter on the flyer. Curvy, equally as glittery letters spelled out "Masquerade Under The Stars". How original. Surely, this whole thing was Annabel's brilliant idea. As if being beautiful, blonde and popular wasn't enough, she had to have all the responsibilities that came with being the stereotypical queen bee of the school. Captain of the cheerleading squad, class president and, of course, head of the homecoming committee. With one quick motion, I swiped the flyer off my locker and crumpled it in my fist.

"So, who are you going with to homecoming? No, what are you wearing to homecoming?" Marty asked me leaning against the locker next to mine. "No. Better yet, what are you wearing tonight? I heard there's going to be a new band playing at Exile. And I also may have heard they're all guys our age." So while I was away, Marty was busy finding new clubs we hadn't been to yet.

A noise somewhere between a scoff and a chuckle escaped my throat as I pulled my locker open and dropped my backpack into the bottom. "Cool," I said sarcastically. "Another wannabe screamo band of seventeen year olds ruining their vocal cords."

"You don't hate it as much as you say," Marty said

with a knowing smile.

I couldn't disagree. I mean, for the most part I was able to get so completely lost in my head that the chaos only added to it. I found myself closing my eyes just then remembering the feeling of euphoria and smiling knowing I would feel it again in a few hours.

"So what are you going to wear?" Marty repeated pulling me back out of my head.

I pictured my closet in my mind. A lot of black with just a few bright colors speckled here and there. I shrugged with a sigh and Marty straightened up, towering over me. No wonder the volleyball coach wanted her to play so bad. "You sure know how to blend into the shadows, *Wyndy*," she said crossing her fishnet-clad arms over her chest.

"Some people don't like to dress like a big neon sign, *Martina*," I sneered back and pinched the leg of her purple leggings.

My friend stuck her tongue out then clapped her green fingerless gloved hands together. "Well if that band is playing tonight at Exile, we need to get you noticed."

I could feel my shoulders sag. "I don't go to clubs for the boys," I said feeling like I had tried explaining this to her a million times before.

"Oh I know. You go to *get lost*." She rolled her eyes. "Just let me dress you this once." Then she stuck her bottom lip out. "My parents wouldn't let me have dolls when I was a little girl. Please be my Barbie just for tonight."

"That's not at all creepy," I muttered then held her pouty gaze for a few moments. Finally, I let out a sigh "Fine."

Marty clapped and let out a squeal as I grabbed my books for English and slammed my locker shut again.

Only a few people lifted their heads and stared when I trailed into the classroom behind Marty. Unfortunately, one of those heads belonged to Annabel. Her pink, glossy lips curled up into a smile as her eyes settled on my black hair. With my books plastered to my chest, I quietly followed Marty to the back and sat down. Annabel immediately swiveled around and rested her chin on her palm.

"So I see you finally decided to embrace your inner vampire," she said with the smug smile still painted on her face.

"And I see you've fully embraced your inner psycho," Marty snapped back at her.

Trying to ignore Annabel as best as I could, I opened my binder and pulled out the English paper I'd very hurriedly typed up the night before. Hopefully, it was worthy of at least a passing grade.

"Alright everyone, settle down" Mrs. Jesson started as she walked into class. Her eyes fell on me and she froze for a second. "Wynn, it's good to have you back." A warm smile lifted the corners of her mouth and I gave her a small one in return. "If there's anything you need, don't hesitate to ask."

I gave a nod as small as my smile and sank down farther in my seat. Annabel turned her head toward me. "If you need to catch the bus to Neverland, just let her know," she muttered quiet enough so the teacher wouldn't hear. I rolled my eyes and dropped my head down onto my folded arms. This was going to be a long day.

Lunch couldn't come soon enough. The cafeteria was too crowded for my liking. Not the way a club was crowded with people dancing and losing themselves in the music. No, this place was filled with more than just bodies. I could feel it in the air. The unforgiving eyes of my fellow classmates nitpicking each other's clothes and hair and lives like mosquitos. The harsh whispers and giggles as they pointed out those things to their friends, gossiping from behind their fingers.

A few times I heard my own name and I tried my best to keep my eyes on Marty's shoes as she marched confidently in front of me. It didn't matter what people said. None of it fazed her. I wished I had her confidence.

Apparently, word had gotten out about Great Gran's love for Peter Pan stories and her final months when she believed it was all true. As the two of us sat down at an empty table, the one next to us erupted in a chorus of bubbly laughter. I turned my head just barely to meet Annabel's sparkling blue eyes. That smug smile was still plastered on her face and she gave me a small wave with her fingers as her friends continued to whisper and laugh.

Marty sneered back at her and let out a scoff. "They really need to find something better to do with their lives," she muttered and took a bite of her pizza.

I turned back around and looked down at my own tray. Along with the people and the classes, I hadn't missed the cafeteria food all that much during my month long absence.

My own slice of pizza looked like it had been cooked, frozen and reheated again about a dozen times. With my mouth turned up in disgust, I used the nails on my thumb and first finger to peel a piece of rubbery pepperoni off and drop it on the plate. Another bout of giggling jarred my thoughts. I couldn't take it anymore. With a frustrated sigh, I pushed my plate away and stood up.

"Where are you going?" Marty asked with her mouth full of pizza.

"I should've stayed home," I muttered then walked quickly past Annabel's table and back out of the cafeteria.

I didn't stop until I was outside on the front steps of the school and, because of the abnormally crappy weather, I was the only one there. For that, I was grateful. The steps were dry so I sat down on the top one and rested my forehead on my knees, listening to the sound of the heavy rain as it hit the pavement. It didn't quite drown out the echo of Annabel and her friends' giggles in my head.

Even in middle school Great Gran and I were the butt end of her jokes but this was just a new low for her. What exactly was funny about losing someone so important to me?

The big metal doors opened behind me but I didn't look up. "Wynn?" It was Marty. "Are you alright?"

"I just don't get it," I replied finally lifting my head off my legs.

"I know what you mean," she huffed. "How can something so evil look so perfect? She's like a freaking demon possessed Barbie."

I couldn't help but chuckle at Marty's remark even as she continued to mutter to herself. Finally, she smiled too and nudged my shoulder with her own. "Just try to ignore her, Wynn. She can only hurt you if you let her." I nodded still feeling a little glum. The bell rang just then signaling the end of our lunch period and the two of us stood up to go inside. "And if Annabel ever lays a finger on you, I'll punch her right in her cute, cupcake face."

For some reason, all of my teachers felt the need to tell me to let them know if I needed anything. Yes, I need you to not single me out.

The day dragged on at an irritatingly slow pace as I tried and failed to avoid Annabel and her cheerleader zombies. It seemed like every time I turned a corner or entered a room, she was there checking on her committee minions or helping put up lame decorations for the stupid dance. There was no way I was going to this thing. I didn't care if Marty got down on her neon legging covered knees and begged. I couldn't go. Annabel would surely find some way to humiliate me and I just couldn't handle it. Not yet. Not until I'd built my wall back up. The barrier I'd been building steadily since fifth grade.

It had tumbled down like the walls of Jericho when we got the call that Great Gran was gone. I remember feeling it the moment it happened. Like someone had wrapped barbed wire around my heart and yanked, leaving it shredded, raw and bleeding. Slowly I'd been stitching it back together.

By the end of the day I could almost feel the heat of every eye burning into me. But at least it was over. I had two days of freedom ahead of me. Not to mention this new club Marty was dragging me to.

She tried talking my head off as we walked to the bus stop. I couldn't pay attention though. I could only think about going to Exile that night and washing away this awful day that seemed to coat my skin like ash.

❧

"So, a large popcorn and a large soda. That will be twelve eighty-six" The guest handed me a twenty and I gave him back his change then the popcorn and soda. "Enjoy your movie," I said quickly then got out of the way so the cashier taking my place could take the next order. As I made my way to the break room to get my purse, I checked my phone. 9 o' clock on the dot. I could feel a smile stretching over my face.

"What are you all cheerful about?" my co-worker, Jared, asked from over in the corner by the snack machines. We had a few classes together, I think. At least Calculus.

"It's Friday night," Caleb said from next to him with a friendly smile. Another guy I'm pretty sure was in my Calculus class. "She's going to hang out with the rest of her vampire friends."

I gave a sarcastic sneer as I ripped the hair tie out of my head and let my dark hair fall down in waves over my shoulders. I grabbed my bag out of my locker. "See you," I said before letting the door shut again behind me.

Exile was already super busy when we got there. We had to stand outside in a long line and wait to get in. That didn't happen very often, but when it did, Marty liked to see how many guys she could get to let us cut in line. As she flirted with a few boys in front of us, I leaned back out of line against the wall and watched the people around us. A small group behind me was already beginning to sway to the music pounding through the walls and out onto the street. One girl was wearing white tights, furry white boots, a light pink miniskirt and a white tank top. The white hat she had pulled down over her ears had fluffy tufts of hair running down the middle and there were two horse ears sticking up on either side. She gripped the strings and swayed from side to side with her eyes closed, making her look like a magical dancing pony. Maybe she was and I would get to see her in her true form tonight. Judging by the way the guy dressed all in black next to her was watching hungrily, perhaps he was hoping to see her in her true form too.

I shoved my hands into my leather jacket pockets and buried my chin into the neck. Marty had done a pretty good job at picking out my outfit, though the bright red mini skirt wasn't doing much to keep this weird March chill out. The thigh high red and black striped socks weren't really doing much for me either. At least I had talked her into letting me wear my combat boots instead of the hooker heels she'd wanted me to borrow for the night.

Finally, the line started moving forward and Marty pulled me toward the door. She had managed to convince the guys in front of us to pay our entrance fee in exchange for a dance. It wasn't really my thing to dance with guys since they liked to get a little too friendly sometimes but maybe if I tuned them out it wouldn't be so bad.

The place was already crazy when I got through the door. The whole room was washed in purple and blue bright lights so I couldn't see anything more than people's silhouettes. A fog machine churned thick, white smoke into the air making it even harder to see where I was going or what was happening. This always made my heart flutter with excitement. The anonymity and not seeing faces but feeling their presence, like each of us altogether was completely alone.

Marty grabbed my arm and pulled me up toward the stage so we could get a good spot. There was already a band up there setting up. They were the only faces I could make out since the lights were shining on them. One of them came forward and put the mic on the stand and I couldn't help but smile a little. He definitely looked out of place in a club like this. Most of the bands we saw were made up of guys in skinny jeans and black band t-shirts or metal heads with dreadlocks and lip rings. No, this boy didn't look like those wannabe bad boys at all. His clothes actually looked pretty normal, which isn't so normal at a place like this. Instead of skinny pants and checkered vans, he wore loose fitting, ripped jeans that sat low on his hips and scuffed up converse. In place of a tight black shirt with the hottest band name on it, he wore a faded orange t-shirt with *Big Bite Diner open 24/7 South Bay* scrawled in white writing under an army green button down jacket. A gray beanie fit loosely on his head matching the gray I could see in his eyes as he scanned the crowd mischievously. Why didn't he have that slight look of intimidation like every other seventeen-year-old singer did when I watched their eyes take in the crowd?

Marty seemed too distracted with one of the guys she'd been talking to in line. That is, until the boy on stage started talking.

"My name's Peter," he said carefully into the mic.

My best friend's mouth fell open. "Was that a British accent?" she hissed at me. "Wow, he is *hot!*" I tried to keep a grin under control as she battered my arm with her elbow.

A smile flicked across the boy's lips for just a second before he continued. "And these are my lost boys."

Cute, I thought. He's playing on the whole Peter Pan thing. Immediately, I thought of Great Gran and the stories she used to tell me. If she were still alive I would call her up tomorrow and tell her about this Peter and his lost boys.

The lights dimmed and I almost chuckled. Usually, right after a singer introduced his band, he would let out some sort of guttural throat scream and the music would erupt into chaos making the crowd go crazy. Instead, this Peter boy pulled the mic back off the stand and took a step toward his guitarist. Taking this as a signal, the guy pressed down on a pedal and plucked a string, holding his guitar close to the amp to create feedback and filling the room with just one note. Letting it carry out for only a few seconds, he then strummed two chords quickly and the drums came in, lights exploding with the sudden beat. Peter was into it whipping his head to the side when the drum hit.

I felt something rise from my feet and tingle its way up my legs and into my stomach like an electric pulse. The cymbals crashed three times along with the guitar then the music turned into a steady, rock beat as Peter began singing.

His voice was smooth with just a touch of gravel as

he sang the verse, hitting every note perfectly. I'd recognized the song almost as soon as his guitarist had strummed the first note. It was one of my favorite songs sung by one of my favorite bands. I almost didn't want to admit this mysterious boy made it even better.

The drums hit two more times and the guitar joined in, blasting heavy notes through the speakers as Peter pressed his lips to the mic. His voice carried the chorus like a tidal wave, louder and rougher as the song intensified and I found myself mouthing the words along with him.

With every riff of the guitar, he stomped his foot, throwing his body forward, getting lost in the music the way I wished I could. But I couldn't. All I could do was watch as this strange boy transformed into a rock star before my eyes. He didn't convulse the way most of the singers did so overtaken by the music, as if demons were possessing their bodies. No, this boy had taken the song by the reigns and rode it like a bucking bronco, keeping control while still letting it course through him.

The music quieted till it was just guitar for only a second before we were all thrown into the bridge, Peter's voice straining, eyes gleaming as he shouted the words that snipped my heartstrings. Each familiar lyric transformed by his voice.

The last word he drew out in an agonizing wail that brought him to one knee. As the band continued, he took his time scanning the crowd through a curtain of sweaty hair. When his eyes hit mine, he held my gaze, a look crossing his face that I couldn't describe. A wicked grin pulled half of his mouth up causing shivers to go down my spine.

And before I knew what had happened, he bounced back onto his feet at just the right moment to start in on the chorus one more time. The drums and guitar held off until the last word then the room exploded again with lights and music all at once. Every hard beat of the drums had the boy throwing his fist, punching it into the air and soon the crowd was punching with him.

Then when the last note hit, he stumbled back with a look of exhausted ecstasy on his face, his arm holding the mic falling limply to his side. Everyone around me began clapping and shouting, girls screaming like banshees in my ears. But all I could do was stand there and stare at this mystery boy, this peculiar, captivating stranger, as he gleamed fiendishly back at me.

I felt an elbow in my ribs. "He's staring at you," Marty yelled in my ear so she could be heard over the crowd. "He's looking right at you!"

Finally, when the applause started to die down, Peter brought the mic back up to his lips. "We're going to take ten," he said between gasps of air. "And then we'll be back. Thanks!"

Another round of applause and then the room was filled with the sounds of lasers, sub-bass and wub-wub-wubbing.

The crowd began to melt together the way it always did, threatening to pull me into its mass. I closed my eyes and let it start to pull me in. But then a hand grabbed my arm, shattering the feeling and causing my eyes to snap open again. Peter stood in front of me, his beanie gone and his dark hair plastered to his forehead. Why had I thought his eyes were gray when they were now so obviously a brilliant forest green?

He leaned in close so I could feel his breath on my ear. "Want to dance?" he whispered. I was surprised I could hear him at all with the chaos around us, but his words came in clear. Usually, I didn't like dancing with people. It always made me self-conscious and I couldn't just get lost in the music like I usually did. I almost wanted to say no. The way he was staring at me, I almost wanted to just find Marty and high tale it out of there. But all I could do was nod. The boy's face was still close to my ear so I didn't know at first if he saw my gesture but before I could step back to nod again, he put his hands on my waist and pulled the rest of me closer to him. He used his hands to move my hips with his to the beat, guiding at first until they moved by themselves. His lips were still near my ear and I could hear his tongue hit the roof of his mouth with each beat like he knew this song. "You can close your eyes if you want," he said. "I know you usually do that when you're dancing."

I'm pretty sure I'd never seen him before so how did he know how I danced? "What makes you think I close my eyes when I dance?" I finally asked into his hair the way he was doing to me.

"I go to The Underground a lot."

The Underground was a club Marty and I frequented the most. I closed my eyes as his grip tightened on my hips. "Then why haven't I ever seen you there?" I said and the music began to speed up like the bass was about to drop.

I could feel the boy's mouth pull up into a smile against my cheek and a sound like a chuckle escaped his throat. "Because you always have your eyes closed."

Then the room exploded and my eyelids shot open again. The crowd around us seemed to disintegrate. Even though I could see the bodies, painted with the purple and blue lights, even though I was watching that pony girl from outside with her hands raised into the air, swaying side to side lost in the music, I felt like Peter and I were completely alone, like all the other people were just holograms projected from the ceiling and if I ran at them, I would just go straight through and smack into the wall on the other side.

I wondered if Peter had meant something deeper by what he said. I shut out everyone else from my little world – with the exception of Marty, but even she was someone I tended to let blend into my surroundings. I always kept to myself. I never let people into my head. I just liked to pretend I was alone all the time. Why did I want to be alone? Whenever I closed my eyes, I imagined I was invisible. I felt invisible and I liked it. But this boy – this boy I had never seen before in my life – had seen me. He noticed me when I thought no one noticed me. Why had I always felt the need to feel invisible? Why did I want to be alone? And why could I feel a tear running down my cheek as I continued to sway with this strange boy with the amazing voice?

I wrapped my arms tightly around his neck and quickly flicked the tear off my face with a finger. Well, I obviously wasn't as invisible as I thought I was. With that, it was time to change the subject. "So what's the deal with your band?" I asked. "Is your name really Peter?"

Again a smile stretched his face against my cheek.

"Yes, but those aren't my real lost boys."

I smiled back and rolled my eyes. This kid really knew the way to make a girl feel better.

"No, my real lost boys are in Neverland."

This time I even let out a chuckle. Alright, I'll play along. "Why didn't you bring them with you?"

"They can't fly like I can," he replied with a shrug like it was nothing.

I let out a sigh. "It would be pretty cool to fly, wouldn't it?"

Peter stopped swaying and the two of us stood there still. Then he pulled back so he was looking at me. I'd already forgotten how green his eyes were. "Want to?" His voice was no longer easy and joking but determined and serious.

Again, I smiled waiting for the smirk to return to his face too. "Sure," I said drawing it out sarcastically. "I'm ready now. Let's go to Neverland." With a nod, Peter took my hand in his rough, warm one and pulled me toward the exit. My stomach did a flip as I realized we were actually going somewhere. "Hang on a second." I stopped once we had gotten out the door and onto the sidewalk. Peter dropped my hand and stood there looking at me. I was shivering in my mini skirt and thigh highs and pulled my leather jacket tighter around my torso, hoping that maybe the warmth in my top half would negate the numbness in my bottom half. "Where are we going?" I asked him realizing he didn't understand why I'd stopped.

"To Neverland," he replied confused.

I narrowed my eyes. Why hadn't I realized this guy was a crazy? "Right," I said. "Is that what you call whatever asylum you escaped from?"

Peter took a step back now too. "You're Wyndy Harper." I could feel my heart skip a beat in my chest.

I hadn't told this boy my name. Had Marty? Had she put him up to this? That girl was going to get it when we got home – which was where I wanted to be at that point. "It's Wynn," I stammered. "And how do you know my name?" I asked backing up until I hit the brick wall of the club.

"You're Wendy Darling's great granddaughter, right?" He took a step toward me and I could feel myself shrinking against the wall.

"Wha-what is this?" I stammered. "Who are you? How do you know all this about me?"

"I knew Wendy when she was your age. You look just like her," he said stepping back again when he noticed how uncomfortable I was. "Actually I thought you were her for a second but then I remembered she's dead."

My mouth dropped open. Who was this crazy person? A couple people passed us on the sidewalk and I snapped my mouth shut again before they saw me gaping like an idiot. I shoved my hands in the pockets of my jacket so he wouldn't see them shaking. "Who are you?" I repeated.

The boy let his head fall back and he sighed. "I already told you," he said looking at me again and stuffing his own hands in his pockets.

"Yeah, you're Peter. I get it," I sneered. "Peter what? Peter Pan?"

He nodded.

"You're Peter Pan."

"Yes."

"Pan," I repeated once more. "The boy that can fly.

The one from the Disney movie."

Peter rolled his eyes. "That thing is riddled with inaccuracies but, yes," then he leaned in close, "the one from the Disney movie," he mocked and I could feel my face go red.

Now I leaned in so our noses were almost touching. "You're a crazy person," I said then pushed off the wall and turned away from him. "I'm going back inside," I muttered feeling like this had been the biggest waste of time ever.

"Hey," Peter said from behind me.

I bit my lip and sighed trying to keep my anger under control. Then I swiveled around on my heel and opened my mouth to yell at him to leave me alone but my words stuck in my throat. My eyes went straight to the ground, to the few inches of space between the sidewalk and Peter's converse. This had to be a trick. There had to have been something wrong with me. Maybe someone pumped some drug into the air and I'd inhaled it. Maybe he crushed a pill and slipped it into my drink. No, I hadn't drank anything since I'd gotten there. Then this had to be real. This boy was actually floating a couple inches off the ground in front of me.

I fell back against the wall and gaped at the boy's shoes like they had turned into aliens right before my eyes. Just then a group of people came out of the club and Peter's shoes were on the ground again like he hadn't just been levitating. He shifted nervously from one foot to the other waiting for them to disappear down the sidewalk. When they finally rounded the corner, Peter met my eyes again and bit his lip like he was waiting for me to say something. I didn't know what to say to that though. Finally, I realized I'd been holding my breath and let it all out in one big sigh.

"Okay then," I whispered. "So, you're Peter Pan."

"Yes."

I shook my head. "Or you're just some psycho illusionist that gets a thrill out of freaking girls out."

Peter grinned. "I'm not an illusionist," he said rocking back proudly on his heels. "Though I do like freaking out girls. Usually, I turn my eyelids inside out like this." And he brought his fingers up to his eyes.

I put my own hands on his, stopping him from attempting to show me. "I think I got it," I said and scratched my eyebrow thoughtfully.

"Do you?" he asked raising his own eyebrow and putting his hand out to me.

I looked at it for a second, at the creases in his palm made prominent by dirt that seemed to be imbedded in his skin. Was that dirt just from something he'd done earlier that day? Or was it from years and years of exploring the woods of some magical land with a band of others just like him.

Oh right, they weren't like him. They couldn't fly.

This was ridiculous. I hesitantly brought my hand up and touched my fingers to the skin on his arm. His own fingers wrapped around my skinny wrist, crinkling the leather of my jacket. He fixed his eyes on mine, holding them with his green gaze. And then I felt the sidewalk fall away, the toes of my boots being the last to leave it. I inhaled sharply and held the air in my lungs as I waited to fall back down to the earth. Instead it didn't happen and I started feeling light headed.

"Breathe, Wynn," Peter said as a triumphant grin

broke out on his beautiful face.

Slowly, I let the air escape my lungs and out of my mouth. It was hard to breathe in again though as I was still anticipating some kind of drop. Instead of falling, Peter carefully lowered us back down until our shoes were flat on the sidewalk again.

Even though it had all been gentle, I was breathing hard like I'd just run a marathon. I pulled my wrist out of Peter's grip and brought both my hands up into my hair. "This is nuts," I gasped trying to get my heart to slow back down. "This can't be happening. None of this can be real."

"Wendy explained all this to you, didn't she?" Peter asked obviously amused by my disbelief and leaned back against the brick wall next to me.

"Sure," I breathed. "But it was all in the form of a bedtime story. She didn't say anything about it being real."

"Yes she did," he said and I could see him staring at me in my peripheral vision.

"She was sick and senile," I snapped knowing exactly what he was talking about. Back before Great Gran had gotten sick I remembered all the fantastical stories she would tell about when she had flown with Peter Pan to Neverland and met the lost boys and Captain Hook. Of course back then he wasn't called Hook, but that was before Peter Pan cut his hand off. That was back when all of them played together and explored the island and the waters around it. But it was all a bedtime story. It was all make believe. At least I thought it was.

Then as Great Gran's mind began to go, it was all she would talk about. She began to forget us. She forgot the names of her children, and my mother and me. She forgot everything about reality until Peter Pan and Neverland had become her only reality. Visits to the nursing home were awkward. We would all sit around her rocking chair while she gazed out the window at the clouds in the sky and tell us about her time in Neverland. The only time she would stop talking about it was when a nurse came in to see how she was doing or when my heartbroken mother tried to change the subject to something else; something like home, or real memories, or my ballet. But she would just jump right back into it and we'd be left trying to figure out the least awkward way to sneak out without her noticing.

Peter kicked at the ground in silence beside me while I slipped further into my depressing memories of Great Gran. Well, if all that were true and this boy next to me really was who he said he was, maybe she wasn't as crazy as we had thought. Maybe she was just scared because subconsciously she knew she was getting sick so all she could do was cling to the memories that made her the happiest.

Finally, I pushed off the wall and faced Peter head on. "Will you take me to Neverland?" I asked him biting my lip to keep it from quivering.

The corner of his mouth twitched up into a half smile but it didn't reach his eyes. He must have been thinking about Great Gran like I was. Of course he was sad. If it all was true, then they'd been very close. How close? Finally, he offered me his hand and I took it.

I expected us to just lift off right there on the pavement but instead he started pulling me down the sidewalk. "Where are we going?" I asked catching up and walking beside him. He didn't let go of my hand even though he didn't need to hold it. I'll admit though it felt kind of reassuring.

"We're not going to lift off in the middle of the street where people can see us."

"Well, we touched off right back there," I replied nodding my head back toward the club.

Peter shook his head. "No one is going to notice a couple people standing a few inches taller. But they might notice if we're floating above their heads."

He had a point. The two of us walked a few blocks in silence before Peter stopped in front of an old, dumpy looking motorcycle. I watched skeptically as he climbed on then sat and stared expectantly.

"You want me to get on that thing with you?" I asked with a chuckle of disbelief. "No way is that safe."

"Better sorry than safe is what I always say," he grinned and dug into his jacket pocket for a key. "Everyone should have regrets, right? It's how you make memories" Then he put the key in the ignition and turned it. The engine coughed and then sputtered to life. Peter held out his hand to me. "So come on, Wynn. Let's make you some memories."

"In a skirt?"

I watched as he glanced quickly at my bottom half and then shrugged. "No one's looking."

It was true. We were the only ones on the street from what I could tell. Before I had a chance to talk myself out of it, I swung my leg over the bike and sat down behind him. The bike let out a satisfied roar as Peter twisted the throttle. "Hang on," he said putting it in gear.

I wrapped my arms tightly around his waist and clasped my hands together in a death grip. I had never been on a motorcycle before but I guess there's a first time for everything. *Tonight will be a night of firsts,* I thought to myself. The first time I've ridden a motorbike, the first time I've actually danced with a boy at a club, the first time I've floated five inches off the ground…

As we took off down the street I started to wonder what other firsts I was possibly going to experience.

The wind was icy and the rain was starting to come down again only having stopped for about an hour. It was back from its lunch break newly rested and ready to downpour. I pressed up against Peter, mostly for warmth but also in an attempt to keep my skirt from showing everyone in Los Angeles the goods. My thigh high striped socks weren't doing a very good job at keeping the goose bumps off my legs and the wind was making my leather jacket cold, which in turn, made me cold. It definitely wasn't meant for this kind of weather.

We veered down an alley, leaning so far to the right I thought I was going to tumble right off, then straightened back out quickly. Peter was actually very good at maneuvering the bike through the streets and alleys. How often could he ride this thing if he lived in Neverland?

Finally, the bike started to slow as we entered a shipping yard and neared the loading docks. Peter brought it to a stop then killed the engine and both of us sat in silence as the roaring faded to nothing. Neither of us said anything for a moment. I probably couldn't have said anything anyway with how frozen my lips felt. I bit my bottom lip to get some feeling back in it.

"So," Peter said, breaking the silence, "are you going to let go of me or do I need to pry your arms off myself?"

"Right," I muttered letting my arms drop to my sides. "Sorry."

Peter stretched his own arms above his head and twisted so his back cracked loudly. "Geez, I think you rearranged my internal organs with your death grip."

I huffed. "Well, if you didn't drive like a maniac maybe I wouldn't have hung on so tight," I said shoving my hands into my coat pockets. I flexed them in an attempt to get some feeling back into my fingertips.

With a chuckle, Peter stood and swung his leg over the motorbike. I pulled my skirt down so I wouldn't flash him. After a second, he leaned in close. "You think I'm a crazy driver, you should see how well I can fly." Then he flicked the edge of my skirt and I smacked his hand away. "You'll love it," he added, his voice and his smile growing softer. Then he pulled the corner of his mouth into a crooked grin, "Your great grandmother did."

I smiled sadly back. "Yeah," I said. "I remember her telling me a bit about it. She said there's no feeling like it in the world."

Peter turned his face up to the sky so the moon reflected in his eyes. "Once you've tasted flight, you'll forever walk the earth with your eyes turned skyward, for there you have been, and there you will always long to return." Then he looked at me again. "She said that to me once."

"And you still remember?"

"I'm a pretty good rememberer." The smile on his face was a sad, reminiscent one that made me want to reach out and touch him. Where were all these feelings coming from? I'd never felt very nurturing toward anyone before but suddenly I wanted to make this boy feel better. Maybe it wouldn't be too weird if I just put my hand on his arm or maybe I could push the hair out of his eyes. That might be a bit too much. Before I could do either of those things, he turned and started toward the end of the dock. I watched as he sat down on the end and stared out at the dark water.

After a few moments of shivering quiet, I got off the back of the silent bike and slowly walked down the dock to sit by him. "I thought we were going to Neverland," I whispered studying his profile in the moonlight.

"We will," he said gruffly after a bit, still looking up at the sky. "Just give me a minute." His eyes still reflecting it so they glowed. Silver studs lined the edge of the one pointed ear I could see. With his glowing eyes and slightly pointed ears, he really did look like an unearthly being.

"Has anyone ever told you that you're kind of beautiful?" I asked tapping my fingers nervously on the wood of the dock.

A smile stretched across Peter's face but he still didn't look at me. "Yeah, a few times."

It stopped raining and now the sky was slowly beginning to clear. Even in Los Angeles, even with all the lights, you could still see some stars, shouting their brilliance to us on Earth. They had to shout. How else would anyone be able to notice them over all the lights and traffic in the city?

What did the stars look like in Neverland? Were there more of them? Were they brighter? Different colors? Did they paint the sky thickly or sporadically pepper the atmosphere like dandruff on the shoulder of a black sweater? I wanted to go. I wanted to leave. So what were we waiting for?

As that thought left my brain and floated off into the atmosphere, Peter stood up and brushed his jeans off. "I'm ready to go when you are," he said cheerily and extended his hand to me. I took it and he pulled me up to my feet. "You're in for a wild ride, Wyndy," he said with a wiggle of his eyebrows. I couldn't help but smile back. "I have to warn you though. It's going to be a mighty cold one."

I didn't know if I could possibly be colder than I was now with the icy wind blowing off the water before us. I pulled at one of my thigh high socks – I often wondered why one liked to sag more than the other – and zipped up my hoodie and then my leather jacket, both all the way up to my chin. Anticipation coursed through my veins like fire, warming my body and causing my cheeks to flush. Or maybe that was the way Peter was smiling devilishly like he had back when he was singing to me on stage. Was that to me? It had to be. He didn't smile at anyone else like that.

I took his icy fingers in mine and nodded. "Bring it on."

The smile widened on Peter's face. "That's what I like to hear," he shouted though no one would be able to hear him out there.

The next thing I knew, we shot off the ground

straight up into the air. I could feel the frigid wind growing stronger the further into the sky we flew. It made my legs quiver and my teeth chatter but it was so exhilarating to be going up and then not back down. Peter let out a whoop of delight as we rose higher above the city and into the black. My own laughter bubbled up and out of my mouth, spilling over as the cold numbed my body and was replaced with an ecstasy that only birds and kites could know.

The wind seemed to take my every doubt and fear and fly with it to someplace far, far away from me. The bitter cold stung my face and my leather jacket didn't help keep me warm either. But I was relaxed, if freezing, and breathed deeply, savoring the moment.

"Do you trust me?" Peter yelled over the sound of the wind in my ears.

"What other choice do I have?" I called back feeling my stomach twinge with nervousness.

I heard him yell out another pleasured whoop before letting go of my hand. As I started to plunge back to earth, a scream escaped my throat. Everything blurred around me as the water below fast approached. Peter was above me, below me, beside me, falling with me with a wide smile on his face. I managed to stop screaming and just watch him as the fear slowly receded.

"Ready?" he yelled over the sound of the wind rushing into my ears.

"For what?" I yelled back. What did he mean? Was I ready to plunge into ice cold water, to have it rush into my ears and freeze my brain? Was I ready to drown at the age of seventeen?

The water was close enough now that I could make

out my blurry reflection in its rippling surface. Here went nothing. I closed my eyes, expecting the cold water to suck me down. Instead I he scooped up into his strong arms and lifted me into the air again. When I opened my eyes back up, Peter's face was only inches from mine and he smiled as we continued to gain altitude. I slipped my hands around his neck and peered down at the world as it fell away again.

"You're crazy," I said breathless from the fall.

Peter took one of my hands off his neck and let his other arm slip out from beneath my legs. I continued to float beside him. It was a weird feeling, flying. I could only describe it as swimming. The air was suddenly tangible and thick like water but I was still able to breathe in and out just fine.

"How long until we reach Neverland?" I asked him looking down to see Los Angeles begin to fade into the distance.

"You know the saying," he replied giving my hand a squeeze.

Second star to the right and straight on till morning was the way to get to Neverland. Now all I could see was sea and sky as we continued away from the city. A few lights from ships peppered the horizon but pretty soon those disappeared too and we were left with an everlasting expanse of dark water.

The moon hung a bit to our left and a bright star shined directly in front of us. Beside that one was a couple dimmer, bluer stars. Peter shifted so we were facing the one farthest to the right. Second star to the right.

"What's it like in Neverland?" I asked after we had been flying in silence for a while. Peter's hand tightened more around my own frozen fingers. I couldn't feel my body anymore. I could've been missing both my legs and I wouldn't even notice until we got to Neverland and I'd discover I was a couple feet shorter.

"Different," he said looking over to meet my eyes.

"How do you mean?"

I watched as he swiveled his body and was suddenly under me, floating on his back. What would happen if I just let go of his hand? I would collide with him, he could wrap his arms around me and maybe I could lay my head on that soft orange t-shirt. I bet I'd be able to feel the ridges of his chest with my cheek. Something told me there was a body of a seventeen-year-old god under those clothes. Wow, maybe a dunk in that frigid ocean below would do me some good.

Peter cleared his throat and a smirk appeared on his face. He must have noticed my eyes trailing thoughtfully down his body. "It just is," he finally said and laid my hand on his shirt so it was flat under his. Yep, I could feel the hard lines of his chest. "You'll see for yourself soon."

"Soon?" I asked giving him a confused look. "I thought the saying goes *straight on till morning*. It isn't even eleven yet."

Peter tipped his head back so he was looking in the direction we were headed. "Think again."

I lifted my head and saw the horizon glowing with morning light. The moon was still high and bright; the stars were still shining brilliantly, yet the sky down far ahead was beginning to fade to a pale blue as the sun slowly rose. In the distance I could make out a break in the horizon. Dips and peaks made up of mountains

and valleys rose up from the water like a tiny hopeful
beat on a heart monitor with a dead line.

   Neverland.

Chapter Three

As we neared the small island, I was able to make out a bit more detail. A large cove with high rock walls spread out like an open door with only a small space between the cliffs for a sandy path onto land. Up on top of the wall, dense, thick forest lined both sides like fur on an animal. Not much else could be seen, even as we drew closer.

We completely cleared the cove and then rocks gave way to the dark forest. Peter rolled over in the air so he was holding my hand from above and I continued to gaze in awe at the trees below us. Before I had a chance to react, Peter took a nosedive toward a clearing, pulling me down with him. It was hard to breathe with the air rushing into my face as we descended down, down, down into the forest. He let go of my hand and I fell the short distance to the ground, landing clumsily on my feet.

"Hey!" I called whirling around to yell at him. Instead, only the trees and the empty sky were there. I searched the air above and around me. "Peter?" I called out to him. "This is not funny!" A twig snapped to my left and I whipped my head around in time to catch a blur of movement in the trees. Then it was gone. "Peter?" I whispered crossing my arms in front of my stomach. A sound on the opposite side of the clearing had me spinning that direction. Something like a snicker came from somewhere else and I heard two hushed voices come from yet another spot. What was going on? "Hello?"

A stick lay at my feet and I quickly snatched it up, holding it out in front of me, brandishing it like a sword. "Whoever you are," I yelled, "come out and face me!"

Something zipped by at the top corner of my vision and I thought at first that it was a huge bird, but then it landed in a tree near me and the face of a giant squirrel peered back through the limbs with its beady black eyes. I covered my mouth to keep a scream from escaping as I gaped at the oversized animal. A whoop sounded behind me and I spun around in time to see a fox jump out from behind a tree trunk and crouch down in the grass. A few feet away, a deer came out from behind another tree.

Wait a second.

Both the deer and the fox stood up slowly, exposing human limbs. These weren't animals. They were people in masks.

Now I could see the shoulder length mousy brown hair behind the fox's orange ears and dark hair cut short on the deer.

"Who are you," I demanded holding the stick out menacingly in front of me. I'm sure I looked ridiculous. Just a schoolgirl waving a twig at these strangers. I wasn't at all surprised when the fox and squirrel clutched their stomachs and started laughing like hyenas. The fox came forward, strolling around me in a wide arc like he was circling his prey and the squirrel dropped from his branch high up in the tree and landed hard, but gracefully, on his feet. I studied the deer wishing I could see the expression on the face beneath the mask but all I could find was a pair of wide, brown, human eyes peering back.

"Well, well, well," the fox finally said, his voice muffled behind the mask. "Has someone gone and gotten herself lost in the Neverwood Forest?"

"I'm not lost," I said then glanced again at the deer. He broke eye contact and kicked at the dirt with his brown boot. "I was dropped here."

"Hear that, Kai?" The fox turned to the squirrel. "Finally, an answer to our prayers."

I raised an eyebrow and glanced at Squirrely. "Prayers?"

Now the fox stopped a few feet in front of me. "Sure." He shrugged. "We've spent many a lonely night on this island."

I tugged my skirt down self-consciously. "Well, why don't you go cuddle a mermaid or something? You have those here, right?"

The fox cocked his head to the side. "They're alright." He shrugged again. "A bit too slippery for my liking though." Then he took another step toward me.

I raised the stick, holding the sharp, pointy end near

his throat so it almost touched his skin. "Well, I think I might be a bit too slippery for you too."

He held his hands up in mock defense and I could see the mask lift a bit as he pulled his face up into a smile underneath. "You've got fire. I like fire."

I rolled my eyes. "Oh please." I muttered. Leaves rustled behind me and I saw the fox's eyes dart in that direction. "What? Another one of your friends here to join in on the fun?"

"Russ," the squirrel said in a small voice. "We should go."

The deer stayed quiet next to him but his hands clenched into fists and then unclenched again nervously.

"Not without her," the fox said through gritted teeth.

I raised the stick more so it left an indent in his skin and then leaned into him. "I'm not going anywhere with you," I spat and then another twig snapped closer to us. Closer than the last one but still somewhere in the trees.

"Russ!" the squirrel boy yelled. This time he stepped back away from my pointed stick and turned to make eye contact with the other two. I stood watching him make a decision in his head.

A terrifying sound like a mix between crunching metal and a foghorn erupted from the trees somewhere behind me. Reluctantly, I turned around, letting fox boy out of my sight so I could scan the woods. While my eyes searched, I kept my body tensed expecting the fox to grab me from behind. He didn't. After a few silent, unmoving moments, I turned around to find myself alone again in the clearing. What had just happened? I lowered the stick and let it drop to the ground beside me.

"Hey."

I turned again to find Peter standing on the ground behind me. He was no longer wearing the faded orange t-shirt. Instead he had on a worn green pirate coat with gold piping, open to expose his naked torso. A piece of leather with little trinkets hung around his neck. Two small silver hoops adorned one of his ears. In place of his jeans, he had on a pair of brown pants, cut off a little below the knee and his feet were bare and dirty. And now in place of his grey beanie, he had a green hat with a red feather poking out of it.

"Really with the hat?" I asked with a grin and a raised eyebrow.

Peter frowned and straightened the hat on his head. "What? I think I look rather dashing with it."

"You're dashing no matter what," I uttered under my breath.

Peter glanced my way. "You say something?"

I shook my head and kicked at the dirt with my boot. "Who were those creepers in the masks? Seemed like real jerks."

Now a smile lifted half his face. "Just a couple of my lost boys. They like to give visitors a hard time." Then he let his eyes trail down my legs. "Which reminds me; you need to change your clothes."

"Oh sure," I said. "Let me just put on the extra outfit I packed for frolicking in the forest."

Peter started circling me, not eying me like I was lunch as the fox boy had. Instead like he was examining me. "You don't want your clothes to be all ruined when you go back, do you?"

Crossing my arms over my chest, I rocked onto one of my hips. "Well geez, I just got here and you already want to get rid of me?"

He shrugged slipping a knife out of his belt and began cleaning the dirt from under his fingernails. "I'm just thinking logically here."

"A seventeen year old boy thinking logically? That may be a first."

Peter chuckled and shook the knife jokingly in my direction like a mother would shake a finger at her child. "Hey, just because we're reckless and impulsive, doesn't mean we don't have rules for when visitors come."

"Do you get many visitors?"

"No, not really," he sighed and scratched the back of his neck with the blade. Another foghorn sound echoed from within the tree line causing Peter to freeze. The two of us kept our eyes locked until it faded again. Once it had, Peter quickly put his knife back into his belt. "We need to go," he said and extended his hand out to me.

"What was that?" I asked and turned my head in time to see a shadowy figure dart behind a tree not ten feet away from me.

Peter didn't respond until we were up in the air and safely away from the clearing. "That was my shadow," he said glancing down again.

I followed his gaze back down to where I'd been standing and saw a dark figure pacing around in the grass below us. Its movements were wild and jerky and its form sputtered like a hologram.

"Why is it moving like that?" I finally asked. The figure lifted its head toward us and I could see a pair of glowing white eyes. I couldn't look away fast enough and two dark dots stained my vision where the eyes had been.

"It got away from me a while ago," Peter explained. We were now far enough away that I couldn't see it anymore. "Darn things are more slippery than you would think."

"Well, what happened?"

I felt Peter's grip on my hand tighten as he remembered. "It wanted to go off and make a life of its own," he explained. I snorted at how ridiculous that sounded. It was just a shadow. Something made by light but then Peter gave me a look and I knew it wasn't such a ridiculous idea. "But it was no longer tied to an identity, my identity, and it slowly went mad."

"Shadows can go mad?" I asked looking back again toward the clearing even though it was way out of sight now.

"Mine can," he said. "Now it's feral and violent. And it's the only thing that can kill me."

"Well, why don't you do something about it? Why don't you catch it somehow and reattach it?"

Peter shook his head. "The thing is almost impossible to catch and even harder to reattach. The only thing that can tame a rabid shadow is a mermaid's song."

I found myself squeezing Peter's hand tighter and took one last look back at the clearing before it completely faded into the distance.

We were only in the air for a few minutes before Peter shifted his body so we were headed back down into the woods. After landing in a dense grove of trees,

I let go of his hand and flexed my fingers. I'd really been hanging on tight. It took me a second to notice where we were but when I did, I couldn't help but gaze in wonder at what was around me.

A huge tree with a thick trunk sat in front of me, its branches reaching high up and creating a canopy over the place. The area was cleared of brush so it was more like a giant room with walls of trunks and a ceiling of limbs. A ramp made of rock, branches and mud circled up the trunk and ended at a tree fort looking thing fixed a good ten feet off the ground. There was a big fire pit off to the right of the tree with dead logs and a few rocks for seating. An old acoustic guitar leaned up against one of the stumps.

"What is this place?" I finally asked turning to see a gratifying smile on Peter's face. He must have found my bewilderment amusing.

"This, my dear Wynn," he said lifting his arms up, "is home."

As soon as he said this, the canopy lit up with a thousand tiny white lights. They danced around in the limbs, twirling around each other. A couple of them drifted down to me, stopping right in front of my face. Two tiny women, with wings beating like a hummingbird's, gazed at me curiously. One of them was clad in dark green moss and the other was wrapped in a red leaf. Fairies.

"You brought another one, Peter?" the one wearing the leaf asked with a tiny, curious smile.

I turned to look at him and raised an eyebrow. "How many girls have you brought here?" I asked him.

"Just you and Wendy," he replied with a reassuring

smile then turned to the two little balls of light. "Don't worry, ladies. You'll each always have a teeny tiny fairy sized place in my heart." The leaf girl scoffed sarcastically but the smile stayed on her face. I cleared my throat just then and Peter glanced at me. "Oh yeah, this is Iris and Aubri." He motioned to the leaf one first. "Iris, Aubri, Wynn."

I gave them a shy nod. Just then, a black bug flew in my face and I stumbled back with a shriek. It took me a few seconds to realize it wasn't a bug but another little fairy, clad in black, shiny armor. She hovered in front of my face. The armor looked really stiff and shined purple and green reminding me of an oil slick. It only took me a few seconds to realize it was made of beetle wings and I tried not to make a face at the thought of wearing clothes made of insects.

"I'm Nyk," she said with a smirk. "Welcome to Neverland."

As if on cue, the other fairies swarmed me, their wings flapping rapidly making them sound like a flock of hummingbirds. Each introduced themselves as they picked at my hair and my clothes.

Ardo, with pine needles sticking out of the cottony hair on her head, lifted a piece of my black hair, curiously. Another, Lyssa, with wings like a butterfly, picked at my short skirt. One with scratchy bark armor mentioned her name was Willow as she pulled at my leather jacket, mesmerized. It was weird that they were all so fascinated with me when they themselves looked just ridiculous. Beautiful but ridiculous.

"She looks nothing like Wendy," A green fairy, Brucie said shaking her head and crossing her tiny, arms. "Are you sure this girl really is who she says she is?"

"For your information," I said, putting a hand on my hip, "I didn't say a word. Peter already knew." Then I turned to him. "Right?"

Peter grinned in amusement. Of course he found all this funny. I would too if I was watching someone argue with a tiny ball of light. "Right," he nodded assuring me.

I smiled and turned back to the little green fairy. "See?"

A few whoops echoed in the distance causing all of us to turn our heads in the direction it came from. "The boys are back," Peter said then looked at me. "You need to get changed before they get here."

"Why?"

Brucie let out a chuckle next to my ear. "It may be the only privacy you get for the duration of your stay," she said and then all the little balls of light floated back up to the canopy overhead, out of reach of the lost boys and their reaching hands.

Peter took my arm and we rose into the air, sailing up past the ramp. Then he set me down gently on the deck of their tree fort. "There are some clothes in there that should fit. Just try to hurry. I could hold one off but not five all at once."

I opened the door. "Why would you need to hold any of them off?" I asked glancing back at the trees where the whooping still echoed.

"Cuz they're boys. And we don't get females around here very often."

I smiled. "Right. Right." Then I put my hand on the cloth covering the entrance.

Peter hesitated for a second in the air biting his lip.

Finally, he shook his head and smiled at me like he'd been deep in thought. "Right. I'll just be down there then," he said pointing to the ground.

I nodded with another smile then pushed the cloth back and stepped inside.

There was so much room on the inside for how small it was outside. The place was divided into two small stories. I found myself standing in a living room of sorts. There were a couple chairs, a couch and a coffee table all made of spindly tree limbs. They looked like they were growing up from the floor, which, in a place like this, could have been entirely possible. There was a shelf to my right with books from a wide range of time periods. Surely, these were books Peter had gotten on his trips to Earth. I ran my fingers along the spines, skimming over the titles to see what was there. Many authors I recognized. Some I'd never even heard of. I let out a chuckle when my fingers trailed over a copy of *Peter Pan* by J. M. Barrie. I wondered how accurate that book really could be. I wondered if he had ever met Peter and maybe the two of them sat and Peter told him all about his life and some of the stories from it.

A loud catcall and laughter pulled me away from the bookshelf. The boys were there. I spotted a pile of clothes on a table next to the bookshelf and took off my jacket quickly. The clothes Peter had left me weren't actually that bad. They fit rather well, only the leggings needed to be rolled up a bit. The shirt was long and made out of soft, gray cloth and fit me like a glove. The leggings were brown and also made of soft material. I slipped my own boots back on. Good thing I hadn't gone with heels like Marty had wanted.

Now that I was fully dressed, I didn't feel panicked that someone would walk in on me. I was able to continue looking around. On the other side of the bookshelf was a ladder leading up to a loft. Carefully, I climbed the rickety ladder to the upper story. There were a few beds up there, all having frames woven from that winding wood. I ran my hand along the edge, feeling the smoothness of it. Lights flickered above my head and I looked up at the ceiling to find millions of tiny dots like stars floating around. At first I thought they were fairies but then when I reached up to touch one, it drifted slowly down, fading to nothing like a fallen snowflake. Another white light formed in its place and floated with the others like it had been there all along.

Where's the girl?" A voice called loudly. "You're not keeping her all for yourself, are you, Pan?" Then laughter from multiple people.

I climbed down again carefully from the ladder and made my way across the room toward the door. What was I going to find on the other side? Were they all going to be skeezy like that boy with the fox mask had been? The one in the deer mask came to mind. He seemed harmless. Shy a bit. At long last I stepped out of the hut and onto the deck.

My eyes went directly to the boy with the fox mask. He no longer had it over his face but pushed back so it lay flat on the top of his head. I didn't want to admit that for such a jerk, he was actually very good looking. His hair was shoulder length and a bit wild. His gray eyes were sharp as well as his nose and his mouth was full and turned up into a bit of a half-smirk when he saw me lock eyes with him. I pursed my own lips and narrowed my eyes before moving on to the next face.

The boy with the deer mask sat on one of the rocks by the fire pit drawing in the dirt with a stick. His hair was dark and just barely brushed his ears. The deer mask still covered his face but when he looked at me, I saw the same, wide brown eyes I had seen back in the clearing. They still looked just as curious.

Sitting not too far from him were two more boys that looked similar enough to be twins, or at the very least brothers. One had a badger mask and the other a rabbit, or I guess it was a hare, mask fixed on his head. Both boys had very short black hair, like it had been buzzed off with a razor. When they looked up at me, I was amazed at how bright their blue eyes were. Like the color of the sky. The one with the badger mask stood up and smiled at me. "I'm Mika," he said waving his hand at me. "This is Finn." The hare boy waved too but just with his fingers.

I waved my fingers back and smiled. "You guys brothers?" I asked him.

Mika pulled his mask off his head, running his hand over his short hair in the process. "How could you tell?" he asked with a grin. Then he motioned to deer boy. "This is Pal and that's Russ," he said and nodded at the boy with the fox mask. When I glanced at Russ I saw he was still looking at me with that smug half smile.

I held his gaze this time. No one said anything as we stared each other down. "What?" I finally asked causing him to jump a little. Then I turned to Peter. "So this everyone?" No wait; there had been a squirrel too, right? Where was he?

Just then an upside down face appeared in front of

me and I let out a squeal as I jumped back. I saw the mask on the boy's head and realized this was the squirrel boy. He had somehow climbed the tree and was now hanging upside down in front of me by his legs.

He dropped down into the space I'd just been standing in. "I'm Kai," he said sticking his hand out. I reached my own out hesitantly and he closed the space, grabbing mine and shaking it vigorously. I couldn't help but smile back at this kid. He kind of looked a bit like a squirrel with his light brown, spiky hair and beady eyes, so dark they were almost black. His two front teeth were just a bit too big. Even with the slight buckteeth and beady eyes, he was still good looking. In fact, all these guys were crazy attractive. Well, physically. For some, aka Russ, physical attractiveness seemed to be all they had going for them. They all looked to be the same age as Peter and I.

"So, you're Wendy's great granddaughter, huh?" Kai asked crossing his arms and leaning back against the railing as he sized me up.

I tugged at the hem of my tunic. "Yeah," I replied. These guys really knew how to make a girl feel self-conscious. At least he didn't have a devious look on his face like Russ.

"So why don't you have brown hair like Wendy?" he asked me.

I picked up a strand of my black hair. "It's dyed."

Kai's beady eyes grew bigger. "It's dead?"

I had to hold back a giggle. "No, I changed the color." I stepped around him and made my way down the ramp. When I hit the ground, Kai jumped from the deck and landed in front of me.

"How did you change the color?" he asked picking up a piece and examining it. "Are you a fairy?"

I snorted and brushed his hand away. "No, I'm not a fairy."

Mika and Finn came to join him now. The three formed a semi-circle in front of me, their eyes filled with curiosity. "Are you some sort of pixie?" Finn asked.

Mika turned to him and frowned, pulling at the ear on his brother's hare mask. "Pixies are smaller than fairies, moron."

Finn batted Mika's hand away and shoved him.

"A mermaid then?" Kai asked nudging the toe of my boot with his own toe.

Now I frowned and pulled my foot back. "Do I look like a mermaid to you?"

"She definitely has the attitude of a pixie," Russ muttered from behind the others.

I threw a glare his way but the rest just ignored him. A smiling Peter, obviously entertained by the boys' fascination with me, sat by the fire pit, strumming the worn acoustic guitar. "You think this is really funny, don't you?" I asked shaking my head.

"Oh, I think this is hilarious," Peter laughed and continued to pluck the strings.

I narrowed my eyes. "So, there really are mermaids here? They actually exist?"

He nodded with a smile on his face "Of course they exist. Not many mythical creatures *don't* exist in Neverland."

"Dragons?" I asked.

"There are a few that inhabit Skull Rock."

"Gnomes?"

Peter scrunched his nose up. "Nasty little creatures in Cannibal Cove. You don't want to have a run in with one of those guys."

I always thought they were cute little men with accents, long white beards and sweet, pointy little hats. Guess not. "What about trolls? Gryphons? Giants?"

"All in Cannibal Cove. All dangerous."

I tapped my chin thoughtfully and looked up at the bright blue sky. Then a smile spread across my face at the thought of a poster hanging on the wall in Marty's bedroom back at her house. "Unicorns?"

I heard Pal laugh from underneath his mask and I stepped past the other three, making my way over to the circle and took a seat carefully next to him. He only turned his head to acknowledge me for a second.

"Where do you guys get these things?" I finally asked him hoping I could get at least a word out of him.

"The Indians," Kai blurted out pulling his own mask down over his face.

Mika shoved him hard. "She was asking Pal."

Kai responded by running over to the ramp, jumping up and grabbing a hold of the deck before swinging himself easily up onto it. Then he leaned down over the railing and cocked his squirrelly head to the side. "Well, she's not going to get an answer out of him. He barely ever talks to anyone."

Mika and Finn came over to join us around the fire pit but Russ stayed standing in the middle of the clearing with his arms still crossed. Then Mika leaned into Pal. "Anyone but *Calliope*." He sing-songed nudging Pal's shoulder.

I turned back to the quiet kid and rocked into his other shoulder gently. "Ooh, who's *Calliope*?" I asked raising an eyebrow and mimicking Mika's sing-song voice.

"His lady mermaid friend," Finn answered also raising his eyebrows.

"Shut up, Finn" Pal murmured and I saw the mask lift a little as he smiled.

"He speaks at long last!" Kai exclaimed from on top of the railing. Then we watched as he jumped, doing a perfect somersault through the air, and rolled onto the ground, landing before me on his feet.

Peter smiled and stood up. Then he held his hand out to me. "Want to come meet the mermaids?"

I put my hand in his. "Of course."

Kai let out a whoop from right behind me, causing me to jump startled. All the lost boys, including Peter, and with the exception of Pal, started laughing. I frowned but couldn't help but laugh as well at their constant giggling. As Kai, Mika, Finn and Russ took off running into the trees, Kai called back to Pal. "Come on, Pal! We're going to see your girlfriend!"

Pal got up. "She's not my girlfriend," he yelled back with his soft, muffled voice, then hurried after them.

As the boys got further away, I could hear them chant, "Pal loves Calliope! Pal loves Calliope!" and I listened until it had completely faded to silence.

Peter turned to me. "Want to race them?" he asked wiggling his eyebrows playfully.

"How? They have a huge head start." Then we lifted off the ground.

"They can't fly like we can," he replied.

We hovered for just a second before shooting

straight up into the sky. It was a weird sensation. Peter wasn't even pulling me behind him. We were shoulder-to-shoulder, elbow-to-elbow, neck and neck, like I was flying all on my own. I knew better though. If I let go of his hand I would drop like a sack full of lead.

When we reached a bit above the treetops, Peter bent at the waist and suddenly we were surging forward like a high-speed train, the forest rushing by below in a blur of green.

I pointed my face downward so I could watch the earth move under us. At one point, I caught a glimpse of white and a touch of reddish brown. Russ sprinted below next to Mika and Finn. Kai wove his way through the woods around them, swinging from limbs and launching himself from trunk to trunk like he was also flying. I didn't see Pal anywhere but I guessed he was straggling behind.

Suddenly, the forest ended and we were flying over crystal blue water. Peter leaned into me and we circled back around toward land. The tree line was abrupt and gave way to a beach that spread out to the water. We leaned again and started following the shoreline. Kai, Mika, Finn and Russ broke out of the trees only a little behind us, still in a dead sprint. Pal appeared moments later, trailing after them at his own quick pace. Soon the sandbar began to slope upward causing the boys to slow down and fall behind again. Peter let out a satisfied chuckle. Up ahead I saw the sand give way to rock and then the rock gave way to a cliff that jutted out over the water.

My stomach clenched nervously as I watched the boys run toward the cliff with no indication of slowing down. We cleared the cliff and circled above a cove that had been cut out of the rock. A waterfall spilled down from a river into the cove and splashed loudly into the sea. Peter dipped and we began to spiral down. The rock walls came up around us and I looked up in time to see Kai launch off the edge of the cliff, letting out a gleeful yell as he sailed through the air then plunged into the water below. Peter brought us down softly on the edge of a rock beach as Mika and Finn cannonballed into the water at the same time, creating a big wave. Russ landed a few seconds after them just as Kai's and their heads popped back up to the surface. They all let out loud laughs surely feeling the thrill of the fall still coursing through their veins. I looked up again to find Pal's deer face peering back down at us.

"Come on, Pal!" Kai called up to him. "The water's fine!"

Pal's head disappeared again and then suddenly he jumped He straightened out and pointed his body down before landing so he slipped perfectly and almost soundlessly below the water. A couple seconds later he broke through the surface to the others clapping the tips of one of their hands to the heel of their other in mock applause. Even with his mask still over his face I could tell he was beaming.

"Where are the mermaids?" I asked after the boys had made their way to shore.

"They will be here any second now," Peter replied lying on his back on the pebbles. "It's almost high tide."

I sat down beside him and wrapped my arms around my knees. "Why do they come in here at high tide?"

Kai, the twins and Pal came and sat around me while Russ stayed down by the edge and threw rocks into the water. Peter put his hands back behind his head. "They like to ride the waves in."

As if on cue, the sound of roaring water grew louder and a wave headed our way from the open ocean. As it neared, I caught flashes of color just before they disappeared again beneath the surface. The air filled with sweet, beautiful music that gripped my heart. It sounded at first like an orchestra, but then as the wave came closer I realized it was a chorus of voices all harmonizing, rising and falling together. By the time the wave reached inside the cove, all the boys and I were standing at attention, listening to the music in awed silence. It slowly faded away and then the water was still.

Chapter Four

I thought for a second that maybe the mermaids had decided to leave without showing themselves but then a head popped up out of the water. She studied me for a second before disappearing again beneath the surface. I didn't even really have time to see what she looked like.

"Come on, girls," Peter called with a laugh. "Don't be shy."

"Yeah, Calliope, your *boyfriend* is here to see you," Kai called too causing Pal to elbow him hard in the stomach.

Several heads popped above the water and eyed me curiously. "Girls," Peter said and put an arm around my shoulder. "This is Wynn."

A couple of them bobbed closer to the shore. Another one jumped up and climbed onto a rock.

Once she was out of the water, I couldn't keep my eyes off her. Her hair, though wet, was long and the color of honey. Her eyes were the same golden shade and a string of pearls decorated her forehead like a crown. Her skin was creamy white as well as her lips, which would have made her look dead, if she were human. Instead they made her look angelic and magical. A tangle of netting and shells covered her chest modestly and then my eyes trailed down her stomach to her waist where the faintest shimmer of scales began. They started out the same color as her skin but then faded into a lemony yellow as it got down to where her knees would be. Finally her tail, which splashed the water lazily, was a burnt color like melted gold. All of her shimmered. She fixed her yellow eyes on me and a smile curled her pale lips.

I looked away feeling a bit embarrassed for being caught staring and I fixed my attention on the ones resting on their bellies in the shallowest part of the water near us. One of them had dark brown, almost black hair and three rubies on both of her temples. Her eyes were red as well and her tail faded from white at the top to scarlet near the middle and then black at the tip of her tail. Next to her was a mermaid with hair the color of blood. Sapphires to match her eyes dotted the bridge of her nose and her lower half faded from the tan color of her skin to a dark, royal blue, the color of the night sky. On the other side of the ruby encrusted mermaid was one with skin paler than the golden girl on the rock. Her hair was silver and curly and purple jewels glittered on one side of her face like a spider web. Her amethyst eyes studied me as I watched the violet tip of her tail float lazily on top of the water.

Peter introduced me to each one of them starting with the golden mermaid. Her name was Harmony. The raven haired one was Lyra, the red head with the blue eyes was Chime and the purple one with the amethyst spider web and silver hair was Aria. Hadn't the boys earlier said something about a mermaid named Calliope?

I turned to see what Pal was doing only to find he was no longer behind me. I spun in a circle searching for the familiar deer face before my eyes finally landed on the shore nearer to the waterfall. A small smile pulled at my mouth as I watched Pal sitting on the ground with his arms around his knees and a mermaid sitting next to him. Her hair was the color of new pennies and shined brilliantly in the sun. From this distance I couldn't see her face but judging by the emerald color trailing down to the tip of her tail, I figured her eyes were just as vivid.

"Nice to meet you," I finally whispered wrapping my arms around my middle. They were all so beautiful. What could they think of me looking so colorless compared to them? What if they didn't like that I was hanging out with the lost boys when that seemed to be their thing?

I couldn't read any of the mermaids' faces. They all looked at me curiously but that was it. Finally, the red one, Lyra, who had been propped on an elbow and tracing one of her fingers in the sand, sat up. "Good to meet you, Wynn," she said in a musical, smooth voice. I caught her ruby eyes drifting down my body and then back up to my face. "Welcome to Neverland."

I hugged myself a little tighter and gave her a small

smile. "Thanks," I said.

"Care to swim?" Aria asked me, ruffling her silver hair as started drifting back out to the water. I shook my head, glancing at Peter.

"I think I'll stick to land for now," I said then sat down.

Lyra shrugged. "Suit yourself," she said then rolled over onto her back and floated back out into the deeper water.

Again, I looked at Peter. He frowned for a second but the expression quickly disappeared from his face. With a shrug he shed his jacket and hat and ran toward the water with Mika, Finn, Kai and Russ following close behind. Peter jumped and soared at least twenty feet into the air before arcing back down with his head pointed toward the water. He did a perfect somersault then disappeared with a ripple beneath the waves. I stayed where I was, watching as Mika and Finn picked up Kai and threw him as far as they could. He crashed into Russ and they both fell into the water creating a big splash. Neither came up right away and I felt worry in my gut at first, more for Kai than Russ, until a flash of yellow caught my eye and then Harmony's tail disappeared under the water. She came back up a couple seconds later with Russ and Kai, shoving them and whining about how she had been trying to let her hair dry.

Peter shot out of the water close to shore and flew up to the top of the cliff next to the waterfall. Kai immediately swam toward the rock wall and, when he reached it, started climbing up expertly. This kid wasn't afraid of anything. I watched in horrified wonder as he climbed up almost as rapidly as he could run, only slipping once and getting a few terrified squeals out of Lyra, Chime, Harmony and Aria.

I glanced over at Pal to find he was still talking to Calliope. The two had their heads together and I watched as Pal's hand twitched a couple times. Maybe he was debating in his mind whether or not to try to hold her hand. I smiled. Pal seemed so different from the other lost boys. While they were all playing in the water, taking turns dunking the mermaids and getting dunked, while Kai scaled the wall to get up to where Peter was, Pal was happy sitting with the girl he liked. Loved? He turned his masked head in my direction and I quickly glanced away, feeling like I'd been caught watching something private. Perhaps I had.

"Wynnie!" Kai called from above us. We all lifted our heads and I shielded my eyes from the sun. I could just barely make out Kai and Peter's silhouettes against the bright sky. "Ready?" he called out and I smiled back at him.

"On the count of three," Peter yelled and bent his knees like he was ready to jump. Kai bent his knees too, though he kept bouncing in anticipation. "One... three!" Then Peter leapt into the air, straightening his body into an arrow. He whooped loudly then curled himself up into a ball right before hitting the water, creating a giant splash. Harmony had finally gotten back up onto the rock and was brushing the tangles out of her hair with her fingers so it would dry easier when the giant wave Peter created came crashing down on her. When I saw her again, her hair was stuck to her face messily and she glared daggers at him when he resurfaced.

"You cheated!" Kai called still up on top of the

cliff.

Peter rose out of the water again. "Sorry, sorry," he called back with a laugh as he made his way up to where Kai was. "Seriously, it will be on three this time." When he was eye level with Kai he crossed his arms over his chest. "Aaand three," he said quickly and fell again doing a back flip in the air before landing and completely drenching Harmony once more.

Kai stood up on the ledge still with his arms crossed. "This is crap, man!" he said loudly.

"Just jump, Kai!" Russ yelled from below just before Aria pushed him into the water. She giggled and dove down after him, splashing her purple tail before it sank after her.

The silhouette up on the cliff disappeared as Kai backed up and then launched off the cliff yelling "GERONIMO!!" This boy was not as graceful of a diver as the others were and his limbs flew every which way as he fell. At the last second he managed to bring his knees into his chest and hit the water in a big canon ball, once again, soaking Harmony. Everyone else laughed in delight except for her. She swam her way to the shore and dragged herself onto the gravel beach only a few feet from me. Immediately, I stiffened and focused my attention on the boys as they played king of the hill with the rock she had been laying on.

"Those boys are ridiculous," she muttered ringing out her golden hair with her hands.

What was I supposed to say to that? "Boys will be boys," I responded quietly.

"Honestly, I don't even know why we put up with them," she continued. I'm not sure if she heard me or if she was even talking to me. Maybe it would be a better idea to just keep my mouth shut. Then Harmony turned to me. "Are they giving you a hard time too?" I opened my mouth for a second as I tried to think of an answer. Then she turned away again and glared at everyone having fun in the water. "Of course they aren't," she muttered. "You're a *human* girl. They haven't seen one of those since *Wendy*." The way she said my Great Gran's name made my mouth taste sour.

"You didn't like Wendy?" I asked her.

Harmony shrugged. "She was alright," she replied smoothing her hair over her shoulder with her hands. "Not a very fun girl though." Harmony wrinkled her nose. "She didn't like it too well when we tried to get her to come swim with us."

My eyes widened. Great Gran had mentioned something about that once. "Didn't you try to drown her?" I asked out loud.

Again Harmony shrugged. "We wouldn't have actually drowned her," she replied. "Just wanted to see how long she could hold her breath." Then she looked me up and down. "How big are your lungs?"

"Oh, they're huge," I replied shifting uncomfortably on the rocks. "Pal and Calliope seem to be hitting it off though," I added in an attempt to change the subject.

Harmony glanced over at the two sitting there, Pal still clenching his hand in and out of a fist. "I guess," she muttered again. "The two just need to make out already or something. They've known each other for how many centuries? And they're still both too shy to make a move."

"I think it's sweet."

She let out a scoff. "I think it's kind of sickening. I mean, how hard is it to just lean over and kiss someone?"

Kai came up onto the shore just then dripping wet and plopped down on the other side of her. Before he could say anything, Harmony put both of her hands on either side of his face and crushed her pale lips against his. It was only for a few seconds but the awkwardness made it drag out forever. Finally, she let go of him and he sat back with a completely confused look on his face. Slowly, a smile formed and then he was beaming ear to ear. Without a word, he got back up and stumbled his way back into the water to join the guys and the other mermaids.

"See?" she said smiling with satisfaction.

I hadn't even realized my mouth was hanging open until she lifted an eyebrow and I snapped my teeth together. How many of the lost boys had these mermaids sucked face with? How many times had any of them kissed Peter so carelessly like Harmony had kissed Kai?

"Hey, Harmony!" Russ called from in the water. "Where's my kiss?"

The two of us looked out at him. I caught myself watching as the sun shined off his lean, muscular stomach. It only took a second though to remind myself of the kid's putrid attitude and a shadow cast itself over him.

I watched unamused as Chime swam up beside him and lunged, their mouths colliding, and their bodies crashed into the water. They came back up a few seconds later, Chime laughing and Russ with a big grin on his face. I rolled my eyes then glanced quickly at Peter. He was sitting on the rock with his elbows on his knees smiling, though his smile looked a bit forced. His gaze met mine and the smile warmed and crinkled the corners of his eyes. I smiled back and gave him a little wave. Harmony scoffed beside me. "You two are just as bad as Calliope and Pal," she said rolling her eyes then scooted back into the water to join the lost boys and the other mermaids.

It was another hour at least before any of the boys even came back onto the beach. Peter was the first and he crawled up from the water and plopped down dramatically on his stomach next to me. I smiled as he stuck his tongue out, pretending to be dead. "You all look like you're having fun out there," I said picking up a few pebbles and dropping them onto his back.

Peter rolled over and put his hands behind his head, closing his eyes against the brightness of the sun. "And you look like you're being a boring little land lubber up here on the beach."

I frowned and swatted at him. "I'm not really a fan of swimming," I muttered.

"Neither was Wendy," he replied opening one eye to glance at me. I opened my mouth to protest but Peter wrapped his wet arms around me and dragged me down on top of him. I shrieked and tried to squirm out of his freezing, wet embrace but he was too strong for me. Our faces were dangerously close and I think the two of us noticed at the same time. Peter let me go and I quickly crawled off of him.

"Get a room, you two!" Harmony called from in the water. I turned my head to glare at her only to find that she was directing her remark at Pal and Calliope down the beach from us. Their hands quickly separated and I felt the urge to slap the fish girl right in her beautiful golden face. How long had it taken Pal to get up the nerve to even do that? Now it was going to take even longer. I scoffed and turned to Peter.

He had a look of amusement on his face. "What?" I asked feeling a little annoyed at Harmony.

"Want to go somewhere else?" he asked me and got to his feet.

I nodded and took his outstretched hand. "Yes please," I said.

The two of us rose into the air. As we climbed higher, I could hear the lost boys and the mermaids calling from below us.

"Hey, where are you two going?"

"We're not your babysitters, Pan!"

"Hey, what do you mean babysitters?"

"Don't wander too far off!"

"Don't do anything I wouldn't do!"

Their voices faded into the distance as we made our way up and over the cliff. I didn't really know where we were going but Peter seemed to have an idea. We sailed over the beach and past the Neverwood Forest. There was another beach on the other side with bright white sand. As we descended, something in the water caught my eye. Two long purple tentacles snaked up toward us before falling with a splash back to the water. I gripped Peter's hand harder and leaned into him as I gaped at the tentacles in fear.

"Don't worry," he assured me with a laugh. "It's just Scylla. She won't hurt you."

"She?" I asked in a squeaky voice that only went

high when I was scared. "Really?"

"Oh, Scylla's like a big, purple puppy dog with a lot of extra legs. She doesn't hurt anyone. Want to meet her?"

I cowered closer to him. "Not particularly," I said swallowing the bile that rose in my throat.

Another couple tentacles came up out of the water and then a giant purple head. One big, yellow eyeball rolled around in its socket before finally settling on the two of us then sinking back below the surface. I swear I could feel the blood draining from my head down into my feet.

"I think she wants to meet you," Peter said and dipped us down toward the water.

"Uh-uh." I shook my head erratically. "No. No way."

Peter squeezed my hand so I would look at him. "Do you trust me?"

I shook my head again. "I don't know!" I exclaimed. "I just met you last night!"

"True," he agreed as we sank further. "But during that time you've followed me out of a club, not knowing at all who I was, and flown with me. All the while I could've easily let go of your hand and let you fall to your death. I'd say trusting me is your only option right now."

If I could cross my arms without breaking contact with him, I would have. I pursed my lips and searched his eyes for any sign that he was joking about getting any closer to the creepy thing in the water. Instead, there was only fascination and excitement in those moss green eyes. "Alright, fine," I spat.

Peter beamed from ear to ear. "Alright!" He dipped

his head toward the water sending us into a nosedive. I didn't even have time to scream before we came to a dead halt about eight feet above the water. I clutched onto Peter's arm like a cat above water and he laughed. Then he put his middle finger and thumb together and up to his lips and let out a shrill whistle. The water bubbled below us and I could see a big dark blob rising up below our feet. When it finally broke the surface, I was able to see just how massive this thing really was. Peter lowered us until our feet were resting on the creature's slippery head and I tried my hardest to keep from getting sick. It felt like I was standing on a big beanbag chair packed tight with Jell-O. Its skin was slick and rubbery and I could see veins and dark spots speckling the violet surface. Just a few feet to my right a slit opened up revealing the big yellow eyeball again. I watched as the dark pupil rolled around before settling on us. With Peter's hand still clutched tightly in mine, I took a tentative step toward the eye, being careful not to slip on its mucus-y skin. I stopped right above it and peered down at the big round crater. The eye itself was actually beautiful, though it would have been even more beautiful if it weren't attached to a giant purple booger. The pupil was black as night and big like a manhole. Like I could fall right down into it. Surrounding the black was a ring of bright orangey gold that seemed to glow with its own inner fire and around that was a ring of opal; blue with little bits of green and white and purple and pink. It reminded me of a ring that Great Gran used to wear on the middle finger of her left hand. She said it belonged to my great grandpa a long time ago and that he got it back when he had traveled around Europe in his younger days. Along side the stories of Peter Pan and Captain Hook, Great Gran liked to tell me stories about my great grandfather. I wondered if she had ever told him about Neverland and all her adventures there.

Scylla let out a loud, low groan and lurched forward causing me to lose my balance along with my train of thought. Luckily, Peter was quick and caught my arm before I could fall and become a slimy mess.

"You alright?" he asked me.

I bent my knees a bit until I felt steady again. "Yeah," I said. "Just clumsy." Then I noticed we were moving. "Where's it taking us?"

"She," Peter corrected me and Scylla groaned again.

"Sorry," I muttered feeling dumb for apologizing to a glob of purple silly-putty. "Where is *she* taking us?"

He smiled and squeezed my hand. "Consider her the S.S. Scylla and I, your tour guide."

We spent the rest of the day circling the island on the giant creature's slimy back. I had actually made myself quite comfortable on her slick surface with my knees drawn up to my chest while Peter sat Indian style in front of me and excitedly pointed out all the different landmarks. There was Cannibal Cove where the most dangerous creatures lived and Skull Rock, which was apparently inhabited by dragons, though I couldn't see any from where we were. I was dying to go in and see them but according to Peter, Scylla didn't like the dragons and she confirmed it with a bellowing moan.

We didn't make it back to shore again until the blue sky had changed to pink and orange and by that time, the lost boys and the mermaids were no longer swimming by the cliffs. When Peter took my hand and we drifted off of Scylla's back, I couldn't help feeling a bit sad that we had to leave the creature behind. Even in that short amount of time I had grown to like her. For a big blob of violet goo, she was pretty alright.

The waves caressed the shore now as Peter and I walked across the sand. We had no intention of hurrying back to the camp and the hyper lost boys. I barely knew this stranger, yet I felt perfectly comfortable strolling down the beach with my hand in his. I didn't understand why. Maybe it was the way Neverland was already beginning to feel like home or maybe it was Peter. Something about him was so familiar. Perhaps it was because I had come to know him so well through Great Gran's stories.

We walked in silence for a while watching as the sky faded to a deep magenta then darkened to midnight blue. Bright stars glittered before us, changing color and winking as if they were alive. And maybe they were. I was enjoying the silence and the way the warm, tropical air blew in off the water carrying the smell of salt and brine with it. Closing my eyes, I breathed in deep letting the wind rake through my hair and whip it around my face. I never wanted this moment to end. But then my stomach growled and I felt my cheeks get hot.

"Hungry?" Peter asked from beside me.

I snapped my eyes back open and glanced at the amused smirk on his face. "Apparently," I muttered realizing I hadn't eaten anything since I'd gotten there. "What kind of food do you eat here in Neverland?"

He shrugged. "Whatever we can pick or catch, I suppose."

"You hunt?"

"Of course we hunt. You don't get muscles like these from munching on carrots and broccoli," he said with a laugh and flexed his arms. I rolled my eyes but couldn't help stealing a glimpse at the hard ridges along his biceps. When I met his gaze again, an amused smile pulled one side of his mouth up. My ears burned.

Then a delightful aroma hit my nostrils and I found myself tilting my head back to catch another whiff. "Something smells delicious," I said with a sigh.

Peter still had the smile on his face but now his nose twitched as well. "Ah yes," he said. "The boys must have already taken care of dinner. Maybe you and I could go another time then." I nodded as the pleasant, barbecued aroma continued to take over my senses. My mouth started to water and Peter held his hand out to me. I took it without a word and the two of us soared into the sky, our noses leading us toward home.

Dinner that evening was amazing. It was some sort of meat but whether it was an animal I'd heard of before or an entirely new creature, I didn't know.

Of course everyone else scarfed down their food in seconds so I was the only one still eating when the sky darkened to bluish black. As I gnawed the last tasty morsel from the bone, Peter grabbed his guitar from behind the log he was sitting on and began strumming and humming softly. I recognized the tune immediately. Without the drums, electric guitar and blaring mics, Peter had transformed the heavy rock song he'd performed at Exile into a beautiful lullaby, amplified only by the acoustics created by the trees that surrounded us. Just a few minutes before, the lost boys had been rowdily pushing at each other, laughing and being loud but now they sat in silence, watching the fire, entranced by the song.

I dropped the bone I'd picked clean into the fire and closed my eyes. The music poured over me like sand and I quickly realized I was humming along. From beside me I could hear Pal's quiet harmonizing and I tilted my head a bit. As soon as I did, he grew quiet again and I cracked my eyes open. Peter's own eyes locked mine in a stare and I was unable to look away. He flashed the same mischievous grin he'd had during his set at Exile and the pace of my heart quickened. The fire seemed to grow hotter and brighter and everything else started to fade away into the shadows around us. I couldn't sense Pal next to me anymore or the other lost boys. It was only Peter and me in that circle. Us and his magical music. Me and those captivating green eyes that shined like stars. Finally, he averted his gaze to the fire and the trance was broken. I shook my head to clear the fog and found that the others were still lost in the music. What had just happened?

Fairies drifted down like little glowing snowflakes and rested on my body and the log I was sitting on. The strong scent of trees danced around under my nostrils as Ardo landed in my lap and started playing with one of the pine needles in her hair. Willow rested her scratchy bark covered body against my hand and let out a soft sigh as she swayed to the music.

I don't know how long we stayed like that listening in silence to Peter's strumming and humming. Time seemed to stand still. Even the forest was quiet as if the trees were captivated along with us.

Finally, the fog lifted when Peter paused to yawn into his arm. With a tired smile, he set the guitar down and rested his elbows on his knees. "I think it's time for bed." The lost boys groaned in protest and the fairies drifted back up toward the forest canopy in a harmonious chorus of sleepy sighs.

"Where do I sleep?" I asked before my own mouth stretched wide in a deep yawn.

Peter stood and held out his hand to help me up. "I can make up that couch for you in the living room since there aren't really any more beds." I took his hand and got to my feet.

"She can have my bed," Kai said as he climbed up onto the deck. The rest of the boys used the ramp.

"Where would you sleep?" I asked him.

The smirk he gave me earned him a jab in the ribs from Pal as he walked by him, "What? It was just an offer," he said rubbing his side. "She doesn't have to take it."

"I think the couch sounds great," I said smiling at Pal. He looked back at me through the eyeholes of his deer mask for a few seconds before disappearing into the tree fort.

The other three boys followed after Pal and Kai leaving Peter and I by ourselves next to the dying fire. I watched him with my arms wrapped around myself while he stamped out the remainder of the glowing coals. "So, Wynn," he said. "What do you think of Neverland?"

I breathed in deeply and the rich smells of the dying coals and the trees filled every nook and cranny of me. The branches overhead swayed and rustled in the soft, cool wind, dancing as if they were nocturnal creatures that were just beginning to stir. A mournful howl echoed through the forest from far away and soon more howls joined in causing the hairs on my neck and arms to stand on end. "I think," I finally breathed, "that I never want to leave this place."

Peter's mouth stretched slowly into a proud smile. "That could be arranged if you really want it to be."

I snorted. "Yeah, I wish."

Then Peter shrugged and started for the tree fort. I followed behind him up the ramp and stopped at the doorway. With one last look back out at the forest, tinged blue from the hour, I couldn't help but wonder what it would be like to call this place home.

Finally, I pushed the curtain aside and stepped through the doorway.

Chapter Five

Sunlight hit my eyelids causing me to roll over and stuff my face into the space between the cushion and the back of the couch. I'd fallen asleep several times in the living room in the past month and every time I'd forgotten to pull the shades closed the night before so this exact thing wouldn't happen. Apparently, this morning wasn't any different. Maybe Marty was awake and wouldn't mind getting up and pulling them shut for me. With my eyes still squeezed tightly shut, I rolled over and put my arm out in hopes of finding her sleeping on the floor like usual.

"Marty?" I groaned before my hand found the rough floorboards. Wait a second. Why didn't I feel carpet under my fingers?

My eyes snapped open and I gaped at my surroundings. I'd completely forgotten where I was.

But now the memories flooded back into my mind as I gazed around the inside of the tree fort. The sunlight filtered in through a window on the wall across from me. A curtain of beads and shells sliced through the light sending splintered fragments in every direction. It bounced off the many trinkets that covered the walls. Pieces of driftwood, small animal skulls, arrowheads, shells and a lot of things I didn't really recognize.

"Who's Marty?"

I snapped my head around to find Mika making his way down the ladder leading up to the loft. Finn followed close behind then dropped to the floor from a few feet up.

"Uh…" I didn't really have time to respond before both of them disappeared out the door.

Kai jumped down from the loft next, completely disregarding the ladder, and walked by. "Mornin' Wynnie," he said cheerfully. "How'd you sleep?"

"Fine, I gue—"

"You look terrible." he interrupted. "My offer still stands if you're interested in a comfy cot." Then he wiggled his eyebrows before scampering out after the twins, leaving me with my mouth still hanging open.

Russ came down next, pausing at the bottom of the ladder to stare at me intently with those gunmetal gray eyes of his. Finally, with a huff he growled up at Pal to hurry and stomped out of the room. Pal appeared at the top of the ladder, still wearing his deer mask – it didn't seem like he ever took it off – and made his way slowly down. As he passed me, his eyes met mine and crinkled as he smiled. I smiled back then watched the curtain sway to a stand still after he disappeared through it.

I swung my legs around so my feet rested on the floor and stretched my aching neck. Kai said I didn't look very good. Well, I didn't feel all that great either. Sleeping on a broken down couch wasn't ideal but look at the world I was in. I'd say it more than made up for it.

Laughter and voices from outside broke through my thoughts. "Last one to breakfast is a codfish!"

I smiled. Guess that's me.

My bones creaked like an old lady's when I sat up and slipped my feet into my boots. I wondered what Peter had planned for us today. Everyone else was already sitting around a crackling fire and stuffing their faces by the time I got outside and down the ramp.

Kai waved the leg of bird meat he held in his hand. "Hey codfish, we thought you fell back asleep."

I folded my arms against the morning chill as I made my way over to them and sat down on a rock between Pal and Finn. "What do you mean codfish?" I asked jokingly. "You were all already out here."

Kai shrugged. "You gotta be faster, I guess," he said and sank his teeth back into his breakfast.

Peter handed me a bird leg with an amused half-smile that seemed to be permanently fixed on his face.

"So what's on the agenda for today?" I asked before biting into the tender meat in my hands. Smoky and delicious.

Peter laughed. "We don't do agendas here," he explained. "The world is our playground. We do what we please, when we please, wherever we please."

"Yeah, even if it doesn't *please* anyone else here," a tiny voice recounted. I looked up to find Brucie drifting down, her little green arms crossed over her chest. She landed on my shoulder and I had to crane my neck back to focus on her.

I offered her a tiny piece of meat. She took it in her delicate little green hands and started eating. "So they like to wreak havoc?"

"Always," she groaned, her eyes widening for added emphasis.

I felt something land on my other shoulder and I turned my head to find Iris fussing with her leaf dress. "One time they convinced a bunch of silk pixies to wrap each of us up in webs while we were sleeping," she said throwing a glare in Peter's direction. "It took days to get all that sticky stuff out of my hair."

"It was hilarious though," he snickered. "They all looked like little floating cotton balls."

The other boys burst into laughter at the memory and I tried to hide my own giggles as I pictured it. Both Iris and Brucie fumed on my shoulders. Finally, the boys' laughter died down and they got back to eating.

A small pile of bones started growing in the fire and by the time the big bird was just a carcass, all of our bellies were full. I lay down long ways on the log and stared up at the blue sky peaking in through the trees. The morning chill had disappeared and now the sun shined down, creating heavenly rays that looked alive and warmed the clearing. I'd never experienced such a perfect morning back in LA. If this was the norm, I never wanted to leave.

"So what do you guys do for fun around here?" I asked after a few minutes of blissful silence. I felt Iris and Brucie stir from their lounging positions on my stomach.

"Besides pick on us?" Brucie asked sarcastically. "Probably nothing."

Finn let out a snort from his place on ground below me. "That's not all we do," he said then cracked on eye open so he was looking at me. "Ever play manhunt before?"

I shrugged and looked at Peter. "What's manhunt?"

At those words, the other lost boys all jumped up from their respective lounging places and started telling me excitedly about this game called manhunt. I couldn't understand a single word so I just stared at the two fairies on my lap.

"Simmer down you bunch of morons!" Peter yelled and the boys immediately shut up. "She's not going to learn anything with you flapping your jaws at her all at once." Then he smiled at me. "It would be much more beneficial if we show her."

I felt my heart falter at the sight of those pearly white teeth of his and tried to play it off but my body betrayed me and I felt my ears get hot. Surely, they were bright red. Luckily, the other boys were far too preoccupied with wanting to play the game.

Before I had a chance to react, Kai stood up, gave me a wink then shot for the edge of the clearing, and disappeared in the dense forest. A beat later, Mika, Finn, Pal and Russ took off after him at an equally inhuman speed.

"Where are they going?" I asked, standing up. Brucie and Iris tumbled down my front until they were both able to catch themselves. "Sorry," I whispered when they both got in my face before shooting up to the canopy again.

"Well, Wyndy," Peter said as he strolled around the

fire over to me, "the game is simple. We're the hunters and Kai is the huntee."

"So, catch Kai?"

Peter held his hand out. "Told you it was simple." I put my fingers in his and suddenly we propelled forward like we'd been shot out of a gun and flew through the tiny space between two trees into the woods. Everything flew by in a blur of green and we quickly overtook the other boys.

"Isn't this cheating?" I yelled over the wind rushing through my ears.

Peter smiled. "Nah, I call it having an advantage!"

The sounds of complaint faded behind us as we pulled further ahead. Pretty soon I saw a small figure fly through the space between two trees and land in the branches of another. Kai really did move like a squirrel.

"There!" I yelled, pointing up at his silhouette. We lifted higher until we were in the thick of the branches, chasing after Kai as he darted from tree to tree. I could see the ears of his mask sticking up above his head. We were almost on him when he suddenly dropped to the ground and Peter had to skid to a halt to keep from slamming into a trunk.

"You alright?" he asked out of breath. I nodded, equally as breathless though mine was out of fear more than exhaustion. "We almost had the little bugger," he growled before gently lowering us back down to the forest floor.

"What now?" I finally asked my legs still quivering.

"Well, usually if they can get away from you long enough to hide, that's when it becomes a real manhunt. Otherwise it's just a glorified game of tag."

"You guys lose him?"

We turned around as the rest of the boys ran up, slowing and coming to a stop in front of us. "How'd you lose him, Pan?" Mika asked whacking him on the shoulder.

"Yeah, you usually catch them right off the bat," Finn agreed swatting him in the other arm.

"Hey," Peter laughed. "Okay I wasn't going as fast as I usually do, because of uh…"

All eyes fell on me and I felt myself go pale. My head snapped around so I could glare at Peter. "Hey, I didn't ask you to go slow," I said crossing my arms. "It's not like you had to worry about me keeping up with you."

"I know," he said scratching the back of his neck uncomfortably. "I just didn't want you to get hurt, is all."

Russ let out an annoyed scoff and rolled his eyes. I furrowed my brow. "I can take it," I said quickly. "I'm not a little girl."

"I don't know," Mika said, pulling his badger mask down over his face. "As far as girls go, you're pretty little."

"And what makes you the expert on girls, Mika?" I asked raising an eyebrow.

Mika shrugged and looked at Peter. "I guess he'd know more than I would."

My stomach twisted again and Peter punched him hard in the arm causing him to shut up immediately. "Alright, so Kai got away," he said trying to change the subject. "What's the plan?"

I listened carefully, trying not to live up, or down, to the fact that I was a lot smaller than everyone else.

Even Pal, who was the shortest, had at least five inches on me. I had some proving to do. The plan was simple enough. Peter would take to the air and scan the forest from a top view while the others would spread out down on the ground. Pal and Russ were to go toward the ocean, Mika was to go left and Finn to go right. That left me with Peter again.

"I want to help down here this time," I said before they could agree and break off.

All of them looked at me in silence and again I felt my ears turning red. It sure is weird being surrounded by a group of guys that could give underwear models a run for their money. "I uh…I want to actually help find him this time."

The corner of Peter's mouth twitched. "Alright, well which way do you want to go, Wynn?"

I thought hard for a second. If I were Kai and wanted to throw everyone off my trail, where would I go? Finally, I looked back up to meet his eyes. "I'll head back the way we came."

"He's never circled back before," Russ said matter-of-factly.

"All the more reason you wouldn't expect it," I replied, matching his condescending tone.

Peter clapped his hands together and we all looked at him again. "Alright, then let's get to it, gang."

"I want to go with Wynn." We all looked to Pal who was looking down at the ground. Slowly, he lifted his head and made eye contact with me through the holes in his mask. "I think she could be right."

Russ didn't even try to hide his disgust as he rolled his eyes and trudged off in the opposite direction. What was his problem anyway? Peter shrugged then gave me a wink and pushed off into the air.

"Hope you're right, Wynn," Mika said clapping me on the arm before pulling his badger mask down over his face.

"Yeah, Russ needs to be taken down a notch," Finn agreed pulling his hare mask down too. Then he cocked his bunny head to the side. "Take good care of Pal. Don't let him get lost."

"Shut up," Pal said digging his toe into the dirt.

The twins laughed then started off in their opposite directions leaving Pal and I alone. I turned to him and smiled enthusiastically. "Shall we?" I asked. Pal's mask lifted a bit as he smiled at me then he nodded and the two of us started back toward camp.

I'd never gone on a hike or visited any of the forests on Earth but I'm sure they were nothing compared to the Neverwood Forest. The trees were all lush and grew high above our heads, creating a ceiling of limbs and fir needles. Down in the depths of it there wasn't much light, just the wide leafy ceiling broken by glimmers of blue sky. Sure there were forests back where I was from, but this one felt different. As we walked through it, creating our own path since there wasn't one already worn into the ground, I could feel the difference. I could feel the magic. Everything glowed a little brighter. Everything was a little greener.

It was a quiet walk, both of us comfortable in the silence. This gave me time to think. To finally process a bit of everything that had happened since I'd gotten there the day before.

I never could have imagined I'd be experiencing Great Gran's stories first hand. I used to love listening to them. The way she described Neverland was so poetic. But now that I was actually there, I couldn't think of any other way to possibly put into words this magical and captivating place. A tree shifted in the distance causing me to focus on it. It was only a sapling, sticking about three feet out of the dirt. A small gasp escaped my mouth when the thin tree pulled itself up out of the ground. The root was big and round and white and I watched in awed horror as arms came up out of the earth on either side, grasping at the dirt. The white thing wasn't just a root, it was the head of the creature that was now wriggling free of the strings that attached it to the ground.

"Pal." My voice was shaky, barely a whisper. "What is that?" I asked gripping his arm tightly.

I couldn't look away from the pale creature as it shook the dirt off its little naked body. It turned its bulbous head to look my way. The thing didn't have a face but somehow it still managed to stare curiously at me.

"A tree spirit," he said, his voice tinkling like wind chimes. "It probably thinks the spot it picked is too crowded and shaded from the sun. It's going to go find a better place to grow."

My eyes didn't leave it as it twirled and danced away, its branch-like arms and twiggy fingers swaying in the wind. Finally, when it disappeared, we started walking again. "Are all these trees like that one?"

Pal kept his head down, eyes on his feet as we went. "Yeah, I think at one point they were," he said with a shrug, the excitement in his voice no longer there. "Peter told me once that when the trunks get too heavy, the spirits detach themselves and go off to find a new place to grow. They're responsible for all the trees here. They were here before anyone else."

It was weird trying to imagine the beginning of Neverland. The forest felt ancient and mysterious like a legend, and I had no doubts it was. But to think that at one point these trees weren't there. That this place hadn't always existed.

"Come on," I finally said after we'd been walking in silence again for a little while. "We'll never catch Kai at this rate." Then I broke into a fast jog.

Pal ran just a few paces behind me. I'd seen him run when we'd raced them on the way to Mermaid Lagoon so I could tell he was holding back. I wondered what it would be like to be able to run as fast as they could. According to the books and the movies – though I didn't know how accurate they were – all the lost boys and Peter had been human at one point. How long would I need to be there before I gained any sort of super speed?

We broke through the trees and into the clearing a few minutes later. The fairies buzzed about like little lightning bugs, glittering in the air around us. One of them drifted down to me and hovered in front of my face.

"Looking for squirrelly?" Nyk asked as she crossed her arms over her black beetle chest piece. It reflected the colors of the trees, shimmering a magnificent bottle green color. "He's up at the top of the tree."

I smiled thanks then looked to Pal. "How do we get up to the top?" I asked him.

His eyes sparkled excitedly. I have a feeling the other boys didn't ask him for help much. "There's a latch in the loft that opens up into the branches. I'll show you," he said and walked past me, an unmistakable bounce in his step.

I followed close behind, making my way up the ladder once we'd gotten inside the tree fort. Pal jumped up and grabbed onto a rope that dangled from the ceiling and a door swung open, flooding the place with dappled sunlight that filtered in through the branches. A rope ladder unraveled, ending in a heap on the floor at our feet. "This way," he said then started up the ladder.

I followed after him, gripping the flimsy rungs and not looking down until I'd made it a pretty long way up the tree. When I did look down, my vision became spotty. The fairies floated below us now like I was looking down at a sea of stars and farther below that was the ground. The hard, compacted dirt ground. One slip and I'd tumble down and surely break every bone in my body. With a quick shake to clear my head, I started up after Pal again, who was gaining distance with every step he took.

The climb went on forever and my muscles started to ache. "Do you really think he's up here?" I called up to Pal, wincing when a stray thread poked into my tender palm.

"Hopefully," Pal called back. "Or else Nyk is in big trouble."

Suddenly, the rope jerked and my eyes shot up toward the upper branches. A blur of reddish, brown fur rushed down to the left of the ladder, bypassing Pal and causing him to almost fall. I gripped the rope harder. "Tag him, Wynn!" he yelled, his voice muffled by the mask over his face.

My eyes locked on Kai's beady brown ones as he

stared at me through his squirrel mask. He wasn't very far above me now but too far away from the ladder for me to reach out and touch him. I had one shot and I needed to make it count. His eyes darted to the branch directly to my left. Surely, this was the one he was going to grab onto next. Trying not to think too much about it, I bent my knees and launched myself off the ladder, stretching my arms out to catch myself on the branch. Kai's eyes grew wide as we drew closer to each other and mine got bigger as I watched the branch graze my fingers. Too low.

Suddenly, I was falling and a scream just barely bubbled up my throat when my arms wrapped around something hard. I don't know when I'd closed my eyes but now I opened them and looked up to find myself grasping one of Kai's legs in a death grip while he held onto the branch above him.

"You alright, Wynnie?" he asked using one hand to nudge his mask up onto his head.

My breaths were quick and shallow and I couldn't stop shaking as I tried to respond but my words weren't coherent.

"What was that?"

"Caught you," I whimpered.

The worry stricken look on his face was immediately replaced with a wide smile and he offered his free hand to me. I took it and let him pull me up onto a branch next to him so I could reach the ladder.

"Wynn!" I looked up to see Pal peering down at me. The blank stare of the deer didn't match the worry in his voice. "Are you okay?"

"Yeah," I cracked. "I'm fine."

I climbed back through the hole first, followed by

Kai and finally Pal and we all walked out of the tree fort together. As soon as my boots hit the dirt, Peter, Russ and the twins stepped out of the woods.

"Well, look who had the right hunch," Finn said with a smile and put up a hand to give me a high five.

Mika put up a hand too and I slapped them both at the same time, pride rushing through me like adrenaline. Peter smiled "Who's up for another round?" he asked and glanced at Russ who silently fumed away from everyone else.

I hadn't had this kind of fun since I was little. All the kids in our cul-de-sac used to meet up in the middle of the road and play until it got dark and the streetlights came on. Back when children actually played together. Back before every eight year old owned an iPhone.

Playing manhunt with the guys brought me back to those times and any time I thought about it, my heart ached a bit with longing. Longing for the innocence. For seeing people as friends no matter what they looked like or how crazy their relatives might seem. If only things could stay that way. In Neverland it seemed they did. What I wouldn't give to take a bit of Neverland back with me. Better yet, if only I could bring everyone I loved there to live.

By the time the sun started to dip from its highest point, we were all sitting around the fire again, Peter strumming on his guitar while the others argued about who won and who lost. I just lay there across a log in exhausted bliss and listened. My muscles ached like I'd just completed a great workout and sweat and dirt coated my skin. I'd never felt like this before. Like there was something wild deep down in me that had finally come out of hibernation. It was only my second day there and I felt like I was home. LA and its lights and smog had nothing on the stars and fresh air.

The boys burst out laughing and I sat up to join them. I smiled as Kai lifted his mask back on top of his head. "So you say you guys got those from the Indians?" I asked.

Kai nodded. "Yeah, Tiger Lily can tell what animal you're like just by looking at you. And they have these masks made up for you already and everything. I don't know why she thinks I'm like a squirrel though."

"Yeah," I agreed sarcastically. "I can't imagine how she could come up with that one."

"Personally, I think I'm more like a panther," he said with a growl. "Or a Komodo dragon."

"Or a codfish," Peter added in between strums on his guitar.

The rest of the boys burst out into more fits of laughter falling backwards off their seats and landing in the dirt on their backs, all but Kai, who glared at Peter, and Pal, who continued to study his hands, though I knew he was smiling. Even Russ was holding his stomach, doubled over.

I smiled too though I guess I didn't find it near as funny as they all did. When the laughter died down, I finally turned to Peter. "Do you think Tiger Lily has a mask for me?" I asked him.

He peered at me curiously. "You want to meet Tiger Lily?"

"Sure," I shrugged. "Then I could be cool like the rest of you."

"Well then," he started and set down his guitar. "Looks like we're going on an adventure."

The rest of the boys whooped excitedly and jumped to their feet, pulling their masks down over their faces. Russ pulled his down too and stared at me with the fox's mischievous eyes. With Kai in the lead, they disappeared quickly into the trees. Pal trailed behind at his own speed. Their hollers faded quickly into the distance leaving Peter and I alone again in the camp.

"Those boys are a handful," I said sighing exhaustedly for dramatic effect.

Peter smiled warmly. "Try putting up with them for a hundred plus years, then we can talk." I smiled back and the two of us started after the others into the woods.

After several minutes, a couple fairies floated lazily between our heads. The glimpse of fiery hair and rainbow wings told me it was Ember and Lyssa. What were they doing out of camp? I looked behind me and saw a line of white lights floating along, reaching almost all the way back to camp. When I turned to look forward again, Ember was in my face.

"You guys don't have to come with us, you know," I said to her, watching as her blazing red hair danced like flames in the wind.

"I know," she shrugged her tiny shoulders. "But we're curious to see what animal Tiger Lily gives you."

"I think it will be something cool," Lyssa added in landing on my shoulder and taking one of her colorful wings in her hands.

I chuckled. "Like what?"

"I don't know," she said shyly. "Maybe it will be like a dragonfly or something."

"A dragonfly?" I asked wrinkling my nose. Peter snickered from beside me. "Why do you think I'm a dragonfly?"

"Dragonflies are spunky," Lyssa said with a smile. "I know a few and I'd say you've got some spunk."

Ember landed on my shoulder next to her. "It's also the animal for purity."

Peter let out a loud snort and I threw him a glare. "Hey, you don't know anything about me," I said.

He scratched the back of his neck and tried to contain his laughter. "I've had my eye on you for a while," he said. "There's nothing pure about the way you dance at those clubs." Then he flicked the bottom of my tunic, "or the way you dress." I swatted his hand away. "What? I'm not complaining. Just saying you're definitely not a dragonfly."

Ember and Lyssa put their tiny hands to their chins as they thought. Then suddenly Ember sprang up. "A lobster!"

My eyes grew wide. "A lobster?"

"Yeah," she nodded excitedly. "They represent nobility and strength." I could feel a smile pulling at my mouth. She thought I was noble and strong after knowing me for only a short time. Then Ember leaned in and wiggled her itty-bitty eyebrows. "And sensuality."

Peter was on the ground laughing and clutching his stomach before I even had time to react. When I finally did swivel around to face him, I jabbed him hard in the ribs with my toe. "What's your animal?" I sneered. "A freaking hyena?"

Finally, he got up and brushed himself off. "Actually, no. But that's a good one." He didn't answer my question though as the two of us continued through the woods

The fairies stayed silent after that, Ember fuming a little on my shoulder at both Peter's and my reactions. Had she been serious? Did she really think I was like a lobster?

Chapter Six

The boys had run so far ahead, that we didn't see any of them on our whole trek. I didn't mind too much though. Sure, Kai, Mika and Finn had been nice enough, even Pal with his very few words but I didn't think I could put up with Russ or his rotten attitude for more than a few minutes.

"So what's up with Russ, anyway?" I finally asked and Ember and Lyssa fluttered their wings uncomfortably.

Peter didn't say anything for a bit but chewed his lip thoughtfully. Finally, he opened his mouth with a smack. "Did Wendy ever tell you about what happened after she left?" he asked turning his head to look at me.

I tried to remember everything she'd said. Great Gran had told me so many stories I couldn't keep track of them all. As I got older, I'd stopped listening so closely so I was having a hard time recalling the details. "You might have to refresh my memory," I finally said.

"Are you hungry?" he asked and slowly rose into the air.

As if on cue, my stomach let out a growl. "I guess I am," I said feeling my cheeks flush.

A warm smile stretched across Peter's face. "You wait here," he said then rose into the air and took off through the trees.

I turned to Ember and Lyssa and saw that they were staring at me. "What?" I finally asked.

"You are kind of red like a lobster," Lyssa said thoughtfully.

Peter sank back to the ground only a few minutes later, his arms full of a bunch of blue, round balls. I watched confused as he sat down on the dirt in front of me, letting them spill out of his arms and roll across the ground. He looked up at me expectantly. "Well? Are you gonna sit or what?" he finally asked. Ember and Lyssa hopped back off my shoulder to join the other fairies above our heads again and then I sat carefully on the ground. A bright blue ball with skin like an orange rested near my hand and I picked it up carefully. Turning the thing in my palm, it really looked like an orange. It had the little dimples and the shine, even the smell of an orange. Though there was also a faint smell of coconut and flowers. "Go ahead," Peter said ripping the peel off his own to reveal darker blue flesh inside. "It won't hurt you, I promise," he added with a smile. Then it quickly disappeared. "Unless you're allergic to suavas."

"I've never eaten a suava," I said still turning it over in my hand.

Peter shrugged. "Well then, I guess it could hurt you. It most likely won't though. I've only ever witnessed one allergic reaction to the fruit before." He popped another piece in his mouth. "It's not pretty," he said with his mouth full.

"What happened?"

Peter wiped a drip of dark blue juice from his chin. "Well, let's just say if you start feeling like your eyeballs are going to melt out of your face after eating the suava, stop eating the suava."

I looked down again at the blue fruit in my hand. He'd only ever witnessed one allergic reaction when someone, whoever it was, ate one of these *suavas*. What were the odds I could be allergic too? There was only one way to find out. I dug my fingernail into the tough skin until I felt it give then I pulled, releasing a fragrant citrus and floral smell and revealing the dark blue flesh underneath. I didn't even want to eat it, just look at it all day. It was such a brilliant blue, I didn't think I would ever see something this color that looked so delicious and wasn't in the form of some hard candy.

I pulled the whole thing apart and it split into segments just like an orange does. Slowly, I pulled a small section from the cluster and brought it up to my mouth. It burst when I bit down, filling my mouth with tropical, natural, sweet flavors. I closed my eyes as I chewed picking out each note with my taste buds. Orange, coconut, anise, honeysuckle. It was all there, all wrapped up in a beautiful blue, juicy package.

When I opened my eyes again, Peter was staring at me with his head tilted sideways. "So? Your eyeballs feel like they're going to liquefy and melt off your face?"

I shook my head. "This is freaking amazing," I uttered around a mouthful of fruit.

He smiled proudly. "Alright," he said. "I'll take that as a no."

"So what were you saying happened after my Great Gran left here?" I asked before popping another piece of fruit into my mouth.

The look on his face turned serious. "Right," he muttered then set down the suava he had been holding and wiped his hands on his pants. "Before Wendy left, the lost boys and I were part of James's crew on his ship."

"Hook?" I asked.

Peter nodded.

My eyes widened a bit. "Really?" I finally asked. "You guys were actually friends like Great Gran said?" He nodded. "Wow, someone needs to alert the media."

"I was actually like co-captain, I guess."

I was already half way done with my first suava. "So, what happened?"

"Your great grandmother happened."

My hand froze half way to my mouth and I narrowed my eyes. "What did she do?" I asked him.

He shrugged exaggeratedly. "I haven't the slightest idea!" he admitted. "Things were great. James was my best friend. We spent our days exploring the waters around the island, flirting a bit with the mermaids. At night I'd take him flying and we would explore the skies. The lost boys were part of the crew and they loved learning the ways of the ship. Kai spent most of his time in the crow's nest or just climbing up the poles and sails. It was all great."

Slowly, I picked apart the rest of my suava. "Well, what happened?" I asked not looking up from my blue juice stained fingers.

"After I took Wendy back home and returned, something changed," Peter explained. "I got back to James' ship and the thing was trashed. It looked like there had been some sort of fight while I was gone. There were wood splinters and bits of blood everywhere. And the sails were all slashed."

My mouth was hanging open at the thought of what he'd seen. "Was anyone dead?"

"I didn't find any bodies," Peter said shaking his head. "But my boys were all missing."

"Well obviously they didn't stay missing or else I never would have met them," I said.

Now he looked up to meet my eyes. "I'll get to that," he said. "Anyway, I searched the ship, I searched the sky. I even had the mermaids search the water."

"Nothing?"

"Nothing."

"So I went on land and followed footprints and drag marks up into the woods and I'd almost reached the tree line when I was attacked."

"You were attacked?" I asked, my mouth still gaping open.

Peter stood up really quick, turned around and shrugged off his pirate jacket. I couldn't help but notice how toned and tan his back was and for a minute I didn't even know what he was trying to show me. Light filtered down from between the trees making him glow. His skin was sun-kissed to a warm caramel color and there was a tiny brown mole on his left shoulder blade. My eyes drifted down from the mole and that was when I saw what he was trying to show me. I stood up too and carefully touched the long, shiny scar that trailed down one side of his spine. It wasn't very noticeable and I would like to say that was why I didn't notice it at first but it would be a lie. The scar was very faint. Just a thin silvery line, almost like the first thread of a spider web.

"Is this from Hook?" I asked still touching the scar.

Peter turned back around and put his jacket on again. "Yeah," he said. "The codfish got me with a knife when I wasn't looking." Then he pulled out his own knife from the sheath in his belt. "But I got him back. That's why we call him Hook now." He said this with a hint of sadness in his voice and twirled the knife in his hand. The blade caught the light and glinted for a second, casting a reverse shadow across his face.

"So what happened to the lost boys then?" I asked unconsciously rubbing the skin around my wrist. I couldn't imagine the pain of getting my hand sliced off.

Peter put the knife away then bent down and picked up a couple of the untouched suavas. "I found them about half a mile inland," he said and handed me another one of the blue citrus fruits.

The two of us continued walking with the fairies trailing silently behind us. "So, whose blood had that been back on the ship? Did any of the lost boys get hurt?" I asked digging my fingernails into the suava skin until it gave.

"Well when I finally found them, they were all kinds of beat up. Pal and Russ took the worst of it."

"Does Pal keep his mask on because of what happened?" I asked thinking of the way he seemed to stay out of the horseplay. Could it be because he didn't want his mask ripped off to reveal some hideous deformity?

Peter nodded. "Yeah his face got cut up pretty bad by another one of Hook's crew. I don't know why he still wears the mask though. It happened years ago and we've all seen him without his mask. It's really not that bad anymore."

I put a segment in my mouth and bit down slowly, letting the juice spray the back of my throat. "What about Russ?" I asked with the fruit still between my teeth.

"Russ almost didn't make it," Peter said and brushed a tree limb out of our path. I hadn't even noticed that the forest was getting thicker and harder to walk through. I couldn't see very far in front of us.

I ducked under a tree branch and stumbled over a root almost simultaneously. It seemed to be getting darker "What do you mean he almost didn't make it?"

"Well, like I said." Peter grabbed my arm to keep me steady. "He was in pretty bad shape. His side was filleted open like a fish and an artery in his arm had been sliced so he was losing a lot of blood."

Again my mouth fell open. "But he's fine now. What happened? How did he survive?"

Peter reached his fingers up to the cord of leather around his neck and gripped a tiny pouch dangling in the center. I hadn't even noticed it there before. But looking closely, I could now see what all the things were. The pouch was in the center, a few different sized teeth, from different animals I presume, hung on either side and then a couple brightly colored beads, one blue, one green, were tied on either end. "What's in the pouch?" I asked and popped another segment of suava in my mouth.

"Tink left me a bit of her magic dust behind."

"Tink as in Tinker Bell?" I asked him raising an eyebrow.

Peter nodded. "Mmhmm. I'm sure you met her."

I shook my head and tossed the empty suava skin over my shoulder. One of the fairies behind me yelped and I looked back apologetically as Aubri glared and rubbed her head. "Sorry," I winced at her then I turned back to Peter. "How would I have met her?"

"She wanted to go back to Earth with Wendy and have a life as a normal person. Find love or whatever. I'm sure you met her. Wendy said they stayed close."

Tinker Bell. Tinker Bell. Tinker Bell. I didn't remember meeting anyone named Tinker Bell. Or Tink. Or...wait. "Tina?" I finally whispered. "Great Gran's crazy friend Tina Belmont from the nursing home was Tinker Bell?"

Peter stopped walking and looked at me with pursed lips and hard eyes. "Was?"

Now I averted my own eyes and bit the inside of my cheek. "Yeah," I finally stammered. "She grew old and got sick and died like eight years ago." Peter's face contorted for a second and he looked down at the ground.

"Was she happy?" he asked me, his voice a little bit rough.

I brushed my fingers against his and was surprised when he clutched onto them. "Yeah, Peter," I finally said. "She lived a long exciting life and she got married and had kids and grandkids." Then I bit my lip again as Marty's face flashed through my mind. "And now I'm best friends with one of her great grandkids"

When Peter looked up again at me his eyes were glassy but then I watched the tears fade away. A sad smile stretched across his face. "Well, I'm glad she was happy," he said and squeezed my fingers.

As the two of us began walking again, he didn't let go of my hand. We were silent for a bit and when I looked back, the few fairies, whose faces I could see, looked sad like they were remembering Tinker Bell. Aubri drifted up near to me and I turned to her. "Hey," I said with a smile. "Do you want to hear about some of the crazy antics my Great Gran got into with Tink?" Aubri's light glowed a bit brighter and she straightened up giving me a nod and a curious smile. "Well," I started, tapping my finger to my chin to get a giggle out of her. "Let's see, there was this one time Great Gran and Tina managed to get a hold of a couple mechanical chairs and raced each other down the main hallway at the home." This got many of them giggling.

"A home as in their house?" Ardo asked playing with one of the pine needles in her hair.

"Not quite," I replied thoughtfully. "It's a nursing home. It's where older people go when they can't take care of themselves anymore."

"That sounds terrible," Brucie said and shook her tiny head sadly.

I smiled reassuringly. "It's okay, really. A bunch of older people live together in a big building and they get to hang out and do stuff together all day."

"So Wendy and Tink didn't get lonely?" Willow

asked from beside my ear.

I shook my head. "Nope. They had each other for a long time."

Aubri sat down Indian style on my shoulder and propped her chin up on her hands. "Tell us more about the things Wendy and Tinker Bell did together."

As I told story after story that my Great Gran had told me, the fairies flew up to join us. Soon, the little balls of light, each one growing brighter as their spirits lifted, surrounded Peter and me. I told about the time the two of them had managed to escape from the home and went on a bit of an adventure. Really it was just a lot of walking around the block they were on and knocking on people's doors. Sometimes they would say they were Jehovah's witnesses, sometimes they would say trick or treat and sometimes they would try and convince the people living there that they were their long lost relatives and they had come to be reunited at last. After a while, I ran out of stories and they began telling me all about the things Tinker Bell did with them there in Neverland. It was weird hearing about this woman I had grown up knowing with a whole different life. A life that had gone on so much longer than her life on earth.

By the time we were finished with our stories, it was almost pitch dark out. The fairies dimmed themselves, lighting us and making the area around us glow with a soft white light. "Why does it get dark so early here?" I asked Peter feeling his thumb make slow circles on the skin on the back of my hand.

"The days in Neverland are a lot shorter than Earth days," he explained. "It keeps things interesting."

"How long has it been back on Earth?" I asked

wondering if Marty was going crazy trying to find me.

He must have sensed the worry in my voice. "There's nothing to worry about, Wynn. It's only been a couple minutes. The song we were dancing to probably isn't even over yet."

"Weird," I whispered under my breath and squinted into the distant darkness. I could see a soft, reddish glow coming from the trees up ahead. "What's that?" I asked pointing toward the light.

Peter squeezed my hand. "We're almost to the Indian camp."

Just a few steps further and I started hearing noises coming from far off in front of us. There was a steady beat like a drum, along with the familiar whooping of some of the lost boys and a couple shouts from unfamiliar voices.

It didn't take us much longer to reach the camp. When we did finally step out of the trees, I didn't let go of Peter's hand. Instead I clutched it tighter. I'm not lying when I say that the Indians were rather intimidating. Almost all of them were men that towered over me. All had big arms like they could wrestle a lion and win and their reddish skin, made even redder with the glow of the giant fire, was painted with dark colored lines that crisscrossed and connected at points. I think what made each of them the most menacing were the masks covering their faces as they danced around the fire.

One wore the face of a bear with giant fangs; the skin on its nose was scrunched up like it was about to attack. Another had on a wolf mask, its teeth bared and eyes still gleaming with the thrill of the kill. As the man made his way around the circle, I saw that the mask actually wrapped all the way around and over his head so it was more like a helmet. The hair on the back of its neck stood straight up while the ears were plastered back to its skull. I didn't know though if this was actually how the thing looked when they killed it or if it was all done artificially to make it look more menacing. Either way, I was terrified of that man and made a mental note to stay away from him. Among the other masks was some sort of cat – I'm guessing a lynx – also an elk head complete with a large tangle of antlers that reached toward the sky like branches, bleached white by the sun and too many other ferocious animals to name.

Almost all the lost boys were dancing around the fire with the Indian men. Even wearing their masks, they didn't in the least bit fit in. The biggest one there was Russ and even he looked like a lanky little kid compared to even the slightest Indian man. It took me a second to find Pal but then my eyes finally settled on him sitting on a log. It didn't surprise me that he had separated himself from the rest of the group. Even being a lost boy for as long as he had been, it seemed like he still didn't know how to be one. Or maybe he was different before whatever happened to his face. I wished I could see what he was hiding. I bet it wasn't something worth being ashamed of.

A man sat on a log near Pal but facing toward the dancing circle, banging out a steady beat on a drum that rested between his knees. Next to him sat the most beautiful girl I had ever seen, and living in Los Angeles, I'd seen some pretty beautiful people. She looked about my age. Her skin was a silky caramel brown and her hair, a richer shade, like dark chocolate syrup spilling down over her shoulders and pooling into a puddle on her lap. Over her head, she wore a white tiger helmet and the mouth was open so you could see her face. Her dark eyes were two perfect almonds and her mouth was small and full. Even under the layers of fur and leather covering her body, I could tell that she had the figure most men dream about. When her eyes locked on Peter, a smile pulled her perfect little mouth up and she stood. I glanced sideways at him and saw his eyes fix on her but not quite with the same "awe inspired" gaze that was in my eyes.

When the girl stopped in front of us, I saw how much taller than me she really was. I shifted uncomfortably as her eyes drifted over me for just a second before settling once again on Peter. "Welcome, friend," she purred, her voice dripping from her lips like warm maple syrup. Then she glanced at me again. "Friends," she corrected herself a tad coldly.

"Hey, Tiger Lily," Peter said easily and put the hand that was not holding mine on her bare, perfect shoulder. "This is Wendy's great granddaughter, Wynn. Wynn, Tiger Lily."

I croaked out a small hi and Tiger Lily nodded at me quickly before turning back to him again. "Well what brings such a beautiful boy to our camp tonight? Are we due for another hunting trip?"

I clutched Peter's hand tighter. I didn't know if "hunting trip" meant something different than actually hunting, but judging by the fire in Tiger Lily's brown eyes and the half smile on her lips, I had a feeling it did.

Not quite," Peter smiled back then turned to me.

"Wynn here wants a mask."

Again, Tiger Lily glanced at me, though now her eyes were cold and dark, the fire that had been in them just moments ago, completely stamped out. Not even coals remained. "Of course she does," she said, then an equally cold smile appeared on her face again. "Won't you come join the celebration, Wynn?" She held out her hand for me to take. I hesitated at first, picturing it more like a tiger's paw with claws that desired to dig into the soft skin of my wrist and pull me into that giant tiger mouth with its giant tiger teeth. Then reluctantly, I put my hand in hers and she closed her warm fingers around mine, pulling me behind her toward the fire and the dancing men. I hadn't even felt Peter's hand slip out of my other one, probably because it was numb from clutching his fingers so tightly. But he didn't follow. Instead, he strolled over to the man banging on the drum and sat down next to him. Tiger Lily finally let go of me when we stood directly in front of the fire.

I could feel the flames warming my face and dancing across my skin. It felt nice after that last bit of our trek that we'd made in the darkness. The night is a bit colder in the Neverwood Forest than out on the beach.

Tiger Lily leaned in close and whispered in my ear. "Look deep into the fire." she smelled sweet and musky and smoky, the way I picture the moon would smell if I could smell it. Doing as she said, I focused my eyes on the flames as they licked the night sky, dancing harshly, violently in the pit. "Look deeper," she said and pointed toward the coals glowing red and white at the base of the fire. I focused my attention on the coals now, watching as the colors shifted over them like cloud shadows over the ground on a sunny day.

"What am I looking for?" I finally asked after watching the shifting colors for a good twenty seconds.

"Your animal."

Just as she said those words, I caught something feathery and dark flit out of my peripheral vision. When I jerked my eyes toward the movement, it was gone. Or maybe it was just the coals playing tricks on me. Either way, my eyes were beginning to water from staring at the bright light for so long and I had to look away. I hadn't even noticed that Peter joined the man with the drum and was now blowing softly into a four-reeded pipe. A soft, raspy sound escaped as he rocked back and forth, his eyes closed, lost in the music. He really was a beautiful boy.

"You saw it," Tiger Lily said crossing her arms over her chest, her voice sounding a bit surprised.

I shook my head. "I didn't see anything," I replied. "It was just the fire."

Tiger Lily's mouth curled into a smile. "I know what you saw. And I know why you saw it." I looked at her to find she was looking at Peter. Her eyes had that glow to them again. "Let us start the ceremony."

The music stopped playing, the men stopped dancing. Everything stopped and all eyes turned to us. Even Pal looked up from his hands and focused on her. I suddenly felt nervous, more nervous, as all the eyes watched me. Tiger Lily put her hand on my shoulder and scanned the spectators. "Let us eat," she said then motioned toward a canvas tent and two

Indian men walked out with a cooked animal hanging on a stick between them. The lost boys all let out a cheer and left the fire to go sit in the circle where the men brought the animal. Tiger Lily took a hold of my arm and pulled me toward the circle as well. She sat down next to Peter and tugged me down onto the seat on the other side of her. I felt a rock form in my stomach. I never should have said I wanted to come.

One of the men took a knife and started cutting off pieces of the animal. Another took the pieces and handed them out to each of us. I held mine in my hand and studied it. The skin was dark brown and crispy and the inside was white and juicy and delicious. When I took a bite, flavors burst on my tongue. Smoke and hickory and sugar and salt.

After we had all eaten our fill and the animal was only a carcass, Tiger Lily whispered something into an Indian man's ear then stood with him. I watched the man walk over and disappear into another tent, only to reappear again a few moments later carrying something under a tan cloth.

"Wynn's animal has been one of the easiest to determine since James was given the crocodile and Peter given the hawk." Then she turned to me with a warm smile. "I could see it the moment I laid eyes on you."

I smiled back, the rock beginning to lift from my stomach. Maybe I had misjudged Tiger Lily. Maybe she really wasn't as vicious as her first name. But rather sweet and delicate like her second. The man holding the object under the cloth came over and placed it on Tiger Lily's outstretched palms. Something long and pointed jutted out from the middle. A beak of some kind. Maybe I was going to get a bird. Maybe she was going to pull off the cloth and present me with something beautiful. A dove? A humming bird? Maybe an owl or a sparrow or a peacock?

"I present you, Wynn," she said still smiling, her fingers pinching the center of the cloth, "with your animal." Then she pulled the cloth off as everyone else cheered and hollered and stamped their feet and beat the drum.

I stared at my mask in her hand as the cover drifted gently to the ground and settled in the dirt. My eyes glossed over the shiny black feathers, over the dark, small pointed beak that was slightly open like it was still trying to call out. Then I looked up at Tiger Lily as she placed the mask in my hands. "A black bird?" Everyone else had grown silent to watch my reaction.

Tiger Lily nodded. "A crow to be more exact." I rubbed my fingers over the glossy feathers. "Are you not pleased with your animal?"

"No, it's not that," I said. "The mask is beautiful. I just don't understand why I'm a crow."

"Crows are intelligent, cunning animals. They exude fearlessness and mystery," Tiger Lily explained more to the crowd than to me. I stood behind her as she paced in front of the crowd. All the lost boys' eyes seemed to be transfixed on the way her hips moved as she slinked like a jungle cat in front of me. I glanced at Peter to find he was beaming at me and I gave him a small smile. He pulled his own mask out of an inner pocket in his jacket and placed it over his face, staring at me now through the eyes of a brown hawk. I slipped my own mask over my head and tied the leather strap over my hair. I gazed around at the whooping crowd through the eyeholes.

"Let us celebrate," Tiger Lily said with a smile from beside me. Then she pulled the tiger head down over her eyes and the Indians followed suit, pulling down their own hoods or fixing masks to their faces.

The following hour was spent dancing around the fire and making cawing noises to the moon. I felt too self-conscious to join in so I sat silently next to Pal and watched through the crow mask as the others partied it up. I watched Tiger Lily twirl and weave her way from one lost boy to the next, brushing one's ear while touching another's waist provocatively. They all loved it of course and just wanted a piece of her. When she got to Peter, she wrapped her arms around his neck and lifted her hood. She touched her mouth to his ear, saying words only he could hear and I watched his eyes, though I couldn't see anything behind his hawk mask. His hands touched Tiger Lily's bare sides and I felt a twinge in my gut. But then he gently pushed her away and shook his head. I watched as he lifted his mask and said something to her. His eyes darted to me for just a second and I saw Tiger Lily stiffen. It only lasted for a moment before she relaxed again, pulled her hood back down and moved on to Russ, clutching now at his waist and wriggling around on him. I rolled my eyes in disgust. Once she was done with Russ, she moved on again to Kai leaving the fox boy to stand there awkwardly.

I heard Pal let out a huff beside me and I turned to find him shaking a bit like he was laughing. I could feel a smile lift my mask a bit as I watched him enjoy himself. Again I found myself wishing I could see the face hiding under that deer mask.

A while later, Tiger Lily sauntered her way over to us and I could feel Pal tense up beside me. My own back went rigid as I stared at those giant fangs. She sat down next to me and lifted the hood off her face. "Having fun, Wynn?" she asked me.

I nodded, afraid that if I lifted my mask, she would be able to read the intimidation on my face. I turned my attention back to Peter as he skipped his way around the circle. He hadn't pulled his mask back down so I could see his mouth open in joyous laughter. It made me smile to see him having fun. Though I smiled wider remembering how he had blown off Tiger Lily when he'd looked my way a bit before.

"You are fond of him," Tiger Lily said quietly.

Again I looked at her, trying to read her dark, cold eyes. Pal shifted uncomfortably next to me. I'm sure he wanted to get up and leave us alone and I wouldn't have blamed him if he did. But instead he just tightened his hands into fists and kept quiet. I was grateful for him staying though I wasn't sure if he was doing it for me or not.

"There is no need to try and hide it, Wynn," Tiger Lily continued and started fiddling with one of the tiger's teeth near her face. "It is understandable. He is a very beautiful boy." Still I kept my trap shut. "It is one of the reasons I knew you were a crow. They are attracted to beautiful things." Now she chuckled, turning her attention to me and narrowing her dark eyes, peering into my own like she could see through the mask. "They are also very well known for picking over other people's leftovers."

Something snipped the string holding up the rock

in my stomach and it crashed back down with a sickening *thud*. All I could do was look down at my lap as Tiger Lily got back up and approached the fire and the dancing boys again. She joined back in, swinging her hips and beckoning for the boys to come to her. I felt Pal's hand touch mine for just a second on the log before I pulled it away and sprang to my feet. I didn't know where I was going; all I wanted was to be away from the fire and safely hidden in the dark, blackness of the forest. As I ran, I pulled the mask off my face, clutching the sleek feathers in my fist. I'd been there for all of two days and all I wanted was to go back home.

Finally, I stopped in a small grove of trees. The sky was dark blue and the moon was bright white. Why were people being so mean to me? First Russ now Tiger Lily. What had I done to deserve it? What wrong did they think I'd done to them? Why had I let Peter take me there in the first place? I brought my hands up to my face, still clutching the bird mask, and rubbed at my eyes. I hadn't even noticed that my cheeks were damp with tears.

"Wynn?" It was Peter. I didn't want to talk to him. He burst through the trees a few seconds later, holding his own mask in his hands. "What's wrong? Why did you leave?"

"I couldn't stay there," I finally said, my shaky voice low and surprisingly calm. "I couldn't stay there with *her.*"

"Tiger Lily?" he asked sounding surprised. "Why not? What did she do?"

I filled him in on what she'd said to me, letting my eyes fall everywhere but on him. At the ground, at the trees around us, at the moon, at the mask in my hands. As I told Peter what happened, a frown appeared on his face.

"I didn't know she was going to act like that," Peter said throwing his hands into the air.

I could feel my ears still burning. "Well, you should have warned me anyway. That was ridiculous," I spat and threw the crow mask on the ground.

"Warned you?" he asked. "About what?"

"That you'd been...romantically involved with her."

"Tiger Lily?" Peter pressed his lips together and blew out hard. "That wasn't anything"

I crossed my arms and rocked back on my heel. "What do you mean it wasn't anything? The whole time we were there she was either trying to make me burst into flames or undress you with her eyes.

"Oh." He tossed his hands out like he was batting away my accusations. "Nothing really happened."

I narrowed my eyes. "Nothing happened."

"Right."

"You were with *that*," I said stabbing a finger back toward the Indian camp, "and you're telling me nothing happened. You've been a seventeen year old boy forever."

Peter looked down at the ground and kicked the dirt with his toe. "Yeah, a seventeen year old boy that's never even kissed a girl."

I dropped my arm. "You've never been kissed?"

He shrugged. "Well," he started, looking up at the sky like he was remembering. "Wendy tried to give me a stupid little thimble and say it was a kiss but I didn't buy into that crap. I've seen movies. I've seen people do it at the places I've performed."

"So then…" I toed the crow mask with my boot. "What did you guys do, if you don't mind me asking?"

"We mostly just hung out," he shrugged again. "Did some hunting. She liked rubbing her nose against mine for some reason.

"Eskimo kissing," I uttered.

Peter looked at me and narrowed his eyes. "No, I'm pretty sure Tiger Lily is an Indian."

I couldn't help but smile at his naivety. "No, when you rub noses it's called an Eskimo kiss."

"I just said I've never kissed anyone."

"Never mind."

Peter took hold of my wrist. "Hey," he uttered and I looked him in the eye again. "I'm really sorry she acted that way."

I shook my head. "She had a right to."

"Why?"

"It's what girls do when they get jealous," I said. "And I'm sure she doesn't get jealous very often."

Peter's eyes searched mine for a bit, his brow furrowed. "Why is that?"

I stepped back, "Well, look at her," I said lifting my hands in a pathetic shrug. "She's what every girl dreams of being and what every guy dreams of doing."

He shook his head, his forehead still crumpled in frustration. "Are *you* jealous, Wynn Harper?" he finally asked, his eyes cutting into mine.

I looked at my mask again on the ground. "How could a wimpy little crow compare to a tiger?"

When I looked up again, I could see the muscles in his jaw moving as he stared at me. "You're right," he finally said. "There's no comparison." Then he grabbed my wrist again and pulled me toward him. I was suddenly only a few inches from his face. Only a few inches from his lips. I watched as he touched his cheek to my own so I could feel his breath on my ear. My heart hammered hard in my chest and the rock in my stomach blazed. Then he wrapped his arms around me, holding me tight against his bare chest, warming me with his body heat.

When he pulled away again, I could feel the blush in my cheeks and I was glad it was too dark out for Peter to see. He smiled then bent down and picked up my crow mask. After brushing the dirt off of it, he carefully fixed it over my face again and tilted his head to the side. "I like it," he said with a smile then used his hand to sweep my hair down over my shoulder. "It fits you well, and not in the way that Tiger Lily told you."

I smiled even though I knew he couldn't see it. Then Peter put his own mask back on and held out his hand to me. "Let us birds take to the sky."

I took his hand and we immediately lifted into the cold air. The rock in my stomach had burned away by now leaving me warmed and light as a crow's silky black feather. From up out of the forest drifted little specks of white light, like snowflakes that hadn't been told which way the ground was. Moments later, Nyk flew past me with a flash of her shiny armor. Lyssa followed, fluttering her rainbow wings. Next came Aubri with a ruffle of moss, then Ember – I only knew because her hair glowed like red burning coals – and then Iris with her red leaf wrap tailed on the end. The rest of the fairies stayed below us while the others twirled and danced above our heads in fits of bubbling laughter.

I looked over at Peter, who had his beaked face pointed at me. Then he raised his head to the moon and screeched, imitating a hawk. I let out a laugh, feeling myself grow more weightless by the second. "Come on, Wynn," he called to me before letting out another screech. "Embrace your inner crow!"

I looked up through the black bird's eyes at the moon, glowing brilliant and bright. Then I tipped my head back and let out a loud *caw*. Peter screeched again in response and the two of us soared through the air calling like the animals we were pretending to be. How could I have ever wanted to leave this place?

Chapter Seven

Someone let out a loud snore causing me to snap my eyes open and sit up with a start. Nothing else stirred. The boys must have all still been asleep. Quietly, I pulled the thin blanket off of myself and grabbed my boots that sat at the foot of the couch before tiptoeing out the door.

The air was crisp and sharp and I could feel the moisture of the evaporating dew. This was going to be another perfect day. Quickly, I pulled my boots on and made my way down the ramp and into the forest.

Birds were slowly waking up and starting to sing as I made my way through the woods. I took my time listening to their music and watching the twinkling of the sunlight on the ground as the leaves shifted in the wind overhead. As I walked, I could feel the air warming and the earthy aromas of the trees and the rich dirt slowly started to fade and mix with the more tropical smells of flowers and ocean. Before long I started to notice sand mixing in with the dirt. Then I stepped out onto the beach.

The sky was perfectly blue and clear and the ocean, calm and shimmering. I took my boots off and dug my toes into the sand. It was warm on top but cool and damp a few inches down. The wind blew my hair back away from my face, and covered my cheeks in salty kisses as I made my way down toward the water. The ocean came up to meet me, washing over my bare feet and making me shiver. I felt a smile tug at my lips as I closed my eyes and stretched my arms up over my head. The wind slid through my hands, caressing my fingers with its sun-kissed warmth and the cold waves lapped up around my ankles encasing me in a beautifully contradicting bear hug. I rose up on my toes feeling my calf muscles ache a bit from my ballet class on Thursday. The sounds of the wind and the waves and the birds flying overhead swirled with my memories of ballet creating music in my head and I soon found myself twirling gracefully to it. If only I could bring this all back with me. I wonder if Great Gran ever danced alone there on the beach. I felt a small stab of sadness in my heart. All those stories she had told me, now experiencing so much of what she had experienced, she must have missed it so dearly. And we had all cast it off as a made-up fairytale.

Another wave came up and crashed against my calves. The tide was coming in. I stepped forward feeling the cold creep up my legs. Maybe Great Gran was experiencing something like this now. I could take comfort in that. I could find solace in the possibility that she was in her own version of Neverland. With my hands still raised above my head, I spun again, the water coming up over my waist.

When I was really little, I'd found an old picture of Great Gran back in her twenties. Her brown hair was wrapped in a tight bun at the crown of her head and she wore a white rhinestone embellished leotard and flowing, gossamer skirt. She stood perfectly en pointe, balanced in a pair of satiny white ballet shoes. As my little six-year-old fingers traced her silhouette, I promised myself that someday I'd be a ballerina just like her. My mom enrolled me in classes a week later.

A wave pushed against my stomach and I lifted my head to the sun, feeling its early morning warmth on my eyelids. My heart swelled as the memories of dressing up in Great Gran's old ballet costumes crossed my mind. I knew she loved seeing me in them. With my small frame and brown hair, I'm sure I reminded her of when she was younger.

"Sure, now you get in the water!"

My eyes shot open as one of my feet slipped in the sand and I stumbled. The water splashed up over my shoulders and sprayed me in the face. With a gasp, I spun around to find Peter laughing at me from back on the beach. I made my way back to shore as quickly as I could trying not to trip and look like an even bigger dork.

"How long were you standing there?" I asked out of breath and shivering.

"Long enough," he replied folding his arms across his tanned chest. I lifted an eyebrow and the smug smile on Peter's face was replaced with an embarrassed frown. "I mean, I wasn't like gawking at you or anything."

The thought of making Peter nervous made my own frown turn up into a smile. "Sure," I said drawing the word out mockingly.

"Look, I was just going to go hunting for some breakfast while the others were asleep and I just came here to see if you wanted to go with me but if you'd rather stay here and do...whatever it is that you were doing, I can just do it–"

"No way," I interrupted. "I want to go."

"Well then, what are we waiting for?" The familiar smirk returned to his face and he held out his hand to me.

"Where are we going to hunt?" I asked once we had taken to the air.

He floated along on his back about two feet below me. Only our intertwined fingers kept me from falling. The morning sun glinted off his light brown hair casting golden inverted shadows on his face. I'm pretty sure something like that couldn't happen to just any ordinary person.

"Cannibal Cove."

I shook my head to clear the fog from my mind. "What?"

"Hunting," he replied with a crooked smile. "In Cannibal Cove."

"Right, right"

Peter twisted sideways and suddenly we'd switched places. I looked up at him with my lips parted, the surprised gasp of air still in my throat. He cocked a flirtatious eyebrow at me.

"Are you trying to make me pee my pants?" I

finally asked breathlessly.

Peter shrugged. "I couldn't see where I was going." I didn't believe that was his reason for even a second. "Though I will admit, I like seeing you from this angle." There we go. "And the look on your face was pretty amusing too."

With my free hand, I shoved Peter's shoulder and the two of us spun again in the air. I hadn't expected that and judging by the surprised look on his face, neither had Peter. Now, it was my turn to smirk.

"You think you're so clever," he uttered with narrowed eyes.

"Yeah actually," I laughed, "I think I am."

Without another word, Peter pulled hard crushing me to his chest and twisted again this time pointing us toward the ground. We spiraled downward and I shut my eyes tight, burying my face into his jacket so I wouldn't have to watch our impending doom come up to meet us. At the last second, he slowed down and set my gently on the ground. I made myself peek up at our surroundings.

It was like we'd flown to a different world. The cool, beautifully haunting forest where Peter and his lost boys lived was nothing like the hot and humid jungle I now stood in. Sure, everything was green but it was all so much brighter. Like light radiated from the plants themselves and not just from the sun streaming down through the canopy of vines and leaves. Breathing in, I felt like my lungs were filling with water though it wasn't like I was drowning. It was much more pleasant than that. I wondered if this was what breathing underwater felt like for a mermaid. Like my lungs were sponges that expanded with the weight then squeezed themselves out when I exhaled.

The damp air smelled heavily of flowers and the kind of scent I'd only experienced when Mom had just mowed the lawn. It was heavenly and made me close my eyes and take in a deep, deep, muggy breath. With a happy sigh, I turned back around to Peter. He was leaning back against a tree picking at the dirt under his nails with his knife. The sound of a waterfall close by filled my head. I guess the name wouldn't really fit the place if there was no cove nearby.

"Why do you call this place Cannibal Cove?" I finally asked after pausing for a few seconds to listen to the strange song of a tropical bird in the distance.

Peter shrugged. "I don't really know. Maybe because of the cannibals."

I felt a cold shutter pass through my body and goose bumps raised the hairs on my arms even though the air was warm. "There really are cannibals here?"

"Well sure," he said with another shrug, then stepped toward me, putting the knife back in its sheath on his belt. "Whoever named this place didn't name it Cannibal Cove for the alliteration."

I took a cautious step back. Suddenly, the way the plants moved seemed too similar to the motion of a person trying to sneak up on us. The shadows cast on the leaves over our heads looked too much like the faces of hungry men. The bird song I'd heard before now sounded more like whispers of strategy like someone was about to give the order to attack. "Isn't this place pretty dangerous then?" I whispered.

Peter took another step closer to me and reached out to place his warm hands on my arms. My eyes darted away from the trees and settled on his. Their color seemed to match the foliage around us. So mesmerizing. "There's no need to worry, Wynn," he said softly and his hands slid down to my wrists. "Don't forget, we've got a bit of an advantage over anyone that could cause us any harm." Then his fingers found my fingers and they interlocked. "Just stick with me."

I nodded as the fear slowly faded. As it trickled out of my body, it was replaced with a sense of peace. Peter wouldn't let anything happen to me. He really did care about me. And I couldn't help but care about him as well. More than I'd ever cared about a boy.

With a final squeeze of my knuckles, he let go of one of my hands and pulled me with the other toward an overgrown path. My Jell-O legs didn't want to go at first but when Peter looked back at me and flashed his amused half-smile, my body came back to life and I followed after him, the feel of his hand in mine assuring me that everything was going to be alright.

We'd been walking for a while in silence and with no sign of any sort of animal worth hunting, when Peter stopped and crouched down low. I followed suit, waiting for him to say something. He didn't.

"What is it?" I whispered trying not to make too much noise.

Peter put a finger to his lips then slowly pulled a leaf back that was in our path. A tiny gasp escaped my throat when I saw what was in front of us. We'd stopped on the outskirts of a small clearing. The ground was covered in spongy moss and overhead, a ceiling of big leaves the size of doormats filtered the sunlight making the whole place glow green. In the middle of the clearing sat a small cluster of lean-to looking huts made of logs and more of the big doormat leaves. A fire crackled only a few yards away from us with a skinned boar turning on a spit. The smell of the cooking meet mixed with the floral scent of the air making my mouth water.

"There's our breakfast," Peter whispered, his lips only centimeters from my ear.

"Isn't that kind of stealing?" I muttered back, my breath shaky with nerves. If I turned my head, our mouths would be touching. I wondered what he would do.

Peter turned away again and I shook my head to clear the fog from my mind. "Don't think of it as stealing," he said. "Think of it more as misappropriating."

"That's the same thing," I hissed.

Peter shushed me again and I tried to suppress a smile as I shook my head in mock disappointment. "What a shame," I said folding my arms across my chest. "And here I thought you were some daring young mountain man. But you can't even get your own food without someone else doing the dirty work for you."

Voices filled the air in front of us just then and I flipped onto my stomach with my face inches from the ground. Slowly, I lifted my head up and peered under a leaf that had been blocking my view. Two men came out of one of the oversized lean-tos speaking a language I'd never heard before. Then again, it's not like I'd heard very many languages besides English in my seventeen years. Both men stood at least a foot taller than Peter and their skin was so dark it looked almost purple. The one with a large, white bone through his nose said something harsh to the other and pointed a crooked finger toward the roasting boar. The other man shook his head, his big, soda can sized gauged ears slapping against his neck, and yelled something equally as loud and equally as unintelligible. Pretty soon they were arguing, their voices filling the clearing and bouncing off the trunks of the trees around them. Then with a huff, bone nose threw his hands up in defeat and turned our way. My eyes grew large as he started toward us with hurried, angry steps. Peter quickly wrapped an arm around my waist and pulled. The two of us rolled out of the way and under the veil of a large, low to the ground, grassy plant.

I watched as the man's big feet snapped a twig only a foot away from my face as he trudged by. Neither of us moved until the footsteps faded to silence. Only when I looked down did I realize that I was laying on top of Peter and he had both of his arms wrapped securely around my waist.

"Uh...sorry," he whispered, his pointed ears turning scarlet underneath his hat. Then his hands unclasped and he rolled a bit, dumping me off of him and back onto the jungle floor.

I didn't respond as the two of us crawled closer again to the edge of the clearing. The remaining man sat on the ground with his elbows resting on his knees in front of the fire. He picked at the rigid hem of his dirty, suede pants, his face contorted in some mocking expression as he went through the conversation he'd just had to himself.

Whatever they'd been fighting about, it must have had something to do with the animal roasting on the spit. Obviously, this one was meant to stand guard or maybe keep it from burning. Either way, I didn't see how we were possibly going to get to it now.

Peter turned to me, a mischievous gleam in his eye. "You want to see daring? I'll show you daring," he said.

I shook my head silently pleading for him to stay put but he got up and made his way along the outer perimeter of the clearing. I was confused at first about how he was staying so silent but then I realized his feet weren't actually touching the ground. Instead, he floated just a few inches in the air, avoiding the twigs and leaves that would surely give his location away. All I could do was stare helplessly as he left the confinement of the trees and stepped out into the open on the other side of the huts. He poked at the fire, oblivious to Peter sneaking up behind him. The flying boy's bare feet didn't quite touch the ground so he was completely silent as he drew closer to the unsuspecting man. I would have felt bad for the guy if not for the fact that he'd eat me if he knew I was there. If Peter didn't get out of there this second, our cover would surely be blown.

I watched in frozen horror as he reached out, hovering a hand right over the man's gauged ear. Peter glanced my way and wiggled his eyebrows then flicked his finger. The man shot straight up, his feet leaving the ground for a second as he jumped, startled. Simultaneously, Peter kicked his legs up so he was upside down above the unsuspecting cannibal. It looked like he was balancing his head on top of the man's head, with just barely an inch of space between them. Though horrified, I still found myself covering my mouth to stifle the giggles I could feel bubbling up in me. The poor oblivious man spun left and right, trying to figure out what had just happened, while Peter stayed above him, moving with him and imitating his bewildered facial expressions upside down.

After a while, the cannibal sat back down, eying the tree line suspiciously. He had just settled back in when Peter, from up above him, reached out and flicked his ear again. This time instead of staying out of sight, he hung down in front of the man's face.

"Hi there!" he exclaimed causing the cannibal to fall back startled. Immediately, he lunged at Peter with his knife just missing him by a hair.

From my hiding place, I watched as Peter let out a loud laugh and circled him, dodging easily to the left and right, just barely out of reach of the deadly blade. The wild, angry look on the man's face, while amusing, made my gut twist. I didn't like the way he lunged at Peter with that killer gleam in his eye. I just wanted to get out of there.

Clumsily, I rolled out from under my leafy cover and stood up tall. "Hey! Over here!" I yelled jumping up and down and waving my arms.

The cannibal spun around to face me, his knife clutched tightly in his hand. While his back was turned, Peter dove at the boar roasting over the fire and tackled it like a football player, sliding into the dirt on the other side. My eyes darted to him for just a second but the cannibal caught on and whirled around in time to see Peter take to the air and soar over his head. He reached a hand out and I grabbed on and let him pull me up into the air with him, then two of us shot out above the trees, leaving the cannibal to yell and jump up and down angrily below us. His shouting grew quieter the farther away we flew. Peter looked down at me with a smirk. "How was that for daring?" he asked, his eyes glittering with excitement.

I laughed. "You definitely earned the title," I said patting the boar under his arm.

We flew on for a while and I watched the trees as they changed from tropical back to the familiar firs and evergreens of the Neverwood Forest. As we drew closer to the lost boys' camp, I felt a twist in my stomach. I'd enjoyed spending time alone with Peter and I wasn't quite ready to be around the loud boys again. Not that I didn't like them. It had just been a peaceful morning and I wanted to bask in it for as long as I could. When I looked up at Peter, he had a touch of a smile on his lips. He glanced my way, noticing me staring.

I bit the inside of my cheek. "Do you think we could go back to the beach instead?"

The smile on his face widened. "Wouldn't it be kind of cruel to keep this delicious breakfast all to ourselves?" he asked nudging his arm up gesturing to the cooked boar under his arm.

I shrugged. "Just for a little while? They can survive a bit longer. Besides, they're probably all still sleeping anyway," I said remembering the deep snoring that had woken me up that morning.

Peter nodded. "Good point." Then he repositioned his body and we arched around until we were heading toward the water. "To the beach!"

As soon as we hit the shore, I let go of Peter's fingers and kicked my boots off, letting the white sand warm my toes. Peter took the boar on the spit out from under his arm and stabbed one end of the stick deep in the ground so it stuck straight up then he shrugged off his pirate coat and let it drop. My eyes scanned over his body quickly, taking in the way his tan skin shimmered subtly in the sunlight before I looked away again so he wouldn't catch me staring. Not that he hadn't already before.

"So, Wynn, what do you think of my homeland?" he asked me and lay down in the sand. He patted the spot next to him and I sat down too.

The wind picked up blowing my hair back and filling my nose with the intoxicating smells of the ocean. I breathed in deep. "It's incredible," I sighed and closed my eyes. "If I could, I'd stay here forever."

"Well, why don't you?" he asked. I opened my eyes again to find a touch of a smile in his green eyes. Then his eyelids drooped and he let out a sigh. "Just kidding," he murmured lazily. "I know you'd miss your family too much."

I didn't respond. Instead I studied his profile for a second, biting my lip and letting my eyes drift down to his own. Those innocent lips that had never been touched. I wondered what they felt like. "So you've never been kissed," I said, looking back out at the water.

Peter put his hands behind his head and arched his spine. "Nope," he said. I couldn't help but watch the muscles under his skin move as he stretched.

"Do you know how?" I asked as I focused my attention back on the waves lapping up on the shore.

He relaxed suddenly, letting his back hit the sand with a soft *thud*. "Like I said, I've seen people kiss before. It doesn't look that hard."

Now I glanced over at him again. "Want to learn?" I asked quietly, feeling my ears get hot.

Peter opened one eye to peer at me. His mouth twitched. "I don't know," he said. "You're not going to try and pull that thimble crap the way your Great Gran did, are you?"

I let out a chuckle and felt my shoulders relax. I hadn't even realized I was tense waiting for his answer. "No," I assured him. "This would be a real kiss."

He looked at me with narrowed eyes for a second like he was debating with himself. "Sure, why not," he shrugged then he sat up.

That caught me a bit off guard. "Really?" I asked feeling the heat wrap around to my cheeks.

"Yeah," he said with an easy smile. "Who knows when the next girl will come along? I've got to take the chance while it's being offered."

I scrunched my mouth "First lesson," I started then smacked him on the arm. "Talking about other girls is no way to get one to kiss you."

Peter rubbed the spot where I hit him. "Right, right."

"Lesson two," I continued, shifting so I could get settled in. "You have to lean in more than she does."

"Why?"

I bit my lip again as I thought of the best way to answer. "Because a girl wants the guy to take the lead. It's like...hunting."

"You want me to shoot you with an arrow?"

"No, that was a stupid example," I muttered. "But you have to be the one to make the first move. Does that make sense?"

Peter narrowed his eyes but nodded like he kind of understood. "So, I have to lean in."

"Right." I could feel my heart beating a bit faster. "Close the gap."

I watched as he scooted a bit closer to me then brought one hand up and placed it on the back of my neck. "Is that okay?" he asked me. I could only nod as I watched his face draw closer to mine.

Carefully, Peter pressed his lips against my own. My heart melted. They were the softest lips I'd ever felt. So smooth, so innocent. They were lips only someone who had never been kissed could have. All too soon it was over and he leaned back away from me again. The look on his face was indescribable. Maybe he didn't really know what to think. I bit my cheek and waited for him to say something. He didn't.

"So?" I finally shrugged.

Peter furrowed his brow for a second confused. "I don't get it," he said.

My shoulders sagged. "Well, usually a person kisses another person because they want to, not just because they never have before."

"Why would a person want to?" he asked in a way that was innocently curious and not at all insulting.

I shrugged. "I guess because it feels good. Didn't it feel good to kiss me?"

"I guess. I mean it didn't hurt or anything if that's what you mean."

I shook my head with a chuckle. "I mean like inside. Have you ever even liked a girl before?"

"Well, yeah," Peter said and lay back on the sand. "I mean, I liked Tiger Lily. But like I said before, all we ever did was hang out and hunt."

I lay back beside him too and closed my eyes, letting the sun warm my skin. The air smelled delicious like salt and trees. This was a place I could really get used to. "And Eskimo kissed."

"I still don't know what Eskimos have to do with anything," Peter muttered sleepily.

I peered at him with one eye open and stared at the way his nose swooped up to a perfect point. The sun made his cheekbones shimmer just a little bit reminding me that he wasn't completely human. Maybe he didn't have human feelings. Maybe he wasn't able to love or get excited. Or maybe it was all too innocent for him. Maybe I needed to start a bit of a fire.

Quickly, I rolled over so I was on top of him and my face was only centimeters from his. His eyes flew open to meet mine and I could feel his heart begin to hammer under my hand.

"Now, how do you feel?" I breathed looking down at his lips, recalling again how soft and smooth they were.

"A little...electric," he whispered with a shaky voice.

"Tingly sensation in your stomach?" I asked. Peter nodded. "Your legs a bit wobbly?" Another nod. "Feel the urge to try kissing me again?" His breath caught in his throat and I saw the tips of his pointed ears get red. Slowly, I lowered my face closer and his own started lifting to meet mine. Right when I could feel the invisible hairs on his lip brush my skin, I sat back up again, my hands on the ground on either side of his face. "*That* is why people kiss each other. *That* feeling right there."

Peter's eyes narrowed and he ground his teeth irritated as he tried to calm his breathing back down. "I don't like that feeling."

"That's because all that electricity is coursing through you and now it has nowhere to go," I said. "It needs some kind of release." Then I leaned back so I was sitting on his stomach and crossed my arms triumphantly over my chest. "Now what have we learned today?"

"A lot. Thank you, kindly," he sneered. "Now, if you don't mind…" With one fluid motion, Peter grabbed my shoulders and rolled, putting me on my back before I even knew what was going on. He leaned over me, his hands in the sand on either side of my head, the tendons and muscles in his arms prominent. "I think I will put some of what I have learned to good use."

I took in a deep breath but before I could even exhale, Peter crushed his mouth to mine. I could feel my own adrenaline surging through my veins, making my heart pump hard in my ears and behind my eyes. The energy tingled its way up from my stomach and out of my lips, soaking into his. And I could feel the same electricity going into mine. My hands clenched into fists in his hair and his breath escaped through his nose in short bursts. He tasted amazing, the way I expected this whole island would taste if it were packed into a little bite sized morsel. Rain, salt, flowers and sugar were on my lips. On his lips.

Then he pulled away and rolled over onto his back and the two of us lay there in breathless silence. Some kind of bird flew above our heads and I watched it drift on the wind like a kite, surfing the invisible waves without a care in the world.

"Now what?" Peter finally asked, his voice shaky.

I turned my head and shaded the side of my face with my hand. "We'll get into that when you're older," I replied jokingly.

Peter closed his eyes and a smile spread across his radiant face. Such a beautiful smile.

I must have drifted off because the next thing I knew, I was being lifted into the air. My eyes shot open to find Mika's upside down face peering down at me. He had a tight grip on my wrists and when I looked down, Finn was holding my ankles. On one side of me, the forest got farther away and on the other side, the ocean drew closer.

"What are you doing?" I asked, my voice cracking with fear.

"We're punishing you for trying to keep our breakfast away from us," Mika answered nodding toward the boar still sticking into the sand. "And for seducing our captain."

"Yes," Finn agreed. "And a crime like that is punishable by death."

"Death?" I shrieked. I tried to kick but Finn had a tight grip on my legs. The grin on his face said he wasn't about to let go either.

"Well okay, not death," he shrugged, struggling against my thrashing limbs. "But it at least deserves a dunk!"

Now they stood ankle deep in the salty water and the spray speckled my back. I craned my neck again to look up at the sand to find Peter and the others laughing. I'll show them, I thought. Mika and Finn started swinging me by my limbs, getting ready to toss me out into the wave. Maybe they thought they could just throw me around like a rag doll because I'm little but they weren't accounting for the fact that I'd been taking ballet for over ten years. And the thing about ballerinas is, we tend to have strong legs.

Mika and Finn made eye contact with each other like that was their signal to let me go. As soon as I was at the top of the arch, I pulled my legs apart, wrenching them from Finn's grasp and quickly brought them back together, clamping onto his slim waist and locking my ankles behind his back. Then I twisted, diving into the water, taking him with me. The sudden movement caught Mika by surprise and he went down as well. Seawater rushed into my nose and ears and I kicked hard, getting my legs under me so I could swim back to shore.

When my head broke the surface, sounds of laughter and applause from Kai and Peter filled the air. I turned around to find my two assailants coming up out of the water, gasping from the cold and I felt pride bloom in my chest like a flower. Peter met me at the shore with his jacket in one hand and my mask in the other.

"My feisty little black bird," he joked and lifted his hand to me. The black feathers on my crow mask gleamed royal blue, turquoise and violet in the sun. The lost boys must have brought it with them from camp.

With a grateful smile, I bowed my head and let him tie the leather strings at the back of my wet hair. When I looked at him again, I let out a shaky, cold "caw" causing a grin to break out on his face. He draped his coat over my shivering shoulders and tugged on the lapel, bringing me closer to him.

Through the crow's eyes, I watched his own, the swirls of green looked like they were moving, dancing inside his irises, igniting with emerald fire. Then he lost his grip on me when a dripping wet lost boy tackled him from the side. I laughed and watched as the rest threw themselves onto the dog pile, burying their beloved leader and mock scolding him for leaving them hungry and helpless back at the tree fort.

While they wrestled in the sand, I went back up to sit by the boar – or rather, what was left of it. The pirate coat on my shoulders was heavy and blocked out the wind while still soaking up the sun's warmth keeping my shivering at bay. I hadn't really looked much at the coat since I got there but now I was able to take the time and really appreciate the handy work. It was obvious that at one point the coat had been a very brilliant emerald green but now it had faded to more of a dark moss color, surely dulled by dirt and sun and salt. The gold piping that traced the edges of the lapel was fraying and altogether missing in other places. I'd never seen Peter button the thing and I don't know if it was because he didn't want to or simply because it only had one button left so he just couldn't. The one button that was still attached down near the bottom edge of the jacket was ornate and burnished like brass. My finger rubbed over the worn image of a crocodile head, the teeth and most of the snout were almost completely smoothed away but the one eye facing me was prominent and bright as ever. As if it was staring at me, staring into me hungrily. Quickly, I looked up and covered the button with my palms suddenly feeling the wind's chill. It was silly reacting like this to an old button but I couldn't shake Tiger Lily's words from the night before. That she had known right away that Hook's animal was the crocodile. I wondered how long she knew his true character. That he could be nasty and evil.

I was so absorbed in my thoughts that I didn't notice Peter come up to me and sit down. "You better get some of this boar before it disappears."

His voice caused me to jump startled and it took me a second to register what he'd said. I lifted the crow mask on top of my head and studied him. He was covered in sand now, his hair wet and cow-licked on one side so it stood straight up. The goofy grin on his face made my heart soar and the chill I'd felt evaporated along with images of the crocodiles still haunting my mind. I wanted to kiss those lips again but it seemed weird with the other boys there.

We spent the rest of the morning there on the beach. I watched them wrestle in the water from a safe distance, wrapped in Peter's coat and hoping none of them would try to throw me in again. Once I was completely dry and no longer cold, I shrugged the coat off and lay back in the sand. My hair fanned out around me in dreadlocked pieces stiff with salt, sand and dirt. It was going to be interesting trying to get it back to its soft state. Or maybe I would leave it like this. I was beginning to like the way my skin had gone from pasty white to a light tan – though I'm sure more of it was dirt than sun. My tunic had some snags and my leggings a few holes. The black polish was almost completely gone from my nails, save for a few bits here and there which I quickly scraped off to reveal dark crescents of dirt underneath. There were scrapes all up and down my arms from playing manhunt the day before. I was beginning to look like I could fit in there. Pulling my mask back down over my face, I realized I felt like I belonged there too.

My mom's face floated to the surface of my mind. Her smile tinged with sadness, her eyes perpetually red and glassy from crying. My own eyes welled up a bit and I closed them quickly to trap the tears. Part of me wished I could stay in Neverland forever while another part ached for my home, my family, my normal life. Obviously, I couldn't have both. And the day was going to come too soon when I'd need to return to LA. Too soon yet not soon enough.

The lost boys slept soundly by the darkened fire pit. They all looked so peaceful surrounded by bones and suava peelings like children napping in a mess of discarded wrapping paper on Christmas. Even Russ looked like an angel with his face relaxed, the perpetual creases in his forehead smoothed out. Peter carefully put down his guitar and put a finger to his mouth. I bit my bottom lip trying to hold back a giggle as I took careful steps over their sprawling limbs. Kai snored on the ramp in front of the door and we had to step over him to get in.

It was pretty dark inside so I could only make out the basic shapes of furniture and the ladder leading to the loft. Peter came up behind me and slipped his arms around my waist causing my heartbeat to quicken and my stomach to flutter like there were a million little snowflake fairies trapped inside.

"Thanks," he breathed in my ear.

I turned slowly, feeling his hands slide along my back. "For what?" I finally asked when my face was only centimeters from his.

With a faint smile, Peter closed the short distance, pressing his silky lips against mine in a short, sweet kiss. When he pulled away, he flashed his pearly white teeth. "For that," he said, his voice low and husky.

"Oh, I was happy to help," I whispered bringing my hands up to touch the back of his neck.

I leaned in again when a loud snore startled me and I jumped backward. Another loud snore was broken by a spattering of incoherent slurs and I brought a hand up to cover my giggling. I had already forgotten that Kai was only a few yards away, sleeping just outside of the door on the ramp. Peter buried his face in my neck and shook with silent laughter. My heart felt like it could sprout wings and fly right up my throat. To think I'd only been there for a few days. Neverland had become home to me. I felt like I belonged there and I never wanted to leave.

"I wish I could stay here forever," I whispered, my throat tightening unexpectedly at the thought of having to go home eventually.

Peter lifted his head back up to look me in the eyes. My vision had adjusted to the darkness and I could see his brow furrow as he bit his lip. Finally, he sighed. "What would be so bad about it?"

I took a step back, keeping my hands clutched in his and looked down at my feet. "I have a life back on Earth though," I said. "I can't leave Marty. My mom…"

"They aren't your responsibility, though, Wynn. You should be able to do what you want. You deserve to be happy." Then he pulled me back against him in a tight hug. "You deserve so much better than what you have."

"How do you know what I have?" I mumbled into the lapel of his coat. I breathed in deep the smell of his bare skin. Sugared spruce with a hint of sea salt.

"I…just know," he replied with a sigh then stepped back so he could shrug off his jacket.

I made my way sleepily over to the couch and fell back on it, taking my mask off and throwing my arms up over my eyes where the moonlight touched down through the window. A hand grasped my ankle and I bolted up to see Peter's half smile and glittering eyes.

"Calm down, there, spazz," he said with a chuckle. "I'm just taking off your boots."

My breath was trapped in my lungs and I watched completely paralyzed as he undid the laces and pulled my boots off my feet. They clunked to the floor loudly causing him to jump and me to snap out of my stupor.

Both of us let out a nervous chuckle then Peter leaned down over me and pressed his lips to my forehead. "Sleep tight, Wynn," he said against my skin then stood back up and started for the ladder leading up to the loft.

I sat up quickly. "Peter." He stopped halfway up and turned to look at me. "Do you think you could…stay down here with me?"

Peter furrowed his brow. "Where would I sleep?"

Drawing my knees up to my chest, I bit the inside of my cheek. "Here on the couch," I said quietly.

"But you're on the couch."

"I know."

The lines in his forehead disappeared and his eyes grew wide for a second. "Oh." Then he quickly made his way back down the ladder and hopped over the back of the couch, wedging into the tiny space between it and me. Light laughter bubbled up in my stomach as he wrapped his arms around me and nuzzled his nose into my neck.

"Thanks, Wynn," he sighed, his voice muffled by my hair.

Again, I felt my stomach clench with a chuckle. "What for this time?" I asked.

He lifted his head so he could meet my eyes. "I've been wanting to share the couch with you since the day you got here."

I felt my ears burn and my insides erupt in a hurricane of butterflies and I opened my mouth to respond but nothing came out. Instead I turned and snuggled up against Peter, his body heat warming my back, his amazing, magical smell filling my head and his soft breathing lulling me to sleep.

Chapter Eight

The next morning I opened my eyes to the beautiful face of a sleeping boy next to me. I sat up carefully so I wouldn't wake him and looked around. The two of us were tangled up on the couch, our limbs twisted together in an unbreakable lock.

My crow mask lay on the floor below me and I carefully bent over to pick it up. In the light I could see the details I hadn't seen by the glow of the fire at the Indian camp. Obviously a black bird's head isn't big enough to make a mask that would cover a person's face but somehow this one was. It didn't look like it had been constructed out of different materials. The feathers were shiny and slick like oil, even though the thing had been thrown into the dirt and crumpled a few nights before. I ran my fingers down the bridge of the beak, feeling the rough ridges under my skin.

The part that connected with the face was covered in light fuzz like velvet. Then the top part of the beak curved down just a bit hooking over the bottom part. I poked my finger lightly to see how sharp it was. I bet this thing could do some damage if I smacked into someone hard enough. Maybe Tiger Lily needed a new hole in her face. Or maybe Russ did. Or maybe he needed a couple. Anything to make his appearance match his terrible attitude.

Carefully, I set it down on the floor again. As I did, my hand hit something under the lip of the couch. I reached under and pulled out Peter's hawk mask. The thing was magnificent. The feathers at the top and around the edges were a dark, chocolate brown and then lighter, almost tan, around the beak and eyeholes. The beak was sharp and curved down into a hook and a peppering of the chocolate brown, tan and white trailed down to the neck.

I heard Peter sigh behind me then felt his lips run up my arm. Still so soft. "This thing sure is regal looking, isn't it?" I asked pointing out the small fringe of goldish feathers along the top of the mask. Peter snorted in response. "What?"

He sat up and rested his feet on the floor next to mine. "I'm no regal figure," he replied and ran his hands through his hair.

"Tiger Lily seems to think so," I said with a small smile. Then I held out the mask to him. He took it carefully and held it flat in his palms. "She made these masks, right?"

"Well she also compared the girl I care about to a creature that likes to eat dead things."

A snort escaped my own nose. "I don't think she

meant it literally," I said and took my own mask from him. "Or maybe she did," I added more to myself. With my dark hair and pale skin, maybe she had thought I was some sort of death eater. "Do you really think I'm a crow, Peter?" I asked him, meeting his moss green eyes.

Peter bit his lip in thought and then smiled an adorable half smile. "I do," he said. "But not for the reasons Tiger Lily said. Crows are known for being intelligent and determined. I think you're both of those things."

I could feel a smile pulling at my own lips. Peter leaned in and touched his mouth to mine, taking my face in his hands and making me feel like I was falling. When he pulled away again, I was dizzy.

"You're getting good at that," I whispered.

He smiled as he took my mask back from me and put it on my face, securing the leather strap around my head. Then he put his own on. "What do you want to do today, my little black bird?" he asked nudging my shoulder with his own.

"I'm up for anything, oh mighty hawk man," I replied nudging him back.

His green eyes gleamed through the holes in his mask like two emerald stars. "I've got it." Then he stood up quickly, pulling me up with him and sniffed at the air. "But first, breakfast."

As soon as I stepped through the curtained doorway after Peter, we were met with whoops and wolf-whistles. My cheeks flamed immediately and I was glad the mask covered my face.

"All you codfish, shut your yap traps," Peter

barked, strolling down the ramp ahead of me. Of course none of the boys took his command seriously and took turns nudging and prodding him, laughing when he swatted back.

All I could do was stand back on the ramp and watch, my face hurting from the smile stretched across my mouth.

Breakfast consisted of fish, freshly caught by Mika and Finn and more of the beautiful and delicious suavas, picked from Cannibal Cove. I don't know how many I'd eaten already just since trying them a couple days earlier on our way to the Indian camp but it didn't seem to matter. The burst of coconut and citrus always took me by surprise and quenched any thirst I might have had. I hadn't had to drink anything since coming to Neverland. The craving for water never came to me. I didn't feel dehydrated or weak; in fact I'd never felt so good in my life. Every morning I woke there feeling more refreshed and renewed than the day before. Like the island was pumping energy into my body the way that nothing else could. It was getting harder to convince myself that I would eventually need to go back home.

Once we were all done eating, Russ mentioned something about getting a game of manhunt going and Kai immediately shot into the forest with Russ and the twins close behind. Pal hesitated at the edge of the clearing, looking back at me through his deer mask.

"Are you guys coming to play too?" he asked.

Peter took my hand and squeezed it. "I think I want to show Wynn Skull Rock today."

Pal shrugged then hurried off into the forest after the others. A sense of excitement welled up in my chest and Peter flashed me a white smile before pushing us off the ground. I closed my eyes as the cool wind rustled my hair and made goose bumps appear on my arms. While the wind was cold, the sun was warm creating a beautiful contradiction on my skin.

We sailed toward the water then along the beach, the wind getting stronger, whipping my dreadlocked hair wildly around my head. Peter caught a piece between two of his fingers. "I like this," he said to me over the rushing sound of the wind. "It makes you look more like–" Then he bit his lip in thought.

"Like what?"

He let go of my hair again and gave me a small, sad smile. "Like a lost girl."

The two of us flew in silence after that, neither wanting to bring up the inevitable. Pretty soon a cluster of jagged rocks came into view, the largest of them rounded like the top of a skull. Two dark holes like eye sockets gave me a glimpse of the pitch black void inside. It wasn't the wind this time that made my hairs stand on end.

The waves crashed dangerously against the rocks below as we sailed toward the opening to the cave. As soon as we got inside, we were enveloped in darkness. The air was frigid and the scent of seawater and charcoal entwined in my nostrils. I never thought I'd smell such a combination but, like all the other smells on this island, it was intoxicating. Peter didn't let go of my hand when we landed, probably so I didn't lose him.

"How are we supposed to see in here?" I asked. My voice bounced off the walls of the cavern causing me to jump and tense my fingers. Peter laughed and squeezed my hand back.

"We're not," he replied, closer to me than I'd expected. I felt the warmth of his face just before our lips connected. His other hand found mine and he pressed into me, backing me up.

"I can't see anything," I said against his lips. "What if I fall off the edge?"

I felt Peter's mouth curl up into a smile. "I won't let you fall," he replied.

He stumbled and my back hit the wall behind me. A chuckle escaped his throat and I matched his smile, lifting my arms to wrap around his neck as he deepened the kiss. My stomach was a hurricane of mixed emotions. Fear, excitement, passion and longing all blended together into the perfect storm making me weak in the knees and short of breath. Peter's hands trailed up my sides before resting against the wall on either side of me. Finally, his lips fell away and he touched his forehead to mine.

"I can't tell you how long I've been dreaming of this, Wynn," he whispered, his voice shaky with nerves. "I think…"

I waited in anticipation for him to finish his thought but instead his lips found mine again in the darkness. His body pressed up against me and his hands tangled into my hair. Wow, this boy learned fast. Again, too quickly, he pulled away and I held my breath, feeling my heart beat rapidly in my temples. "You think what?" I finally gasped.

"I think," he started again, trailing a finger from my ear lobe, along my jaw and then the ridge of my bottom lip. I closed my eyes, savoring the feeling of his touch on my tingling skin. "I think it's time to show you some dragons."

The smile on my face widened even though I knew he couldn't see it. "Really?"

Peter squeezed my hand and pulled me away from the wall. "Really," he replied and then our feet were no longer touching the ground.

We flew through the air blindly. I couldn't tell you how high above the water we were or how fast we were flying, as it was absolutely pitch dark in Skull Rock. As we flew, Peter drew me to his chest and touched his lips to mine in a long, savory kiss. I relaxed in his arms. I felt like I could slip right through his grasp and drip down like melted chocolate into the water below us but his arms were secure around me. He wouldn't let me go.

A low, distant rumbling from somewhere ahead of us had me pull away and crane my neck back. A soft, reddish glow lit the cavern far off in the distance. "What's that?" I cracked.

Peter cleared his own throat. "That's the dragons' den. The fire in their bellies makes their bodies glow. Pretty cool, huh?"

I couldn't do anything but stare ahead as the deep red light drew closer to us. Pretty soon it was all I could see until finally, we turned a corner and found ourselves in a huge cavern. The ceiling disappeared into the black making the place look endlessly tall. Cliffs of different heights jutted out from the walls like shelves all the way up and surrounded a floor of rock. Giant, sleeping creatures lazed everywhere, each one glowing like a big, red lantern. I gaped in awe as we neared one perched on a cliff higher up. Peter touched down soundlessly in front of the dragon and put a finger to his lips to signal me to stay quiet. I nodded in understanding as I took a cautious step away from him and toward the big monster. It lay with its tail wrapped around its body like a dog curled up on a bed. The whole thing was covered in iridescent, red scales that shimmered in the light like each one had its own tiny flame trapped inside. The dragon's pointed snout was only an arm's length away. I followed the wide bridge of its nose up to a pair of closed, black-rimmed eyes. As I wondered what color those eyes could be, Peter walked past me right up to its long, pointed snout.

"What are you doing?" I hissed at him.

"Just trust me," he replied then swatted the creature hard on the snout. "Rise and shine, napalm breath!"

I felt my jaw drop as the big beast snorted, sending a cloud of smoke out of its nostrils. What had Peter done? The two black-rimmed lids flew open like blinds over windows revealing big blood red eyes. The yellow pupils in the middle dilated to the size of dinner plates as they fell on me.

Uh oh.

I stood frozen in fear watching as the dragon lifted up onto its four pillar like legs, towering way above us. It stretched its long neck up toward the ceiling then sucked in a deep breath and roared. Hot air hit me like wind from an industrial fan. I could just barely see the glow of fire making its way up the throat through my squinted eyes. The flames were coming our way.

Quickly, I dove at Peter, knocking into him hard and wrapping my arms around his chest. The two of us fell from the cliff just as the fire stream hit the rock we'd been standing on. Peter quickly recuperated and we were no longer falling but sailing through the air. A pair of glimmering red and black wings opened on the dragon's back and flapped once, lifting the giant beast into the air. It let out another bellowing roar and a dozen more echoed from all around us. I watched in horror as more dragons set their red and yellow eyes on us and took to the air.

This was it. This was how I was going to die. I'll admit I'd wondered in the past how my life was going to end. I'd contemplated it a lot more recently with Great Gran's passing but I won't lie when I say that the thought of death by dragon had never even crossed my mind. Now it looked like that's what was going to happen. This was how I was going to go. In a literal blaze of glory.

The dragons flew together in a circle high above our heads, creating a whirlwind of hot air with their flapping wings. My hair danced wildly around my face making it hard for me to see. I was frozen in place, clutching Peter's jacket in terror.

Jets of fire shot at us from all directions and air rushed out of my lungs in the form of a scream. I felt the heat as it came closer, as it burned my skin, as it cooked my eyeballs then suddenly, I was enshrouded in cool air. I hadn't even realized my eyes were squeezed shut until the muscles in my face began to cramp. Finally, I cracked open a lid and watched the red glow fade off into the distance. Peter shook silently and I quickly realized he was in a fit of soundless laughter. I felt a fire begin to blaze in my own belly.

When we landed softly on a ledge just inside the mouth of the cave, I pushed away and smacked him hard on the arm. "What were you thinking?" I yelled and pushed him again.

Now Peter's laughter bounced off the walls in bellowing fits and I watched in the dim light as his body fell to the ground. I could almost see him clutching his stomach, eyes tearing from laughing too hard. "Oh Wynn!" he cackled. "You should have seen your face when I woke that dragon up." I crossed my arms over my chest. This was not funny. "I haven't seen someone's eyes get that big since Finn stuck a snapper beetle down the back of Mika's pants."

"Yeah, I bet it was hilarious," I muttered. "We could have been roasted alive back there!"

Peter stood back up and put his hands on my shoulders. "I said you could trust me," His words were serious and assuring but his eyes still sparkled with amusement.

I shook my head and put a hand on his chest to keep him away. "I felt the heat. They could have killed both of us."

A small smile played on his lips as he studied my face. "Just trust me, Wynn. Let me show you. You'll see. We'll be alright." And he took my hand, tugging me gently toward him.

With the hurricane building back up in my stomach, I bit my lip and let him pull me into the air again without a word. This time as we neared the glowing red room, I felt nothing but fear in my gut. No fascination. No awe. Just fear. Fear that made me grip Peter's fingers almost to their breaking point. Fear that had me breaking out in a cold sweat and shivering even as the air grew warmer. He wanted me to trust him, sure. But with my life?

We turned the corner into the cavernous room again. The dragons were back on their ledges but were restless and focused their attention on us the moment we came into view. When our feet touched the rock floor in the middle of the room, I clung to Peter, watching as one of the big, shimmering beasts took to the air with a flap of its mighty wings.

"Peter," I whispered but couldn't say anything else.

"It's okay, Wynn," he said with an easy smile. "You're safe with me."

The dragon settled down in front of us and I had to crane my neck to see its face. Those red and yellow eyes as big as dumpsters stared down at us curiously. Peter's hand that wasn't wrapped around my shoulders went up to the cord around his neck holding the little pouch of pixie dust.

"Watch this," he whispered to me. "Hey, Scaly!" he yelled up to the dragon. My body tensed in anticipation. "Why don't you show me what you got, you tail-turning, frogspawn-swallowing, scale-buffing bonfire-sniffer?"

The creature in front of us let out a bellowing roar that would put Godzilla to shame and rose up into the air. I pressed myself into him more, wishing I could shrink until I disappeared. The other dragons joined this one and I found myself in the same situation I'd been in before. They flew in a circle above us, creating the vortex of hot air that made my hair whip everywhere. Then with a loud chorus of roars, a pillar of fire came down toward us. I shut my eyes tight again and buried my face in Peter's neck as he clutched onto me tightly. I could feel the heat, the intensity building. Singeing the hair on my arms, threatening to annihilate me on the spot. Then the heat faded to an absolutely delightful warmth. Slowly, I peeked out from under Peter's chin only to find that we were standing in the middle of the vortex. The eye of the storm. Fire burned on all sides and above us creating a dome over our heads. Like a snow globe caught in an inferno.

"How?" I gasped taking a step toward the fire.

Peter chuckled. "Tink's pixie dust makes for a great creator of force fields."

I lifted my hand and touched it to the wall in front of me. It felt like there was a layer of glass separating us from the flames but it kept the intense heat out as well. The warmth moved across my hand as if I were touching something alive.

"Hey."

I turned around again to face Peter. He bit his lip, a spark of sadness in his eyes. "I told you, you could trust me," he said taking a step my way. His hands came up to cup my face and his lips pressed against my forehead. "I'd never let anything happen to you, Wynn." He placed a kiss on the bridge of my nose. "I'll never let anything hurt you." Then he pressed his lips against mine and I felt my feet lift off the ground. I kissed him back as we rose into the air, the anger and fear in me leaving my body to be burned up by the fire surrounding us.

I felt a different fire welling up in me, scorching through my veins and heating my heart until I thought I was going to burst into flames.

I think…I think I love this boy.

Chapter Nine

That night Peter and I sat by the fire alone while the other boys were off doing their own thing. "I'm going to miss all this," I said looking up at the sky through the trees.

Peter stopped strumming and I looked down to meet his frown. "Then why don't you stay, Wynn?" he asked, a hint of irritation in his voice. "I know, I know. We've had this discussion before. You can't stay here because you feel like you belong back with your mother and your friend in your world."

I looked down at the ground as sadness washed over me like an icy tidal wave. We had talked about this. I already knew what he wanted. I knew what I wanted, but what I wanted and what needed to happen weren't the same. If only he could come back with me.

That was it. "Why don't you come with me?"

Peter's face fell and he just stared at me like he was trying to process what I'd said. "What?"

"Come with me back to LA," I said scooting closer to him on the log. "You can meet my mom and Marty and go to my school with me and we can graduate and grow up together. It'll be perfect."

"Grow up," he repeated, the words leaving his mouth in a whisper. I could almost see the internal struggle as he considered it. This boy that had stopped aging at seventeen would suddenly have to deal with it again.

"What's wrong, Peter?" I asked feeling the spark in my heart slowly die.

"I can't go with you, Wynn," he said shaking his head. "I can't grow up."

"Why not?"

Peter stood up and paced to the other side of the fire. I sat silently, watching, my heart hammering against my ribcage as I waited for him to answer me. Finally, he turned back around to face me. "I used to go and visit your great grandmother. I'd fill her in on everything that was going on, everything she was missing. My visits became fewer and further between. She didn't even look like Wendy anymore. I had to watch your Great Gran get old," he said. Then he sat down on the rock across the fire from me. "And I couldn't do anything about it. Humans can only come here once and then when you leave, once you've been gone for twenty-four earth hours, once you start aging, you can't come back, Wynn. Whenever I left, I was never gone for more than a couple hours."

I shrugged sadly. "So what do you want me to do then?"

Peter bit his lip then let out a frustrated growl and dropped his head into his hands. "I don't know," he muttered. "I want you to stay."

"And I want you to go."

Neither of us said anything as we sat there. My eyes stayed locked on the flames licking at the air in front of me but I could feel Peter's eyes on me, like he was waiting for me to give in.

Maybe Disney hadn't been completely wrong about everything. Maybe Peter was just an unrelenting, stubborn boy. Though I didn't really have any room to talk. Both of us were asking the other to give up their home, their family, their life. And if neither of us was going to crack, where did that leave us?

"I need to take a walk," I whispered, getting up and leaving my crow mask sitting on the log next to me.

I heard Peter jump up. "Let me come with you."

"No," I said, my voice coming out harsh and abrupt. "I just need time to think." Then without turning around to meet his stare, I slipped between two trees, leaving him to watch as I disappeared into the forest.

The sun was setting and the branches overhead blocked out most of the dimming light but still I was able to see clearly without tripping and it took me a minute to realize that the fairies were following behind me, silently illuminating my path with their soft white glow. I caught a glimpse of Lyssa's gauzy wings in my peripheral but my heart was too heavy for me to say anything or give her a smile. Instead, we continued in silence, the fairies keeping me on a straight path toward the beach.

Of course Peter wouldn't want to come with me.

How could I be stupid enough to ask that of him? Especially, when I didn't even know his true feelings for me. So we'd kissed a few times and I had slept curled up in his arms, his breath on the back of my neck, his nose buried in my hair…his heart beating so steadily like a soft drum against my shoulder blade. He'd told me I could trust him and that he'd never let anything hurt me, but what does such an eternal promise mean to someone that is themselves' eternal? How easy is it to forget about something you said years ago? Decades? Centuries? On his life's timeline, I was just a speck growing smaller with every passing day until I was so small I wouldn't even register in his memory. But with just these past few days, he had become the biggest mark on my own timeline and things would never be able to go back to normal for me. And with every passing day, the sadness would just get bigger until he's not just the biggest part, but the whole thing, and life would no longer matter.

"How pathetic am I?"

It was dark by the time I got to the water but the fairies' soft glow helped light the way. I sat down on the sand and wrapped my arms around my legs, hugging my knees to my chest. The moon was full and bright white and stars twinkled brilliantly around it and across the sky reminding me a bit of when I used to look out my window when I was a little girl at the skyline. Lights would go on and off in the buildings making them look like they were twinkling stars.

A wave climbed slowly toward me, threatening to get my feet wet but I didn't move. Instead, I watched as the water filled in the dimple my toes were in.

Slowly, I rose up to my knees and made my way down into the water, sitting down again so it reached just barely below my waist. Immediately, I was warmed and I closed my eyes, smelling the salty air. I was glad my Great Gran had decided to come home, otherwise I wouldn't be here, but smelling the air, feeling the water surround me like an embrace, how did she not fall in love with the place and never want to leave?

"Are you here all by yourself?"

I opened my eyes quickly to find an auburn head sticking up out of the water in front of me. "Calliope?" She drifted closer to me, riding in on the tide. I looked around to find that the fairies had left and I was, in fact, alone. "I guess I am," I said with a shrug.

Calliope came to sit next to me and the two of us looked up at the moon in silence for a moment. "I didn't get the chance to really meet you the other day," she said at last, her voice barely louder than the waves.

"It's okay," I assured her and the wind caused me to shiver. I hugged my knees closer to my chest. "You were with Pal." When I glanced over at her she had a small smile on her pale lips like she was thinking about that day. "You really like him," I said with a grin.

"He's not like the other lost boys."

I chuckled, thinking about how loud and uncaring they had been to Harmony and her desire to have dry hair. "No," I agreed. "Pal does seem different."

"He's very sweet," she added with a smile. "Though, I wish he would take that mask off so I could see his face." I straightened my legs out so my toes were just barely visible above the water. Calliope's tail rose up above the surface and hit the water making a soft slapping sound. I lifted my legs up out of the water to try to do the same and she snickered when they hit with a hollow *ka-thunk*. "Do you think he'll ever let me see his face again?" Calliope asked me, the smile replaced with a look of uncertainty.

I bit the inside of my cheek as she hugged her knees – or whatever mermaids have – to her chest. "Hey," I said and she rested the side of her face on them so she was looking at me sideways. "If Pal is going to take his mask off for anyone, it will be you."

Her mouth drew up into a smile and she closed her eyes. "Thanks, Wynn," she said then rested her chin on her hands again and looked out at the water. "You're really kind, you know."

"Thanks," I said feeling shy all of a sudden.

"Who cares what the others think."

This caused me to sit up straight and look at her. "What do the others think?" I asked suddenly feeling sick to my stomach.

Calliope shrugged. "Harmony just says you're a bit boring."

"Boring?" I huffed. "How am I boring? How would she even know if I was boring?"

She smiled at my reaction. To be honest, I didn't see what was so funny. "You didn't get into the water and swim with everyone else."

"Neither did you," I said, putting my chin back down on my arms and glaring at the moon.

The smile didn't leave Calliope's face and I could hear the amusement in her voice. "But I'm always in the water. What's your excuse?"

I sighed and closed my eyes. "I guess I don't have one," I said. "This is all just too new to me. I think I was still in a bit of shock."

"Shock?"

"I just met Peter a few days ago and this is all just too…out there."

Calliope turned so she was facing me. "You don't know do you?" she asked with excitement in her voice.

I turned to face her too and crossed my legs so I was sitting Indian style in the water. "Know what?"

Her shoulders lifted in a shrug of excitement like she was the one who had the privilege of revealing a big secret. Maybe it was a big secret. "Peter has been searching for you. For *you*, Wynn!" she said taking my hands in hers. They felt slick and a bit slimy like I was holding onto a fish.

"He's been searching for me?" I asked, repeating what she had just said.

Calliope clutched my hands even tighter. "Oh Wynn, you have no idea what this boy feels for you." My heart fluttered with excitement and pounded with fear at the same time. How had Peter had feelings for me if I'd never even met him before that night at Exile? "He's been making a lot of trips to your world lately and we all wondered what was so special about you. He would come back from his trips and tell us about what you were like and what you were doing.

I couldn't help but feel flattered. Peter was there in Neverland, surrounded by beauty and beautiful women that seemed to just fling themselves at anyone and he could have any of them, judging by the way they all – except for Calliope – looked at him, and he chose me. Some quiet girl that did ballet and danced like a schizophrenic person at clubs on Friday nights. The fear in my chest immediately disappeared, leaving just the floating feeling in my heart. All those times I had thought I was invisible, he saw me. I had to go back to him. I was so lost in my head that I hadn't realized I was staring at Calliope with my mouth hanging open like an idiot.

"Wynn?" she said with a look of confusion on her face.

I shook my head to clear it and squeezed her hand. "I have to go," I said quickly and stood up, almost falling over when my feet moved through the water like it was mud. Leaving her sitting there, I scampered out of the water and back up onto land. "Thanks, Calliope!" I called back with a wave as I ran.

She waved back then disappeared beneath the surface with a ripple. The fairies were gone so the forest was pitch dark but I was still able to follow the path back to camp. I couldn't wait to get back to Peter. I needed to tell him how I really felt. I needed to touch him and kiss those lips again. Those lips that tasted the way Christmas trees smell.

I broke through the trees, my lungs burning and my hair plastered to my face with cold sweat and looked around the clearing. It was dark and silent and empty. Everyone must have still been gone. Then something stirred in my peripheral vision and my eyes landed on a shadow sitting by the fire pit.

Russ stood up and brushed off his pants slowly when I started walking toward him. "What are you doing out here?" I asked him, crossing my arms against the cold. Why was the weather so weird here? It was so warm out on the beach but always so cold in the woods.

"I just need to talk to you," Russ said stuffing his hands in his pockets and looked down at the ground.

"I feel like we got off to a bit of a rough start."

I let out a laugh. "You think?"

He kicked the dirt with his toe. "You heard about what happened last time Pan brought a girl here, didn't you?" he asked and moved his eyes but not his head up to look at me.

"Yeah, I guess."

"He and Hook were friends before that whole mess. Don't you see, Wynn?" he asked now lifting his head and holding it high. "Your great grandmother ruined everything," he continued and took a step toward me. "If she hadn't come here, none of this would have happened and everything would still be okay."

I began to back up now as the look in Russ's eyes turned to anger. "What are you doing?"

"I'm sorry, Wynn," Russ said pulling a knife out from his back pocket. "But Hook wants his revenge."

He lunged at me and I stumbled back in time as the blade sliced the air in front of me. My heart pounded hard in my chest. I needed to yell for help. I needed to get out of there. As I whirled around and sucked in my breath to scream, Russ grabbed me, wrapping one arm around my face, covering my mouth and holding the other one across my collar bone. The edge of the knife rested against my throat. "You will not breathe a word," he whispered into my ear. Then he buried his nose in my hair and inhaled deeply. "Too bad we're in a hurry," he said and I arched my back to try and put as much distance between us as possible. It wasn't very effective but he seemed to get it. With a growl, Russ pulled me back and used his body to push me forward. His hand didn't leave my mouth, and I could taste the

165

dirt and sweat on his palm, and the knife pressed into my neck as the tree fort and Peter got farther away. I quickly glanced up at the canopy. Where were all the fairies?

After we had been walking for a while and were well out of sight of the camp and covered in the shadows of the trees, Russ's grip on me loosened a bit. He took his hand away from my mouth and spun me around to look at him. With one hand still holding the knife to my throat, he brought his other hand up and trailed his fingers down the side of my face. "You really are beautiful, Wynn," he breathed, though his eyes were still wild.

"I thought you were Peter's friend," I said coldly, trying my hardest to keep my face completely unemotional, though my insides were writhing at his touch. His thumb brushed over my lip and I had to fight the urge to bite it off. The knife felt like ice pressed against the skin of my throat.

Russ let out a chuckle. "Sure I was," he said. "Until Wendy came and ruined everything."

"And now you're blaming me for something you *think* is my great grandmother's fault?" I asked finally turning my head away from his hand.

With a twitch of his lip, Russ reached around the back of my head and grabbed a fist full of my hair, pulling back so I was forced to look into those cold gray eyes of his. "This has nothing to do with you," he spat, "and everything to do with what Pan did to Hook." Then he let go of my hair and dropped both his arms before stepping back. "It's what all you women do! You weasel your way into our hearts then rip them out without a second thought."

"How do you know what we apparently *do*?" I asked crossing my arms, wishing I could rub my throat with my hand.

"I saw what Wendy did to Hook. I see what you're doing to Pan." Then he turned the knife letting the moon glint off the blade. "Maybe I should save everyone the heartache and just end you right here."

A shudder went through my body. Did Russ really want to kill me? Would he go through with something like that? I had to run. But he was so much faster than me. I'd seen the way he sped through this forest when he was racing Peter and me. I needed to hurt him. My eyes darted down to his side. The moon flashed off his skin and for a second I saw the long white scar left there so many years ago when they had escaped Hook's ship. Peter said it still ached. Before Russ could see what I was focused on, I turned my attention back to his face.

"Are you sure you're not just jealous?" I asked him trying to keep my voice from quivering. The muscles in his jaw moved under his skin as he ground his teeth and glared at me.

"Jealous?"

I took a tentative step forward then another. "Sure," I shrugged. "You just said you see what I'm doing to Peter. Are you sure you don't wish something like that could happen to you too?" Then I stopped in front of him. My body only inches from his. "Don't you wish you could feel what they felt?" I asked putting one of my hands around his neck and tangling my fingers into his hair. My face was dangerously close to his and I could see the pores in his nose. "Or maybe experience what he's experienced?" Russ's breath was shaky and hot on my face as I lifted up onto the balls of my feet to get closer. Just when I could feel the warmth coming off his lips, I jabbed my hand forward, keeping my fingers straight and dug them into his side with the scar.

Russ keeled forward crying out in pain. When his knees hit the dirt, I kicked him hard in the ribs and took off running, pumping my legs as fast as they would go. I wasn't following any sort of path so I had no idea where I was going. As long as I wasn't running parallel to the water, I would eventually reach the camp or the beach. Either way there was someone that would be able to help me, whether it was a lost boy or a mermaid. I didn't care which. I just needed to run. Run. Run. Ru-

Suddenly, I was slammed from behind and went crashing to the dirt. I could hear Russ cursing at me under his breath as he tried to get his arms around my squirming body. Somehow he managed to get me on my back and then the last thing I saw were his cold gray eyes before something hit the side of my head hard and I was plunged into darkness.

When I was able to open my burning eyelids, I shut them again immediately. My head pounded and the light, wherever it was coming from, only made the pain worse. I tried to lift my hands to cover my eyes but they were stopped halfway to my face. I opened my eyes, slowly this time, and squinted at my surroundings. I was in a small room, lying on a very scratchy blanket on a very uncomfortable bench. I sat up and rested my back against the wall. The place was smaller than I had thought. More like a large walk in closet. There was a locked cabinet above my head and a small window with smudged glass next to that. I wasn't quite high enough to reach it so I just kept scanning the room. A net was hooked on all four corners to the ceiling and ropes and a couple beat up looking lanterns hung from it along with the skeletons of a few different types of fish that I'd never seen before. At least I'm assuming they were fish.

There was a shelf at my feet and I stood up so I could take a look at it. When I tried to move, my arms were pulled back again. Looking down at my wrists I saw there was a piece of rope as thick as my thumb wrapped several times around them. The end was secured to a metal loop sticking out from the wall. I pulled hard a few times with no success, leaving the skin on my arms burning and the rope still tied securely.

Maybe I could stand up on the bench and see out the window. I managed to get up onto my feet and had to crane my neck to be able to see out of the dirty glass. Nothing but ocean as far as I could see. I could feel panic rising up in my throat like salt water as I searched for anything that could resemble land. Just some break in the straight line of the horizon. Anything. Just then the whole room shifted and I was sent sprawling onto the floor. My shoulder hit the ground hard and I cried out in pain. Movement caught my eye and I whipped my head around. In the doorway stood a boy my age. His hair was dark and shaggy and his wide eyes were as blue as Chime's tale. He looked a little worse for wear. He had on a loose white shirt that hung off his lean frame. It was ripped and stained with dark smudges. Some dirt, some blood. His pants were also ripped in a few places but he himself didn't look hurt. Was the blood staining the shirt not his?

"Are you alright?" he asked, his eyes still wide.

I got up as carefully as I could. My arms were stuck above my head, held up by the short rope. It was rather difficult and I was slightly embarrassed as I tried to right myself again. A pain shot through my shoulder and I tried not to wince. It obviously didn't work because the boy rushed forward to help me get all the way to my feet. I wasn't able to completely straighten up, again, because of the rope.

"Thanks," I muttered once I was on my feet and stable. "I'm Wynn."

"I know," the boy said with a crooked smile. When I narrowed my eyes skeptically, he continued. "People around here seem to know who you are. You're Wendy's granddaughter, right?"

"Great granddaughter," I corrected him, softening my hard stare.

The boy stuck his hand out, the other one, I noticed, was wrapped and in a sling. "Well, it's a pleasure to meet you," he said widening his smile. I moved my hands together to show that I couldn't return the shake and he brought his own hand up to scratch the back of his neck awkwardly. "Sorry," he muttered then pulled a knife out of the back of his pants. I immediately tried to take a step back when the memory of Russ holding his knife to my throat flashed through my mind. The boy held his hand up. "I just want to cut the ropes off your hands."

Hesitantly, I held out my arms to him and he grabbed hold of my wrists. Then he took the blade and started sawing the ropes between them. My bindings broke after a few strokes and fell to the floor. "Thanks," I said and rubbed at the raw skin on my wrists. "What is this place?" I asked after looking around again for a few moments.

"You're on the Jolly Roger," he replied and put his knife away again.

I could feel my heartbeat stammer for a second and I started feeling sick to my stomach. "The Jolly Roger?" I asked quietly. "Hook's ship?" So Russ had been serious when he'd said Hook wanted to get Peter back for letting my Great Gran leave. My eyes landed on the boy's wrapped hand again. The pain in my head kept me from putting two and two together.

He peered at me a bit worriedly. "Wynn?" he said putting his good hand on my arm. I flinched. "Are you alright?"

I tried to focus on steadying my breathing again as the edges of my vision began to get black. I couldn't pass out. I had to find a way to get out of there. "I need to go," I whispered, my wide eyes matching his.

"You can't go," he replied shaking his head. "We're out in the middle of shark infested waters. There's no way to leave without a life boat."

My vision was beginning to go dark and after a few seconds, I could only see shapes and outlines. I had to get out of there. I pushed past the boy and stumbled through the doorway not really sure where I was going. I could barely see anything so I stuck my arms out in front and to the sides, feeling the walls with my hands as I hurried down the short hallway. Just a few seconds later, I hit a staircase going up. Up was a lot better than down. I took the steps two at a time and my vision was already getting a bit better.

Once I hit the top of the stairs, I found myself in another hallway. This one was bustling with people. All of them boys, all of them menacing looking. One caught me hard in the shoulder. He wore a thick dark sweater with the sleeves pushed up past his elbows and I caught a glimpse of a skull tattoo on his forearm. Another one, skinny with greasy hair and a long scar running down his face glared at me as I passed him, mumbling something to someone else. I caught the word "girl" and knew he was talking about me. I really needed to get out of there. My eyesight was beginning to darken again as the air grew thinner and hotter. I could see the end of the hallway and another flight of stairs. So close. So close.

I was so focused on the staircase, I didn't notice the boy standing next to it in the dark corner with his head down. Not until he lifted his head and I saw the pointed nose of a fox. I couldn't help it. I felt a scream rise up in my throat as Russ lunged at me, tackling me to the ground.

My vision was almost completely black by now. Russ stared down at me through the fox's eyes. I'm sure he was smiling at me from behind that mask. "Step aside, Russ," I heard someone yell harshly. "She's mine now."

"But Hook," he argued.

"I said step aside!"

It all continued to darken and I could barely make out the boy's face as he pushed through the crowd that had formed around me. The arm that had been in a sling was now hanging down at his side. The last thing I saw was the glint of a shiny metal hook as he brought his hand down toward my face.

I woke up again to ocean blue eyes only inches from mine. With a start I backed up as far as I could, my back hitting the wall behind me. An amused smile spread across the lips of the dark haired boy as he stared at me. "How'd you sleep?" he asked me, almost kindly.

"You – you tricked me," I stammered bringing my knees up to my chest. I looked around as best as I could. I was in a different room than the first time I'd woken up. This room was bigger and less cluttered. A giant window looked out at the ocean and a desk sat in front of it. I could picture him pacing back and forth behind the desk, eyes on the horizon as they cut through the water. Against the adjacent wall was a big, wide bookshelf that covered the whole wall. There were a few books on it. All really old. And a globe, along with more of those weird fish skeletons and finally my eyes settled on a crocodile head. The thing stared menacingly at me with its vacant, black eye holes. Then I realized it was a mask. A mask from Tiger Lily? It had to be.

"I never tricked you," Hook said as I tore my eyes away from the crocodile mask.

"You're Hook," I said and slowly got to my feet. I was still light headed so I had to put my hand against the wall to steady myself.

He smiled a crooked smile that made him almost look charming and innocent. That was when I noticed he was no longer wearing that ratted old shirt. Now, instead his clothes were cleaner. He wore a black baggy shirt, tied loosely right on his chest bone and a black coat that looked similar to the tattered one Peter wore. Though this one was in much better shape. The hook in place of his hand gleamed menacingly. More like hematite than metal.

"It's quite fitting, isn't it?" Hook asked, his smile widening as he noticed my eyes rake over him. He probably thought I was ogling over how attractive he was.

"I can think of a few names that are more fitting."

He leaned in close. "You can call me James if you'd like."

"What am I doing here?" I finally asked.

He went over and sat down at the big desk and put his boots up on top of it. "You're my bait," he said scraping the tip of his hook against his thumb. I couldn't tell how sharp it was but I bet if he pushed a little harder it would break the skin.

"Bait?" I watched the metal glimmer in the sunlight.

"I want Peter Pan on my ship," Hook explained, the amused look having been replaced with anger. "And the only way to get him here was to take something valuable to him."

It took me a second to figure out what he was saying. "Me?" I asked surprised. "I haven't even been here for very long. How do you know I'm valuable to him? Why didn't you take one of his lost boys?"

Hook shrugged. "I think this will be more effective," he said with a click of his teeth.

I crossed my arms and bit my lip. This couldn't be happening. I really hoped Peter wouldn't fall for this. He couldn't. He must have known what Hook was up to. I had to get off this ship myself. "Well what am I supposed to do till he gets here?" I finally asked trying to sound like this didn't affect me.

The look on his face only wavered for a second before he regained composure. "Just sit tight," he said and stabbed his hooked hand into the wooden top of his desk. "It's not like you can get off this ship anyway." He sat there and whittled in silence for a few moments as I stared at him. A strand of his glossy black hair fell into his eyes when he looked up again at me. "I hear Russ is looking for someone to keep him company," he added with a knowing smile.

I clenched my hands into fists. "No thanks," I uttered through gritted teeth. I remembered all too well the way he'd eyed me when I first met him, then how he had grabbed me and held that knife against my throat and pressed his body against my back in a way that definitely made me think he had ulterior motives.

Heavy boots stomped down the hall behind me and I snapped my head toward the door as the guy with the bulky sweater and skull tattoo appeared. "Cap'n!" he grunted. "We're ready to set sail."

A crooked smile curled one side of Hook's mouth up. "Ah good," he said then glanced my way. "Put her out, Smee! Draw anchor and hoist the sails!"

Smee gave a strong nod. "Aye, Cap'n." Then he hurried back down the hall. I stared again at Hook and the two of us listened as the footsteps faded into silence.

Finally, he let out a chuckle as he strolled toward the door. Just before disappearing through it, he turned to me and leaned in close, a grin on his face as wide and wicked as a crocodile's. "Welcome to the

Jolly Roger, Wyndy."

Chapter Ten

I stayed there against the wall for a few more moments and stared out the wide window behind Hook's desk. Through the far edge of the glass, I could see Neverland's white sand beach. The ocean stretched on forever next to it. Slowly, I walked toward the window, taking careful steps that were drowned out by the commotion overhead. This couldn't be happening. This couldn't be real. But then I guess that would mean Peter and the other lost boys wouldn't be real either. The whole week I'd spent there wouldn't be real. Even though I'd never felt more alive or awake than I had in Neverland. At least not ever since Great Gran's death. My brain had been so clouded for the past month.

The room lurched just then and I fell to my knees in front of the glass. I scurried forward and peered sideways out the window as the land began slowly drifting away from us. I was really going to be trapped on this ship with this awful guy and his mangy crew. I had to get out and now was my only chance.

Without another thought, I scrambled to my feet and lunged for the door. The hallway was dark but I sprinted forward anyway, my boots squeaking along the polished wood floor. My feet hit stairs and I quickly climbed, taking two at a time. I bypassed another hallway, now empty thanks to everyone being up on the deck. Finally, I saw another set of stairs illuminated by sunshine and dove for them, using my hands to pull myself up faster.

The deck was a mess of bodies, all doing their jobs to get the ship away from shore. None of them seemed to notice me as they tended to their tasks and I took the opportunity to make my way toward the nearest edge. My fingernails dug into the wooden rails as I looked down at the churning water far below. The beach wasn't too far away and I knew how to swim well enough. I could make it. I could make it back to shore and run back to Peter. As quickly and carefully as I could, I pulled myself up onto the railing, my eyes never leaving the water below me.

All it would take is a step.

Just step off, Wynn.

I lifted one foot at the same moment strong arms wrapped around my thighs and tugged me back. I almost fell forward and smacked my head but the arms loosened enough so I'd slip. "What do you think you're doing, love?" I recognized the throaty whisper and tried to squirm out of Russ's grasp but he just squeezed me tighter.

"Let me go!" I screamed as I thrashed and threw my head back. Finally, he brought one arm up to brace against my neck and I was unable to move.

"She was trying to jump ship, Captain!" Russ yelled as he turned to face us away from land.

Hook sauntered down the steps from the upper deck, the crooked smile still on his face, his eyes gleaming and his shaggy black hair blowing in the salty ocean wind.

He walked right up to us and brought a hand up to snatch a piece of my wild hair between his fingers. "Now, Wyndy. Is that any way to treat your Captain?" he tsked.

I reared back and spit. Since my mouth was dry from fear, nothing more than a pathetic shower of spittle came out but I figure he got the gist of it. "You're not my captain," I snarled and Russ's arm tightened across my chest.

Hook calmly swiped his thumb across his top lip where I'd hit him. "I am while you're on my ship."

"Well then just let me off. Problem solved."

He met Russ's eyes for a moment before giving him a small nod. With a hard push, Russ propelled me forward, keeping a strong grip on my body. "Where are you taking me?"

"Somewhere you can't cause any more trouble," he growled leading me back into the dark depths of the ship.

I stayed quiet after that as I tried to pay attention to every turn we took and every stairwell we descended but this place was a maze and I soon lost track. Finally, we entered a dimly lit room with a grimy iron-barred cell. The air was frigid and smelled like mold and mildew. This had to be the lowest part of the ship. I imagined only the slimy wall separated me from the icy ocean on the other side. A small, circular window up above my head confirmed my suspicions.

"Well, Wynn, I hope you enjoy your stay on the Jolly Roger," Russ said as he shoved me through the little doorway into the cell and shut the barred door.

I turned and watched him make his way back toward the hallway. "How could you do this, Russ?" I asked quietly as I wrapped my fingers around the cold iron bars. He stopped mid-step. "How could you betray Peter like this? After everything he's done for you?"

Russ didn't respond at first. Just kept his back to me. Then with a heavy sigh he turned and took two quick strides to close the space between us. His cold gray eyes glared into mine, shining like a sharpened blade. His lips were parted slightly as if he was wanting to say something and I thought he was about to. Instead he gave me a sadistic smile and reached up for the mask on top of his head. "They don't call me the fox for nothing," he responded and pulled it down to cover his face. Then with a taunting nod, he turned and started back out of the room.

"I wouldn't call you a fox," I said quickly, my breath fogging in the air. "You're nothing but a coward."

Russ hesitated for only a second before slipping out of the room, closing the heavy door behind him.

The only light was that from the sun where it penetrated the ocean surface and came in through the little circular window. It barely lit up the tiny room though it had been enough to glint off Russ's steel eyes and reflect the evil within. Or maybe his soul was so toxic, it radiated out of him, creating its own malicious glow.

I couldn't keep my teeth from chattering in the cold and my hands did nothing to keep the frigid air from soaking into my body and freezing the blood in my veins. I'd been pacing back and forth for a while, trying to keep warm but I soon noticed my movements growing more sluggish the colder I got. This was it. I was going to die down there.

Feeling my chin tremble, I bit down on my bottom lip and sat on a wooden box in the corner against the wall. With my forehead resting on my knees, I focused on keeping my breathing deep and my heartbeat even. A hot tear slid down my cheek cutting through the ice for only a second before dripping off my face and soaking into my leggings.

If only I hadn't gone by myself to the ocean to talk to Calliope. If only I hadn't gotten into that argument with Peter. If only I hadn't kissed him on the beach the other day or let Tiger Lily's words affect me so much or even left Exile that night with Peter. None of this would have happened if I hadn't been at the front of the stage with Marty which wouldn't have happened if I hadn't gone to school that day and agreed to go to this new club with her. And absolutely none of it would have happened if Great Gran hadn't died, which wouldn't have happened if she'd stayed in Neverland like she'd surely wanted to do. Which means I wouldn't have happened. And I wouldn't be there freezing to death, trapped in the belly of this evil ship run by an evil captain.

Another tear escaped trailing fire down my cheek as

I hugged my shaking knees even tighter. A low moan made the wall behind me shutter and I got to my feet to see what it was. The room was completely dark now. My eyes went directly up to the window. A large shimmery orb filled the hole and a dark pupil darted left and right before finally settling on me.

My numbing lips still quivered but somehow I managed to get them to form a word. "Scylla." The whisper materialized into a white cloud for a second before dissipating again. With achy, sluggish movements, I climbed up on top of the wooden box and touched my flat palm to the glass separating me from the big purple monster. "Scylla," I wheezed again.

The creature moaned in response and rolled its giant pupil.

I touched my teeth down on my bottom lip as I tried to form another word but the cold stole my breath leaving me stuttering incoherently. "*Ffff…fff.*"

Again Scylla whined like a helpless dog. I tried harder to push the words out. "*Ffff…fffindd…*" My knees cramped up and I fell, landing on the concrete floor. It didn't even hurt. My whole body was numb. My vision blurred but I could just barely make out the monster's eye darting from side to side. Still my mouth continued to move and my body tried to spit out the words. "*Fffind…P…*" The cold darkness crowded in and my eyelids grew heavier. My cheek rested against the damp floor and I forced my frozen lungs to pull in one more breath of icy air. As they finally collapsed in on themselves, I was able to whisper his name. "*Peter.*"

Chapter Eleven

I felt warmth soaking into my skin before anything else. Then the pain started. A groan escaped my throat as I rolled over, my shoulder throbbing in rhythm with my heartbeat. Somewhere above me, I heard the captain swear and call for Russ.

"Are you trying to ruin my only chance at getting Pan?"

"I thought you wanted me to take her to the cell."

Finally, I was able to crack my eyelids open enough to see two silhouettes against the sun. Hook let out a growl and poked his hooked hand under Russ's chin, forcing him to stand taller. "Only until she learned her lesson. You left her in there for three hours, you bilge rat!" he yelled shoving him. Russ's back hit hard against the mast. "She could have died!"

Russ furrowed his brow and clenched his teeth until

the lines showed in his jaw. "Well, clearly she didn't, alright?" he yelled flinging his hand in my direction. I cringed feeling my body curl up tighter as if he'd physically hurt me. "What would have been so bad about that anyway?"

Ouch.

The captain lunged at Russ wrapping his good hand around his throat and backed him into the mast again. The tip of his hook dug into Russ's cheek. "Listen here you worthless, pathetic excuse for a pirate!" Spit shot from his mouth on the last word. "This isn't about you! If you even *think* about doing something so stupid again, I'll sling a rope round your neck and keelhaul your land loving butt till you bleed dry! Aye?"

Russ didn't respond. I didn't know what keelhauling was but it didn't sound pleasant.

Hook squeezed his throat harder and Russ's head sagged, his hate-filled eyes landing on my own "Aye," he finally wheezed. Hook released him from his grip and Russ fell to the ground, slumping back against the mast. Blood slid down his cheek where the captain's hook bit into his skin but he didn't move to wipe it away.

The sound of Hook's heavy boots finally made me rip my eyes away from Russ and I lifted my head to meet his blue-eyed gaze. "Doing alright there, deary?" he asked cocking his head to the side in mock concern.

I shivered though I don't know if it was because Russ was still glaring at me or because I hadn't quite thawed out all the way yet. "Yeah, just peachy," I managed to whisper as I sat up. My one whole side still ached and I could feel a bruise on my cheekbone where it had struck the cold floor in the cell but the ocean air was warm and the sun felt glorious on my skin. I could have been worse. Though at the same time I also could have been a lot better. I glared back at Russ. "Just keep him away from me," I growled then stood up slowly and painfully. Russ didn't move from his spot at the foot of the mast but I could feel his eyes on the back of my head as I shouldered my way past Hook. "You stay away from me too."

He wrapped his metal hook around my arm to stop me. "Ah, don't worry, Miss Wyndy," he purred in a low voice only I could hear. "You'll warm up eventually." Then with a wink, he took his metal hand away from my arm and strode up the stairs. "In the meantime, let's put you to work," he said then spun around to face me. "Morgan!" he called. A spindly looking kid, shorter and younger than me, scurried over. Judging by the mop and bucket in his hands, and the way the bottoms of his frayed pants were soaked, he'd been cleaning some part of the ship.

"Yes, Cap'n?" he asked in a high voice. He couldn't be any older than thirteen.

"Why don't you have Wyndy here help you clean the upper deck?"

"Aye, Cap'n."

"It's Wynn," I uttered hoarsely. "Wyndy is an old person's name."

Hook shrugged. "I like it."

"You would."

Without another word, he turned back around and sauntered away leaving me to babysit bucket boy. Morgan glanced over at me then averted his eyes again as his ears turned red. I peered at him with an eyebrow raised.

"Uh," he stuttered. "I'll show you what to do."

I followed behind him across the deck as the rest of the crew went about their duties. The boy with the long scar down his face sat on a wooden crate peeling potatoes with an oversized blade. A large pile of peelings sat at his feet. When he was done with this one, he tossed it over his shoulder and it landed among others in a barrel. Judging by the look of the barrel, I didn't think I wanted to eat any of those potatoes come dinnertime. Then again I wasn't even sure they were going to feed me.

"This way," Morgan called and I realized I'd stopped walking to watch Scarface work. He looked up and winked at me with the eye that wasn't scarred. I quickly moved on after Morgan, and he got back to peeling.

By the time I got to the upper deck, the kid had set down his bucket of water and mop. He got down on his knees and pulled a dripping rag out of the bucket. Water slopped out all over the sealed wood.

"See all those black marks?" he asked purposefully not making eye contact with me.

I nodded before realizing he couldn't see the motion. "Yeah," I muttered.

He started scrubbing at them with the grungy rag. "Hook don't like boot marks on the boards of his ship so we gotta scrub 'em off."

I looked down at my own boots and kicked at the floor. Sure enough, the sole left a black streak on the dark wood. "Don't you think this is kind of pointless?" I asked. "You're never going to be able to get them all off."

"It don't matter," Morgan said and rubbed the one

away that I had just made. "It's what Hook wants."

I rolled my eyes. "And what Hook wants, Hook gets."

"Aye."

I couldn't help but smile as I watched the kid work himself into a sweat over the black marks on the floor. Wrinkles appeared in his forehead as he scrubbed, making him look older than he was. "How old are you, Morgan?" I finally asked as I got down on my knees with him. Another rag lay next to the bucket and I dunked it in the grubby water.

"Don't really remember," he replied still keeping his eyes down.

"Don't you celebrate a birthday every year?"

Morgan stopped scrubbing and finally lifted his chin to meet my eyes. "What's a birthday?" he asked genuinely confused.

I threw my rag down letting it splat on the floor. "It's a day to celebrate your birth, of course. Haven't you ever had a birthday?"

Morgan shrugged. "I don't think so."

"Well how do you know when you turn a year older?"

"We don't get older here."

Oh right.

We continued scrubbing the deck in silence until my arms ached and my fingertips looked like raisins. "It doesn't even matter than you don't get older here," I muttered. "I already feel like an old lady." Morgan finally looked up at me. Then I held my hands up so he could see them. "I'm even beginning to look like one," I said and wiggled my wrinkly fingers. A childish giggle escaped his mouth and he lifted his own prune-y fingers to wave back at me.

Then, just as quickly as the smile appeared, it wiped clean off his face and he bent his head back down to scrub at an invisible black mark. I was about to ask him what was wrong when I heard footsteps coming our way.

"This girl distracting you from your work, Morgan?" Russ asked with his arms folded over his chest.

I peered up at his face, squinting against the sun as it made a halo around his head. The irony was almost too much. I wouldn't call any of these dogs angels. Maybe Morgan.

"No, sir," Morgan replied keeping his head down and the rag in his hand scrubbing at the clean floor.

I shook my head in disgust. "We were just talking," I said. "Besides, we're done up here anyway."

Russ looked down the bridge of his pointed nose at the deck, steel eyes searching for anything he could reprimand us for. When he couldn't find anything, he put his toe up on the edge of the bucket and rocked it until it tumbled over. The grimy water splashed across the wood, soaking into my leggings and Morgan's pants. "Clean that up," he said before waltzing away.

"What a tool," I muttered as I got up and tried to shake some of the water off my wet legs.

Morgan let out a heavy sigh before standing up as well and grabbing the mop. "It's alright," he muttered as he moved the mop back and forth. "I'm used to it."

My heart ached for the kid. This was no way to live. He shouldn't have to be on this ship working when he could be out with the lost boys eating suavas and playing manhunt and swimming with the mermaids.

Something needed to be done.

Just then a bell rang off somewhere on the other side of the ship, pulling me out of my head. "What's that?" I asked watching Morgan throw the mop down onto the wet ground.

A small smile pulled the corners of his mouth up. "Dinner time."

I followed Morgan across the deck, down a flight of stairs and into a cramped room with a table running almost the entire length. The place was a madhouse. An old chandelier hung from the center of the ceiling, giving the place a dim but warm glow. Not that the room needed any more warmth what with all the bodies crammed in. Morgan took ahold of my wrist and tugged, leading me toward the far end of the table. Guys scrambled, trying to find a place to sit. A couple had gone for the same chair and were now in a loud pushing fit. The volume in the room kept rising as everyone tried talking over each other. I barely had time to jump out of the way when one of the ones fighting picked up the other by the neck of his dirty shirt and slammed him down on his back on the tabletop. Cheers and curses erupted from all corners of the room as everyone coaxed the two on. Even Morgan joined in, yelling for the one with his back on the table to throw a punch. I hunched back against the wall and covered my ears to try and dull the deafening chaos that filled the room.

If I closed my eyes, I could almost imagine I was on the beach again. The screaming and shouting was actually the sound of the waves crashing against the shore and the wind whipping my tangled hair. The smell wasn't that of unwashed bodies and moldy wood, it was fresh and salty like the sea with a hint of tropical flowers.

"That's enough!"

The image shattered and I opened my eyes to find everyone else frozen with their attention on the doorway. I peeked around one of the bigger guys in front of me. Hook stood at the end of the room, his metal claw stabbing into the wood millimeters from the ear of the guy still on the table.

The anger in Hook's eyes quickly dissipated and his face broke out in a grin. "Is this any way to act in front of a lady?" Everyone turned to look at me and I felt my whole face flame up. A flicker of amusement sparkled in his eyes when he saw me cower. Even with embarrassment still obvious on my face, I straightened up hoping it would help. It didn't. The air was thick with the awkward silence and the body heat and pretty soon I felt a bead of sweat roll down my forehead.

Then the lanky guy with the scar tripped through the doorway and I jumped startled. "Clear out the way, ye dogs!" he yelled shoving through with a big metal bin piled high with some kind of meat. I couldn't tell what it was but it smelled fishy and garlicky and I suddenly couldn't swallow. Scar-face slammed it down on the table and everyone around me immediately dug in, pushing me toward the back to the far corner of the room. I was lost, letting the current drag me back when a hand clamped down on my wrist and tugged. I squeezed between a couple of nameless pirates and hit my shin against the bench under the table.

"Sit!" Morgan yelled over the chatter and I quickly did as he said. Now I had a front row seat to the ruckus. The bin slid down the table toward me and

Morgan nudged me in the ribs. "Grab some!" As the bin flew past, he snapped his hand out and snatched up a handful of the slimy meat. "You gotta be quick," he scolded. "It's okay though. You can have some of mine." I watched as he plopped it down on the table in front of him. No plate, no napkin, just directly onto the table. My stomach churned violently as I stared at the mushy meat. I was going to be sick.

"I need some air," I gasped and stumbled away from the table. Blindly, I pushed through the crowd, my head swimming with the smell of over-seasoned rotten fish and body odor.

I think I heard Morgan call my name from back in the corner but I'm not sure. I couldn't distinguish all the different sounds I was hearing anyway. The conversations; the yelling, the singing, the laughing. The sounds of eating; the slurping, the crunching, the belching, the tearing. None of it made any sense as I made my way to the door. When I finally reached it, I turned to look back at the chaos. Instead of focusing on the mosh pit, my eyes landed on a fiery blue stare and I paused. Hook sat calmly at this end of the table, his mouth curled into a mischievous smirk, his expression radiating his smugness. His enjoyment at seeing me so distraught.

Finally, I managed to tear my eyes away and rushed into the hallway. I didn't stop running until I'd made it up the stairs and onto the deck. My heart was pounding and a layer of cold sweat coated my skin. I was going to be sick.

Flinging myself at the railing, I threw my top half over the edge just as my stomach flipped and I heaved, sending vomit, tinged blue with suava juice, into the ocean below.

I stayed like that, staring at the water through blurry eyes until I couldn't stand the pain that throbbed in my skull. My bones felt like putty and my muscles like cotton so when I finally did straighten back up, my legs gave out and I sank to the floor.

I didn't try to get up. I didn't try to fight back the tears or the sobs that racked my whole body like a kick to the ribs. I didn't acknowledge Russ when he came to stand by me at the railing.

"You're being ridiculous, you know," he said matter-of-factly.

Slowly, I lifted my eyes, my aching head following until I was glaring up at him. I'm sure I looked like a mental patient with my hair sticking to the sweat on my face. "I was dragged here at knife point, almost froze to death, tackled countless times, forced to do some meaningless grunt work, thrown around by a bunch of grubby teenage boys and had this terrible smelling fish shoved in my face, "I snarled. "I think I'm handling it pretty well."

Russ stared down at me, his expression absolutely unreadable. What would it take to get through to this kid? I didn't understand him. What was his objective? What was he trying to accomplish here? Did he want to make me miserable? If that was the case, he was doing a bang up job.

Finally, I got up so I didn't feel like a bug he was about to squash. "What do you want from me, Russ?" I finally asked, my voice steady even though I was shaking.

His brow furrowed. "I want you to leave."

"And how do you expect me to do that?" I spat

back at him. "Just jump overboard and swim to shore? In case you've forgotten, I already tried that once. *You* stopped me."

Russ turned so his whole body was facing me. "No. I don't just want you to leave the ship. I want you to leave Neverland." I opened my mouth but I didn't know what to say. It didn't matter though because he kept going. "Leave so that when Pan gets here, he'll see that you're just another stupid broad that didn't really care about him anyway and then Hook will feel better about losing his girl and everything will go back to the way it was before."

Aha.

"So it was never about whose side you were on," I said. I leaned on the railing now too and looked out at the sun as it touched the horizon. The days were so short. "You don't care who you have to hurt as long as everything goes the way you want it to." Russ made a sound in his throat to confirm my suspicions. "Well, let me enlighten you," I continued, the bitterness in my words overshadowing the weak volume of my voice. "Life isn't always going to be the same. I don't care if you live for five years or five hundred but just because you stop getting older doesn't mean you're done growing up. The fact that you're alive means you're going to deal with crap you don't want to have to deal with." I turned my head to look at him as I continued. "It's time to get over it, Russ. Besides, you can't expect everything to return to the way it was. Not when everyone figures out what a pathetic little worm you are." His eye twitched and I felt pride spark in my chest.

A look passed over his face just then. Something

crazy, something evil. I didn't know if he wanted to say something or strangle me but just as quickly as it appeared, it was gone. Without another word, he pushed away from the railing and sauntered toward the stairs leading down to the dining hall. I stood there frozen until he was gone. Once I was alone, all the pride that had been holding me upright evaporated and I slumped back against the railing.

Again, my eyes glassed over and I looked up at the billowing sails to try to get the tears to go away. It didn't work. Instead, one broke free and slid down my cheek, leaving a hot trail in its wake. Russ's words echoed in my head. *I don't just want you to leave the ship, I want you to leave Neverland.* If I thought that would help, I would try and find a way. But if anything that Calliope had told me the other night was true, and if Peter felt the same way I did then it didn't matter. It was too late for me. This place had gotten into my brain, my blood. Peter had made his way into my heart. And the pain of losing someone you love doesn't just go away over time. Sure, it gets a little easier to deal with as the years go by but nothing can ever return to the way it was before because you're not the same person you were before.

Life keeps going forward. It doesn't wait to let you catch your breath or try to heal. It pushes on whether you want it to or not. And at that moment, I wished time would just stand still.

Chapter Twelve

Hunger stabbed at my stomach. I couldn't tell though if that was what kept me awake or if it was the feeling of the rough, wooden crates I'd been given as a bed. Or maybe it was the awful snoring coming from the sleeping pirates all around me. I'd been a bit surprised when Smee led me to the sleeping quarters instead of another freezing cold room in the bottom of the ship. Maybe Hook didn't actually want to treat me like a prisoner. He could have at least given me something a little softer than these boxes to sleep on, though.

My one side started to ache from laying on the hard surface, so for the thousandth time, I rolled onto my back. I lost count of how many complete rotations I'd made since laying down. If it wasn't the scratchy wood underneath me, it was the loud snoring around me. I didn't know which was worse. Either way, I wasn't going to be getting any sleep tonight.

As quietly as possible, so I wouldn't disturb the sleeping beauties around me, I got up, dragging the thin blanket with me and tiptoed barefoot out of the room. The hallway was dark but the stairwell at the end glowed in the moonlight like a beacon.

The loud snoring faded with every step I took and by the time I hit the deck, everything around me was still and silent and a lump formed in my throat as I stared at the scene around me. The sky was a brilliant mix of blue, violet and black, all swirled together and sprinkled with a net of glittering stars. The moon was full and bright, covering every surface of the Jolly Roger with a silvery dusting of light. The wind was calm and the sea was still and the whole scene was lovely.

But none of it could dull the ache in my chest or get rid of the rock in my stomach. In fact, it just made it worse. Being out there on the ocean with no land in sight. With Peter so far away and everyone else I loved even farther. My mom, Marty. Sure, only a few minutes had passed back on earth. But time was different in Neverland. It wouldn't matter if I was gone for another month. That almost made it worse. While my mom thought I was still at Exile with Marty and while Marty thought I was still dancing with Peter to whatever techno song that was playing, I was on Hook's ship, possibly never to see them again, hurting and missing them. And they had no idea. Not a clue that anything was wrong. Yes, that made it so much worse.

A small gust of wind blew past me, soft as a whisper but cold as if I'd just opened a freezer and I shivered, wrapping the thin blanket tighter around myself. I took careful steps to the edge of the ship, my bare feet silent on the polished wood of the deck. My elbows rested on the railing and I peered down at the water below, inky black and rippling softly. A dim glow like an echo shined up from far beneath the surface. Shadows of different sizes and shapes passed over the light sporadically and I squinted to try and make out what they were. Then something massive passed over the top of it, winking it out like a light and I didn't see it again after that.

There had to be a whole other world down there. One with mermaids and sea monsters and who knew what else? Creatures I'd never seen, never heard of before in my life. Too many things were unknown, it made my head hurt. What other things lived in Neverland? What other places had I not gotten the chance to see? What was Peter doing right this second? Was I ever going to make it back home?

Was Peter still upset about our argument?

The lump in my throat grew bigger and I closed my eyes to try and keep the tears from coming. He thought I didn't care enough about him to stay. Maybe he wasn't going to come for me. Maybe I was going to be stuck on this awful ship with these awful people forever and I'd never get to see anyone I loved ever again. Marty or my mom.

Or Peter.

Why did that last one hurt the most?

I lifted my eyes up to the sky. To the two stars just left of the moon that shined brighter than all the other ones. I wondered if Great Gran could see me from wherever she was. From whatever Neverland she'd ended up in. I wondered if she was looking up at the stars too, knowing where I was, knowing my situation and wanting to tell me something.

"I'm listening, Great Gran," I whispered, my voice hoarse from having not used it in hours. "If you have any advice for me at all right now, I could really use it." A wave slapped against the side of the ship softly. "Anything at all. Any hint at what I should do."

Still nothing. The stars winked at me and I blinked back, wishing I knew some sort of secret language or way to communicate with them. But they were just stars and I was just a girl. Not as brilliant, not as bright, but just as useless in this situation.

A low, sorrowful moan sliced through the silence causing shivers to trickle down my spine. It was pretty far away, too far for me to really tell where it was coming from but it sounded like Scylla. I wondered if there were more big purple blob monsters like her or if she was the only one. If that had been her, she sure sounded lonely. Maybe she was. What if she'd been there since the beginning like the tree spirits but didn't have anyone to share her days with. What if Peter was her only friend? I felt a flutter in my stomach. Peter cared so much about the creatures in this place. It was his home. They were his family. I could see that he cared just in the way he treated them, treated the lost boys, and treated me. He did care for me. He would come. Any doubt that I'd had just moments before dissipated into the cool night air and rode away on the wind. He would come for me and we would beat Hook and then we'd be together again. Everything else we could figure out later. It didn't matter. All that mattered was that I got him back. And if I wanted to get him back, I needed to be prepared. Prepared to help. Prepared to fight.

I woke up to the ear shattering, obnoxious clanging of a bell and my eyes flew open like shutters. I'd snuck back down to the cabins after staying up on deck until I was unable to keep myself from shivering and curled up in the corner on a sack. Now I sat there in the corner and watched the others as they scrambled about, shoving each other up the stairs until finally it was just me and Morgan left.

"How'd you sleep?" he asked running a hand through his greasy dark hair.

I shrugged and watched him tie a bandana around his head. "About as well as anyone can in this crap hole," I finally muttered and stood up. My body complained and my bones creaked but I managed to get to my feet and straighten up somehow.

Morgan looked down at his boots as he slipped them on. "I don't figure you'd want to go eat breakfast, would you?" He didn't lift his eyes from the floor.

My stomach grumbled loudly and I winced hoping he hadn't heard it. The way he smirked when he finally looked up at me told me he had. "I guess I don't really have a choice."

The food Scar-face threw on the table this time looked significantly more edible than the night before and when the bin came sliding down toward me, I was ready. As quickly as I could, I reached my hand out and snatched up the first thing my fingers wrapped around. This time is was a big hunk of bread with bits of meat and beans baked right in. While it was stale and salty, at least it wasn't slimy.

Any time one of the pirates shoved into me, I shoved right back so I could keep my place at the table. I wasn't about to let them throw me around again like they had before. I was done cowering. If Hook wanted me on this ship, I wasn't going to be pushed around anymore. And that included taking abuse from Russ.

I think my words the day before had gotten to him because I didn't see much of him for the morning and most of the afternoon. Even as I helped Morgan scrub the decks and polish the railings, I never caught one glimpse of Russ's smug smile or cold gray eyes.

When Hook wasn't in his quarters, he was up on the top deck, steering and barking orders at his crew. I didn't understand how they could all just let him treat them the way he did but even Morgan didn't complain. I guess if someone has been your captain for this long, they must be doing something right.

I was beginning to get the hang of how this ship was run. Even having just gotten there a couple days before, I was beginning to feel more comfortable and almost like I knew what I was doing. While Morgan and I sat on the deck, the sun warming my arms, the scar-faced pirate approached me. I instinctively cowered at the sight of his sneer as his head blocked the sun but when I focused on his eyes, I saw that they weren't menacing at all. I felt my shoulders relaxed.

"Hook says you could help me with dinner," he said to me.

With a quick glance at Morgan, who gave me a shrug and an assuring nod, I put the net down that I'd been helping him mend and got to my feet. Scar-face was already across the deck and heading down the stairs to the dining room so I had to hurry to catch up to him. My stomach churned at the thought of having to work down in some hot grubby kitchen and when I crossed the dining room and went through a doorway, a wall of wretched smells hit me. Garlic and fish invaded my senses and immediately brought me back to dinner the night before. My insides twisted, threatening to make me sick at any minute.

Counters lined two of the walls while a big tank that held some ugly looking bug-eyed fish took another up. Over in a corner was what looked like the sandbox I used to have in my backyard as a kid. It was pretty simple looking. Just four pieces of wood with sand in the middle. I was confused until the boy walked over to it and started layering logs on top of the sand to make a fire. Interesting.

Once the fire was lit, he filled a pot with water from a bucket and hung it on a spit over the fire so it could boil.

"So what's your name?" I asked feeling awkward and useless in the doorway.

He stomped out of the sandbox and started toward the fish tank. "Jonas," he said and grabbed a net that hung on the wall. "Come help me."

Quickly, I made my way over to him, tripping over the empty bucket. "I'm Wynn," I replied once I was standing by him.

"I know," he said and that was it.

I watched in silence as he plunged the net down into the fish tank so the water came up to his elbow. He didn't seem to care that he was getting the sleeve of his shirt all wet. "Get your arms ready."

I didn't really know what he meant by that but I bent my knees and braced my arms like I was getting ready to catch something. Then he jerked, snagging a fish in the net. In one fluid motion, he ripped it out of the water and dropped the flopping thing into my unsteady arms. I teetered for a second as I wrestled the fish but luckily I regained my balance before the thing went onto the floor.

"Bring it here," Jonas ordered as he rushed over and started clearing a place on a nearby counter. As I brought it over to him, I felt a hard wet slap against my cheek and then a couple more. "Set it down, quick!"

With a grunt, I dropped the fish on the counter in front of Jonas and stood back. He grabbed hold of the thing with one big hand and a huge knife with the other then reared back and brought the knife down hard. The blade cut through the fish's neck and suddenly the head was gone and the creature lay still.

Blood spilled out onto the counter and black dots started creeping into my vision like spiders crawling across glass. *No, Wynn,* I told myself, *you can handle this. Suck it up.* With a shake of my head, the spots were gone and I breathed in deep, embracing the fishy smell as it filled the room like smoke. I hadn't even noticed that Jonas had left the headless fish there next to me and was now back over at the tank with his arm in the water.

"Get ready to catch," he grunted and swooped a big one with bulging eyes into the net. I'd just barely gotten down into my football stance when he flung his arm out and the fish sailed through the air toward me.

The thing smacked against my chest, pushing the air out of my lungs before slipping through my arms and onto the floor. "Grab it, Wynn!" Jonas yelled at me. I scurried after it as it flopped across the floor, it's bulging eyes moving erratically in their sockets, its mouth opening and closing as it tried and failed to breathe. I managed to get my hands around its slimy, brown body twice but both times it just slipped right out of my grasp and splatted back onto the floor. Finally, I bent down and dug my fingers into its flesh, praying my fingernails didn't break the skin, and hugged the thing upside down against my chest. I carried it quickly back over to the table, fighting it the whole way. The fish managed a few good slaps with its tail, soaking my face with water and slime before I threw it down onto the counter next to the other fish. I didn't know what Jonas wanted me to do next so I grabbed the knife and sliced the head off the thing so it would stop squirming. The blade cut through its soft, fishy skin like butter and the body went limp.

With a heavy sigh, I dropped the knife on the counter and slumped back against the edge. The corner by the fish tank erupted with hearty laughter and I whirled around to find Jonas clutching his stomach. Giggles spewed out of his mouth and tears rolled down his face. He couldn't even get a word out and pretty soon I felt laughter bubble up in my own throat as water dripped down the side of my face. It took a while for either of us to be able to say anything, let alone breathe.

Jonas shook his head and wiped the tears from his face. "Oh man, I haven't laughed like that since…" Then just as quickly as he'd started, he stopped and turned back toward the tank.

"Since when?" I asked pulling a wet strand of hair back behind my ear.

"Er, nothing." The humor in his voice was gone. "Try to catch one this time."

I bit my lip feeling a hollow spot form in my stomach, like I'd done something wrong, but what? I tried to shake it off and prepared myself. This time I kept my eyes on the fish as it flew through the air – surely thinking it was making its way to freedom – and right into my arms. I'd braced myself for the impact so it didn't knock the breath out of me, then I used its momentum to swing around and drop it on the table. With a quick motion, I picked the knife up off the counter and brought the blade down on the fish's head, cutting clean through. It slid across the counter and joined the other two.

We worked like this in silence after that until I had six headless fish sitting in front of me. The water and slime and sweat had dried on my face leaving my skin feeling coated and stiff and I wished for the first time since coming to Neverland that I could take a shower.

My arms ached and my lungs hurt from having fish hurdled against my chest and I was relieved when Jonas finally hung the net back up on the wall and came to join me at the counter. "You done good, kid," he said giving me an impressed nod.

"Kid?" I asked and cocked an eyebrow. "Last I checked, we were close to the same age."

Jonas shrugged. "Sure," he said. "But I've been this age for longer than you."

I guess he had a point.

He showed me how to butcher the fish and pull out

all the bones. Then we dumped the meat into the pot of boiling water along with chopped up onions, carrots and garlic. The whole thing smelled a bit rank but I tried to keep a straight face as I stirred everything around with a wooden spoon.

"Not too impressed with my cooking skills are you?" Jonas asked from beside me.

Finally, I let my nose scrunch up in disgust. "What gave it away?" He cocked a crooked eyebrow, split in half by the scar running down his face. "How'd you get that scar?" I asked quietly. His face fell and he turned toward the pot, taking the spoon from me.

"I uh…got it when we attacked Pan." Oh. Way to welcome the awkward silence, Wynn. "Why don't you go get the dining room ready?"

I backed away from the pot, relieved to get out of the hot, stuffy kitchen. "How do I do that?"

Jonas gestured over to the corner with his head. "There's a bucket and a rag over there. Just go in and wipe down the table. Just get all the gunk off it."

With a nod, I grabbed the bucket and rag and made my way out into the dining room. It was weird being in there alone. Almost eerie. The place was big – bigger than I thought – and all the corners were darkened thanks to the dim light coming from the chandelier overhead. The bucket made a loud, hollow thud as I set it down on one of the benches and dipped the rag in. It was stiff with dried sea salt. So, this was ocean water. No wonder everything tasted so salty. We were basically eating off a mineral lick like a bunch of animals.

What I wouldn't have given for something sweet like a suava or savory like a wild boar. Anything else would do.

As I scrubbed away at something crusty caked onto the table, Jonas stomped in carrying two steaming bowls of salty fish stew. "You should eat before the stampede comes and tramples you."

I sighed and tossed the rag into the bucket then sat down at the bench. Jonas sat across from me and set our bowls down on the table. I muttered a thanks before scooping up some of the briny broth with a spoon.

"Hey, it may not be any fancy meal, but it's somethin'," he said with a shrug.

My eyes lifted from my bowl to meet his own and I noticed a hint of sadness. I guess I hadn't really thought about the fact that I was insulting his cooking. Really, he could only do so much with what he had, which wasn't a lot. "I'm sorry," I finally said. "I didn't mean—"

"No, no, it's alright, Wynn," he said with an easy chuckle. "You're right, it's pretty gross."

I met his smile then looked back down at my soup. "Then don't get offended if I don't lick the bowl clean."

Again, Jonas chuckled, his scarred eye sparkling. Man, even through the dirt and grime and greasy hair I could tell he was a handsome guy. Seriously, someone needed to bottle up some Neverland magic and give it to a few of the grubbers back at my school.

As I shoveled spoonful after spoonful of the salty fish soup into my mouth, I tried convincing myself it was just energy, just fuel to keep me going. Now if my taste buds could just understand that I would be set. It took a lot of willpower to choke it all down but eventually the bowl was empty and my hunger was gone. Jonas and I stood up and grabbed for each other's dish at the same time. An awkward second passed before he pulled his hand back and let me take the bowl from in front of him. Without another word, I carried our dishes back to the kitchen to wash out in the sink.

Everything there was caked with sea salt and the sink was no exception. Out on the ocean there was no way to get fresh water but having been there for a few days already, I remembered that while I'd felt hungry, I never actually got thirsty. Something I could add to my list of things I'd never understand about this place.

As I rinsed the soap off the bowl, a bell clanged from in the dining room. *Here comes the hoard.* Jonas barged in just then causing me to drop the bowl I'd been washing. It clattered into the sink as I spun around to face him.

"I'd get outta here if I was you," he said, his voice rough. "Quickly, before you're flattened like a fishcake."

I nodded and hurried out of there, the sound of pounding boots already resonating in my ears from overhead. By the time I got out into the dining room, the guys were on the stairs coming down and I flattened myself against the wall just in time. They all flooded into the room, massive like a wall and filled the large space quickly. Jonas's rough voice rose above the commotion as he told them all to quiet down. When I saw a gap appear in the crowd, I dove through the doorway and out into the hall with a laugh. Sure this place was hectic and the pirates were rowdy but they added to the charm and reminded me of the lost boys who – according to Peter – used to be pirates too. No wonder it all felt so familiar.

A soft chuckle made me whip around and press my back to the wall. Hook stepped off the last stair and strolled toward me. I don't think I'd ever seen someone walk as arrogantly as him. The guy could strut sitting down.

"You seem to be fitting in just fine here, Miss Wyndy," he purred leaning in. I shrank back and satisfaction flashed in his blue eyes.

"It's Wynn," I corrected with a glare.

"Yes, of course. Would you like to join me for dinner?"

"No thank you," I said, "I already ate."

He stood there in silence for a moment, studying me like I was an abstract painting. Finally, he took in a sharp breath and let it out quickly. "Well then, I better get in there before the dogs devour everything."

"Yeah, you better."

When he disappeared through the doorway and into the dining room, I slumped back against the wall and let my head fall forward. I wished Peter would hurry up and get there. At the same time, though, if he did, Hook would kill him. I didn't know how he planned to kill Peter since he was immortal but Hook seemed to think there was a way. At the very least, Peter was going to get hurt and I didn't want that either. The safest thing was for him to stay away.

With a sigh, I pushed off the wall and started up the stairs, the conflict in my mind causing my head to throb.

Chapter Thirteen

The sun was setting as I made my way up the stairs and onto the deck. The sky was a symphony of color. Streaked with orange, green and pink like sherbet ice cream. Everything looked techni-color and my body felt weightless as I drifted toward the railing. I was a ballerina spinning across the stage.

I closed my eyes, the crazy bright colors tattooed on the insides of my eyelids, painting the darkness like watercolor. Music played in my mind, the songs we were practicing for our upcoming recital, Swan Lake. Just like Great Gran back in her ballet days.

She'd played Odile, the black swan. We kept all her old costumes up in the attic and used to spend hours up there standing in front of an old, cracked full length mirror holding the dresses up in front of me, imagining that I was wearing those costumes, starring in those roles, dancing those solos. My favorite had always been her black swan costume. Even sixty years later, the thing was in perfect condition. I'd looked at it so many times I could imagine it perfectly, down to the last detail.

The bodice was made of rich, black satin. A swirling starry array of silver rhinestones adorned the feathered sweetheart neckline. It wasn't a traditional ballerina costume. Instead of the traditional tulle, the skirt was made of feathers, black and shiny like motor oil. It was shorter in the front, coming down to her knees but brushed the floor in the back like a train. I could almost picture the way the feathers would flutter and float with every pirouette.

When I opened my eyes again the sky was dark and along with the sun, the euphoria I'd felt before was gone. The lonely, hollow feeling of sadness had taken its place.

What was it about the nights there that made me feel extra homesick? The smooth surface of the water mirrored the moon and stars. I couldn't tell where the ocean ended and the sky began. Like the ship floated in a cave full of diamonds.

Memories of my first big recital drifted to the forefront of my mind. I'd won the lead role in The Nutcracker over Annabel. I felt like I'd earned it. Great Gran had played Clara in her ballet days and I wanted to be just like her. So, I'd worked hard, memorized and perfected all the solos. It was an all girls class so the part of The Nutcracker went to Marty. I think that's how we became such close friends, and how Annabel came to despise me.

Great Gran had come to every showing of that

performance. Every chance I got, I would sneak a peek at the audience and search for her face. Whenever our gazes met, she would beam at me proudly and the corners of her eyes would crinkle.

A breeze picked up, ruffling my hair and I breathed in deep. If I tried hard enough, I could almost smell the bouquets of pink roses Great Gran would have waiting for me after every performance. Afterwards she and Mom would take me out for ice cream and she'd tell me stories of her days doing ballet. It became one of my favorite childhood traditions. One of the many I missed as I grew older and she grew sicker.

"Enjoy the sunset?" Morgan came up beside me and folded his arms across the railing. His fingers dangled over the edge, dancing as he fidgeted.

I let out a heavy sigh and looked up at the moon. "Not particularly," I muttered resting my own elbows on the railing and balancing my chin on my fists. "I'm ready to go home."

Morgan laid his head down on his arms so he peered at me sideways. "Not a big fan of the pirate life?"

A puff of air escaped my nose in a humorless chuckle. He took that as an answer and lifted his head to stare out at the horizon. "Are you happy here?" I asked him after we'd been quiet for a while.

"It's hard work," Morgan admitted. "Sometimes the others pick on me. The food ain't all that great." I smiled. "But it's not all bad. This here makes it worth while."

Again, I looked up at the moon. He was right; I'd never seen anything like it in my life, especially living in the city. The two of us didn't say anything else as we enjoyed the scenery. The only sound was that of the water lapping the ship and the distant howls of Scylla.

Breakfast the next morning was more of that fish stew. It didn't seem to taste as bad this time though. In fact, nothing seemed as bad as it did even just the day before. Maybe I was really getting on there. I needed to remember though, I wasn't there to make friends, I wasn't there to be a pirate; I was there because Hook threatened to kill a person I cared about and I couldn't let it happen.

I found I was much less likely to be trampled if I waited until the pirates had filtered back out of the dining room before I even rose from my own seat. When I offered to help Jonas clean up, he gave me a kind smile and assured me that he could take care of it. So, I took reluctant steps up the stairs to the deck, knowing and dreading that I'd have to face Hook when I got up there.

"Hoist the anchor!" he bellowed from above my head. "I'm ready for a change in scenery."

Morgan hurried past me as my boot hit the deck. "Come on, Wynn," he called excitedly over his shoulder. I smiled and started after him. Then a shadow stepped in my way, a shadow smelling of the Neverwood Forest.

"You seem to be fitting in nicely here," Russ uttered. His tone didn't seem very congratulatory.

"Stay away from me, Russ," I sighed. I was done dealing with him. I'd given my two cents the other night and that's all he was going to get. He pressed his lips together into a hard line before slinking away, his hands clenched into white knuckled fists. When I turned around again to go help Morgan, Hook stood in my path. "You stay away from me too," I said hitting his shoulder with mine as I stepped around him.

I heard him chuckle from behind me. "Just wait, Wyndy. You'll see I'm not the bad guy."

Finally, I turned to face him again. I could only watch as he strolled up the stairs to the upper deck and took the wheel. Smee started jabbering at him, his chubby cheeks flapping as he talked. What did Hook mean he's "not the bad guy"? *He's* the one that turned on Peter. *He's* the one that tried to kill him and his lost boys, after they'd been friends for who knows how long. What had happened to change him? What did Great Gran do? Whatever it was, according to Russ, I was doing the same thing to Peter. With my eyes still fixed on Hook, I watched as he glanced my way. Even from there I could see how blue his eyes were. Though dazzling, they were nothing compared to the shocking green of Peter's eyes. My heart sank a little. I never got the chance to say I was sorry after talking to Calliope. I hadn't even seen Peter since our argument. Maybe he wasn't going to come rescue me after all. Maybe I was going to be stuck there forever and I'd never get the chance to tell him that I did love him. The way I knew he loved me.

That's it.

Keeping my eyes fixed on Hook, I marched my way toward him. Just before my boot hit the first step to the upper deck, a greasy, blackened hand wrapped around my arm.

"You can't go up there, Miss."

I turned to meet the eyes of another one of Hook's pirate's. It was a burly one, built like a football player with eyes as black and ominous as the inside of Skull Rock.

"Let her up, Eddie," Hook said from above me. "You shouldn't interrupt a woman on a mission."

I pulled my arm from his grasp and glanced down at the dark smudges he left on my skin. I didn't even want to think about what could leave residue like that. With a disgusted grimace, I turned back around and made my way up the stairs. The captain didn't look at me, just kept his eyes locked on the horizon and used the hook on the end of his wrist to grip one of the handles. "Come to help me steer, deary?" he asked.

I leaned back against the railing next to him and crossed my arms. "You loved her, didn't you?"

The sly smile fell from his face but other than that, he didn't respond. I watched for a few silent minutes as he continued to teeter the wheel from side to side.

"You didn't want her to leave and then when she did, it broke your heart."

Hook brought his fisted hand up and slammed it down against the railing in front of him. "It was that blasted *Pan!*" he growled, spitting out Peter's name like it was a swear word. "He made her leave. I'd almost convinced her to stay and then I woke up one morning and she was gone."

A gust of wind blew my hair back away from my face and a seagull cried overhead. Again neither of us said anything for a while. Finally, I let out a sigh. "Peter wants me to stay too."

"But?"

"But," I continued. "I can't. I have family and friends and a life there."

Hook let out a pathetic chuckle. "Typical Darling," he uttered shaking his head.

I shut my eyes as another gust of wind filled my nostrils with salty ocean air. "Harper," I corrected.

The creaking sound of the wheel stopped. "What?"

Cracking my eyes open again, I found him staring at me now with his wide blue eyes. "Unless you were just being sweet, which I doubt, you think my last name is Darling," I explained. "It's Harper."

The confusion didn't leave his eyes. "But you're Wendy Darling's great granddaughter."

With a sigh, I propped my elbows on the railing. *Here we go.* "Wendy Darling married Jeffry Harper. They had a son, James Harper. James Harper married Jeanine Tenny and had James Harper the Second. James Harper the Second married Cindy Evans and they had me, Wyndy Harper," I said annoyed listing it all off with my eyes pointed to the sky.

Hook was silent and when I finally looked back down at him, he was staring at me with his lips slightly parted. Like he wanted to say something but couldn't spit the words out. His hooked hand dangled loosely from one of the spokes of the wheel and the sun gleamed off the metal menacingly.

"Wendy," he finally breathed, "named her son James?"

I shrugged. "Yeah. It's a pretty common name."

"Could it have been after me?"

Again, I shrugged. "I suppose so."

He straightened up and pushed past me, sending my elbows off the edge of the railing. I barely caught myself before my chin hit the wood. "Where are you going?" I asked following him as he started toward the stairs.

"I must know for sure! I must go see her!" he called back to me and disappeared down into the ship.

My boots thudded against the polished wood as I trailed after him. He was already almost to the end of the hall by the time I jumped off the bottom step. "You can't do that." I called pushing past a mangy pirate with a scruffy beard and terrible body odor.

"There's always a way, my dear!" his voice echoed back to me.

I started down the next set of stairs, squinting into the darkness to find his shadowy silhouette. Finally, I turned the corner at the end of the hall to find the doorway to his quarters illuminated by the sun. I stepped carefully into the light and peered into the room. Hook was busy rummaging through an ornate cabinet against the wall. The sound of papers rustling and his cursing under his breath filled the room.

"No, you don't understand, Hook," I said quietly.

He let out a frustrated growl and slammed the doors of the cabinet shut before stomping across the floor to a bookshelf on the other side of the room. There he continued searching for something.

"What are you looking for?" I finally asked stepping cautiously over the threshold. I had to lean to the side to avoid getting hit by a flying book. It clattered against the cabinet and fell to the ground, the pages spreading open like a blooming flower.

"Before Pan made Wendy leave, Tink left a little bag of pixie dust for emergencies," he explained as he continued tearing the room apart. "I can use it to get to your world and see Wendy. I knew she loved me back. I knew it!"

"Hook," I said quietly as a rock settled in my stomach. He ignored me, sending an animal skull my way. I knocked it quickly out of the air and watched as it fell, shattering on the floor. Finally, I sucked in a deep breath. "Hook!" I screamed.

This caused him to finally stop and jerk his head my way. His face was red and shimmering with sweat and his eyes blazed with blue fire. "What?" he screamed gripping my arm tightly. I could see the veins in his eyes, bright like they were about to burst. Deep lines creased his forehead.

"You can't go see her," I said. "She's...not there anymore."

"What do you mean she isn't there anymore?" he asked. His fist clenched and unclenched as he waited for me to answer him. Surely, he already knew what I was going to say.

"She died," I finally said.

The fissures in Hook's brow smoothed and his lip twitched before he let go of me and whirled around to face his destroyed bookshelf. "How?"

"Alzheimer's."

Without turning around, he cocked his head slowly to the side as if he was studying something on the wall in front of him. "What is that?"

I bit my lip to keep it from quivering. The worst possible way to go, I thought. "It's a disease that makes you forget everything."

When Hook turned around again, all the color had drained from his face. Immediately, my eyes darted up to the chandelier over his desk as I felt them glass over with tears. "Everything?" Without looking away from the chandelier, I nodded. "What a horrible way to die," Hook whispered.

"And a horrible way to live," I finally choked out.

When Hook didn't say anything, I lowered my gaze again to look at him. The tears had dried up leaving my eyes burning like I hadn't slept in days. Hook was silent, his head lowered, his raven hair covering his face. "Hook?" I breathed. What was going through his mind? Had I broken down a barrier? Was he feeling hurt and confused the way I had when I'd first heard the news? After all, Great Gran really meant something to him. He loved her. Maybe more than I could even imagine. Maybe Hook wasn't such an evil guy. Maybe instead he was just a broken soul in need of a friend. I could be his friend. I could help him through this loss. Maybe we could help each other.

Slowly, I lifted a hand to place on his arm. "James?" I whispered this time using his name. My fingers barely grazed the material of his coat when, in a flash, his hand came up and his fingers clamped around my wrist. He lifted his head slowly to meet my eyes. Any thought I'd had just before this flew out the window as I stared into those two whirlpools of darkness. Then the ship lurched hard to the left and I fell against the wall.

"Cap'n! We need you on deck!" Smee yelled from above us.

Hook kept a tight hold on my arm as he pulled me behind him back up the stairs. It was no use trying to fight him. He had an iron grip. Once we were up on deck, it took all my concentration just to keep from getting trampled by any of his crew as they scrambled around and tried to regain control of the ship. I had no idea what was going on but it was obviously something bad. I didn't really get the chance to look around though as Hook was still dragging me along behind him. Smee scampered around him, barking orders at the crew like a hyperactive puppy.

"Where are you taking me?" I shouted over the madness.

When he didn't respond, I tried yanking my arm free. As soon as I pried my arm out of his fingers, I spun on my heel to run. Instead, Hook caught me by a fistful of my hair. I let out a yelp as he continued dragging me across the deck only now by a much more painful leash.

Finally, he flung me to the ground at the foot of the mast.

"You're going to stay put," Hook snarled as he yanked my hands behind my back and slipped a loop of rope over my wrists. He pulled it taut and it bit into the skin on my wrists. I gritted my teeth against the pain.

"Peter will come for me," I said the words bitter in my mouth.

Hook leaned close again and I pushed down the bile rising in my throat. "I'm counting on it, deary," he said before tapping his hooked hand against the mast above my head. Then, he turned and waltzed away, leaving me alone.

With a frustrated scream, I tugged hard at the ropes, thrashing my arms like a crazy person until my muscles ached too much to move them. I slumped back against the mast, my hair stuck all over my face with sweat. This was no use. I couldn't get the ropes off.

In a tired, frustrated slump, I eyed one of Hook's unnamed crewmen as he scurried speedily up a rope ladder toward the top of the mast I was tied to. Shielding my eyes from the blinding sun, I watched him hop from the ladder into the crow's nest. He extended a telescope he'd attached to a string around his neck and peered through it out at the calm water surrounding us. If the water was so steady, why was the ship bucking and rocking like it was?

"See anything, Wayland?" Hook barked up to him from his place at the wheel.

The guy above me turned in a slow circle, scanning the sea from above. Then he froze, his telescope pointing at water on the left side of ship. "Somethin' big and dark, Cap'n!" he yelled back. "Right beneath us!"

I turned my head to look again at Hook and was surprised to see his mouth curl into a wicked grin. "Perfect," he purred and his eyes fell from Wayland up in the crow's nest and landed on me. They flashed with a blue spark causing my stomach to churn. What was he up to? "Retrieve the nets!" he bellowed, his eyes still locked on mine. "It's time to go fishing."

His crew wasted no time running to the side of the ship. Jonas hurried over to a big wooden and metal contraption and pulled a lever sticking out of it. The big spool looking thing began to spin as ropes pulled out of it and disappeared over the edge of the ship. I heard a splash and then everyone gripped a part of the rope still attached to the pulley. "Lay your back into it, boys!" Hook ordered as he strode down the stairs.

I tried getting up but the binds on my wrists were

220

too short so I craned my neck. That obviously did no good either. It was no use. I couldn't see anything as the crew chanted "heave, ho" in unison, pulling the rope in quick swift motions.

Russ sauntered over and leaned his shoulder against the mast. I glared up at him. "Do you know what this is all about?" I asked. He didn't respond. No surprise there.

Finally, the crew managed to pull whatever was in the net up and over the edge of the ship. I still couldn't really see what it was since everyone quickly surrounded their catch the second they dumped it onboard. Hook walked up to me still grinning triumphantly.

"What is that?" I asked wishing I could punch that smile right off his face.

He kneeled down next to me and rested his elbows on his knee. "This, Wynn, is our secret weapon."

I narrowed my eyes. "For what?"

"Well, you see," he started, straitening back up. "There's only one way to kill Pan. If I'd known this back when he betrayed me, I wouldn't have gone through all that trouble trying to gut him with my sword and I probably wouldn't have lost my hand." By now he was ranting. Then he turned to me again. "But, now I have it and there's no stopping me."

"What?" I yelled. "What do you have?"

Hook walked over to his crew and they parted before him. "The one thing that can destroy him," he said before stepping out of the way of whatever was squirming underneath the net. A terrifying sound like a mix between crunching metal and a foghorn erupted from behind him. Immediately, a shudder passed through my body. I hadn't heard that noise since I first got to Neverland and I hadn't thought about it since then either. But now I watched with wide eyes as a darker than black form rose up slowly onto all fours. There was no detail, no features to it. The whole thing was just one mass that seemed to change size and shape at will. Even as it contorted, it kept to a basic form. Two arms, two legs, a body and a head. The net moved on top of it, keeping it down on all fours. Then, it slowly lifted its head with a mechanical groan. Two glowing, white orbs where its eyes should have been locked into mine and my mouth fell open.

I couldn't look away as it gazed at me. The light wasn't even that bright but everything around me began to fade away and I felt like I was floating. I couldn't breathe. I couldn't blink. I couldn't look away from this creature's beaming white stare. Finally, the creature jerked and looked away, releasing me from its mental hold. I collapsed, pulling air deep into my aching lungs. The creature glared up at Hook who had apparently just hit it hard with the butt end of his sword.

"Not her, you idiot," he growled at it, keeping his gaze away from the deadly white stare.

My chest still burned but finally I was able to cough out a few words. "Why do you need Peter's shadow?" I asked breathlessly but then I understood. The way it had stared at me with those two intense eyes, I couldn't breathe, I couldn't move, I'd been frozen in place. It was sucking the life out of me and I hadn't been able to do anything about it. That was what Hook wanted to do to Peter and now he was going to be able to. "No, Hook, you can't!" I yelled. "Please,

222

you can't kill him."

Again a grin pulled only one corner of his mouth up. "Oh I can, deary." Then he stepped carefully around the captured shadow and made his way past me. "I can and I will."

Chapter Fourteen

Numbly, I watched as Jonas and Eddie each grabbed a hold of one side of the net and began dragging Peter's shadow across the deck. My eyes followed the black figure, keeping away from its deadly white stare until the three disappeared into the ship. I could hear their captive's eerie protests all the way down the stairs until the sound finally faded away.

Russ shifted beside me and I felt his leg brush against my skin. Automatically, I flinched away, my head snapping up to meet his eyes. "You know, you're worse than Hook," I spat disgustedly at him.

A smile tugged at his lips. "How's that?" he asked without even the slightest hint of curiosity.

"At least he's open about what a terrible, wretched guy he is. You've spent the past however many years pretending to be someone you're not. There's something wrong with you," I said as I narrowed my eyes to slits. "Something in your brain. Were you dropped on your head as a baby or exposed to some bacteria that only ate the good parts of your personality?" A burst of air escaped his nose and he shook his head amused before pushing off the mast to walk away. "You can't let Hook do this, Russ!" I called after him. He stopped mid-stride. "He's going to kill him!"

I thought he'd turn around, meet my eyes, give me a nod, anything. He didn't even clench his fists. No, he just started walking again, leaving me by myself, trapped at the foot of the mast.

It felt like there was a big ball of raw dough – cold and hard – sitting in the pit of my stomach. Every time I tried to swallow, the ball just got bigger, filling my gut until it started pushing up my throat and crushing my lungs. Even as my insides grew tighter, I still somehow felt hollow, like a jack-o-lantern that just had its insides scooped out with a spoon.

I could never fully describe what it had been like staring into that creature's eyes as it hungrily sucked the life out of me. I felt violated. I felt helpless. I wouldn't wish that on anyone. Not Annabel, not Russ, not even Hook who was planning to do that very thing to Peter.

The day continued like every other day I'd spent on the Jolly Roger. Smee stuck by Hook's side like a puppy, and Wayland stayed up in the crow's nest with his telescope and used it as a bat whenever a seagull tried to perch on the crossbeam near him. Most of the other pirates were polishing the wooden floorboards or the railings or repairing nets and Russ looked on like he was warden of a highway work crew.

I was invisible to them all it seemed. The only one that acknowledged me was Morgan. He kept glancing over at me, worry creasing his young face. I was still there when Jonas rang the dinner bell and the others rushed down to the lower deck, leaving me alone again with the setting sun for the third night in a row.

Apparently, I wasn't getting any dinner this time. Whatever. It was probably more of that gross fish stew, anyway. I wouldn't have been surprised if I developed high blood pressure after eating the food I'd eaten the last couple days.

The rope binding my wrists, and fastened to a metal eye-hook, was so short I had to arch my back and now I shifted uncomfortably as the mast ground into my spine. The wind blew softly, catching the fly away strands of hair around my face making them tickle my forehead and cheeks. And I couldn't scratch. Ugh, this was almost as bad as being stuck down in the bilge. I was more comfortable down there on the icy floor than up here on deck. At least I got some kind of sleep. So, what if it was due to hypothermia setting in?

My wrists burned from the scratchy ropes and I had that pins and needles feeling in my limbs from sitting in the same position for so long. When I wiggled my toes, it sent an annoying tickling sensation shooting up my legs. I shifted again, trying to get some feeling back but it was no use and I finally slumped back against the mast in defeat and closed my eyes.

"Wynn?"
My eyes snapped back open and I sat up to find

Morgan standing at the top of the stairs with a blanket in his hand. "What are you doing up here?" I croaked. Apparently, I had managed to doze off. He stepped forward slowly, balling the blanket in his fists. "Is that for me?"

"I thought you might be cold."

I shifted again, wincing at the bruises that had formed along my spine. "It's not exactly on the top of my list of worries right now, but yeah I guess I am." Morgan took that as the green light and hurried forward, unfolding the blanket to drape over me. "Actually." He froze. "Could you put it behind my back?"

With a solemn nod, Morgan balled the blanket back up and kneeled down to stuff it in the small space between my lower back and the mast. When I slumped back down again, the cushion eased a bit of the pain. "I guess that'll work," I muttered then gave him a small but grateful smile. "Thanks."

"Sure," he said backing away. "I wish there was more I could do for you."

I shook my head. "No, it's alright. The blanket helps."

Morgan gave me a small nod before disappearing back down the stairs to go to bed. I could tell he felt bad for leaving me there. He was a nice kid but I knew where his loyalties lay.

I woke the next morning with a painful jolt. Images from my dream flashed through my mind. A black bird trapped in a crocodile's mouth – a cage of teeth –

thrashed, gasping for air as the monster dove farther down into the dark water.

My shoulders ached and I ground my teeth together to keep from yelping as I rolled them. Even moving my hands just a little bit made the skin on my wrists throb under the ropes.

The deck was empty. Everyone else must have still been asleep, comfortable in their bunks. Well, maybe not super comfortable but more so than I. Gray, cottony clouds covered the early morning sky making the water look pale and icy and the chilly wind caused the inside of my nose to hurt when I breathed in deep. If I closed my eyes and didn't concentrate on the varying aches and pains, I could almost pretend I was somewhere else. I was sitting on the beach with my toes digging into the sand or around the fire with the lost boys listening to Peter play his guitar.

"How'd you sleep?" I opened my eyes slowly and glared up at the captain, angry more for the fact that he pulled me back into reality than for the fact that he was the reason I was tethered to this pole. "So you're not speaking to me then?"

"How do you think I slept?" I growled back. The memory of him grabbing me by my hair made my head ache. A smug smile appeared on his face and I wished my hands were free for the sole purpose of smacking it back off of him. "Are you just going to keep me tied here forever?"

Hook brought his metal hand up and tapped it against his chin like he was caught in an internal debate. What had Great Gran ever seen in this weasel? I seriously hoped he'd been a different person back then. More for Great Gran's integrity than anything else. Finally, Hook looked back down at me then puffed out his chest. "Swear your allegiance to me and my crew and I'll release you from your bonds," he bellowed dramatically.

I rolled my eyes. "Oh please."

"Though I do enjoy begging as much as the next person, your sarcasm will get you nowhere, deary," Hook said then strolled back toward the stairs and disappeared down into the ship.

I don't know how long I sat there alone after that. Time didn't seem to be going at a very steady pace. One second, the gray clouds above stretched on as far as I could see, hiding the sun and its warmth then suddenly the fog burned off and the sky was clear and bright.

The ship slowly came to life as the pirates made their way up from breakfast – another meal I didn't get the chance to partake in. Thanks, Hook. Morgan came up last, still chewing a mouthful of whatever Jonas had cooked up. When his eyes met mine, his jaw stopped moving and he swallowed hard, wincing as he struggled to get the food down his throat.

"How'd you sleep?" Morgan croaked.

I shifted sending pain shooting up my spine and down my legs. "Better with the blanket," I said trying not to show how much discomfort I was in. "Thanks for that."

"Cap'n!" Wayland yelled from up in the crow's nest. "Off in the distance! It's Pan!"

A grin stretched across Hook's face as his eyes blazed with blue fire. "Finally," he snarled. "Finally I'll get my revenge."

I spotted a silhouette, black against the perfect, clear blue sky. My stomach clenched and it felt like someone had grabbed my intestines and twisted. "This isn't a fair fight, Hook!" I yelled, panic taking over my body and crushing my lungs as I yanked hard on the ropes around my wrists. "You can't!"

"This isn't about fair!" he yelled back at me, his voice cracking. He sounded demon possessed. "I have one goal here, Miss Harper, and that is to cut Pan's heart out like he did mine."

My eyes darted back to the sky and I watched with clenched teeth as Peter drew closer to us. There was no way he'd be able to take on Hook and his crew – and especially not his shadow. I remembered how I felt looking into the eyes of that creature and shuddered. This was it. There was no way out. There was no hope.

A low roar shook the ship just then and I craned my neck around to see where it came from. I felt a holler rise in my throat and my boot struck the ground in a triumphant stomp. Three huge beasts headed our way from Skull Rock, riding the wind with their wings extended like sails. Their red scales gleamed like rubies in the sun. As they got closer, I could see a little figure on each of their backs. The lost boys each had knives in their hands and masks sitting atop their heads. They and their steads were ready for battle.

Hook had turned around too and his smile fell, only for a second though before he regained his composure. There was no way this was going to end well for him, especially when the only thing that kept him from going into the water was a highly flammable, wooden ship. With the help of the dragons, the Jolly

Roger would be destroyed in no time.

"Surrender now, Hook," I called over the ruckus surrounding me. "You're outnumbered in strength. You can't win."

The captain took quick, confident steps toward me and I found myself scurrying to back up against the mast. My confidence disappeared when he grabbed my shoulders, his face inches from mine. "You underestimate me, deary. Do you really think I wouldn't take into consideration the fact that Pan has the creatures of the island on his side?" His eyes burned into mine and my knees trembled. "He may be the king of the land but don't you forget, Wynn Harper. The waters are my domain. I rule here."

As if he'd said the magic words, water shot up out of the ocean creating a wall on all sides. My mouth dropped open as I turned my head to watch this amazing, horrifying fete. The water climbed higher, engulfing the sails, the mast and finally coming together at the top to create a dome. It reminded me of the force field Peter had generated to keep the dragons' fire from burning us. This was for the same purpose.

Just then Peter shot through the water barrier, did a flip in the air and landed on one of the crossbars up near the top of the mast.

"Nice tent, Hook!" he called down to us. "Did you have your fish friends pitch it for you?"

"Nice dragons, Pan!" Hook yelled back. "What fire fairy did you have to seduce to get those dogs?"

"Your mother!"

"Oh geez," I muttered with a roll of my eyes. These two sounded like a couple of high-school rivals.

Then all at once, the other lost boys broke through the water dome, rabid and fierce versions of the animals their masks portrayed. Kai somersaulted through the air, tackling Wayland out of the crow's nest. As Wayland tumbled down, arms flailing, grasping for anything to catch him, Kai followed, bounding between the main masts. The two collided and rolled down the rope ladder, sprawling onto the deck. Kai drew his knife and Wayland immediately knocked it from his hand. His knuckles caught Kai in the mouth and the two wrestled to beat the other to the cast off blade.

Mika and Finn landed second and third, slashing out with their knives to connect with Jonas and Eddie's swords. I watched in horror as these boys that, just a few days ago, had swung me by my limbs over the water, now swung their blades. The usual goofy grins replaced by twisted grimaces, their thick eyebrows drawn tightly together as each concentrated on dodging the pirates' sharp edged swords. A spray of blood arched high above them like a fan and I looked away before I had to see who it belonged to.

My eyes searched the deck frantically until I caught sight of Pal in his deer mask. His eyes met mine for a second then he looked back at his assailant just in time to dodge a swinging sword that could have easily sliced him in half. My head was swimming, black creeping into the edges of my vision like mold. I wanted to rush to their aid but I couldn't get to all of them. I was helpless. Useless in this war. In this fight over me. Over Great Gran. Over love.

The battle raged on around me in a big blur of metal and speckled light as it filtered in through the watery shield. I could no longer make out who was who or what was what, and I was glad for that. I didn't want to see my friends getting hurt. A curse cut through the commotion behind me and I couldn't tell if it had come from a pirate or a lost boy. I couldn't wish for one over the other.

Long, purple snake like arms burst through the water barrier, sweeping across the deck and taking out anyone in their way. A low moan shook the ship and those left standing held on for dear life to whatever was closest to them.

Kai let out a holler from somewhere behind me. "Yeah, Scylla!" And Hook roared, cursing the high heavens.

So much for ruler of the waters, I thought to myself.

Suddenly, my wrists were free and I scrambled to my feet and whirled around. Morgan stood back, a knife in his hand. I mouthed a thank you as I rubbed my sore wrists and he nodded back before diving to the side to keep from getting hit by one of Scylla's giant noodle arms. Another low wail shook the ship.

Peter let out a warrior cry from atop the crossbeam and I craned my neck as he ascended, fury gleaming, in his green eyes. He dove right toward me and Hook. In one quick motion, Hook shoved me out of the way and drew his sword. Peter pulled out his knife at the last second and the two blades collided, sending a shower of sparks spraying onto the deck.

I stumbled back and twisted out of the way just as Wayland threw Kai down at my feet. A glint from the knife in his hand caught my eye and I lunged without thinking. My body hit Wayland from the side, a searing hot sensation shooting up my arm and he staggered sideways, the knife falling from his grip and clattering onto the deck. Wayland shot me a bewildered look as if he'd forgotten I wasn't on their side. This gave Kai the chance to roll to his feet and lunge at the confused pirate. I quickly snatched up the blade on the ground.

A loud growl came from behind me and I turned just in time to see another one of Scylla's arms hit a pirate that had apparently been coming at me. He flew back and crashed into the railing. If I made it out of this alive, I'd have to remember to thank her.

The sound of metal on metal crashed in my ears and I spun around to find Peter and Hook caught in a fighting embrace, their weapons crossed. With gritted teeth, the two struggled until Hook overpowered Peter and threw him back. Neither of them even saw me as I stood there with Kai's knife clutched in my fist. Hook made his way toward Peter slicing through the air with his sword for dramatic effect. He was only a few feet away when I lurched forward. My one hand flew up to wrap around Hook's chest and pull him down to me while the other pressed the knife against his throat.

"Drop the sword, Hook," I breathed into his ear.

His Adam's apple bobbed as he chuckled against the blade. Then he tossed his sword away. The motion caused me to stumble. Why did I feel so lightheaded all of a sudden?

Peter looked at me wide eyed. "Wynn, your arm."

Keeping the one hand grasping the knife firmly to Hook's neck, I lifted the other from his shoulder so I could look at it. A gash ran the length of my forearm from the inside of my elbow to just above my wrist. I must have grazed it when I hit Wayland. It looked kind of deep. With Hook pressed against my chest, I could feel my heart hammering against my ribcage and my breaths became short and made me dizzy.

Everyone around me faded as I stared, mesmerized by the bright red that oozed from the cut. Glints of silver speckled the wound like glitter and my delirious mind remembered something about how Neverland changes a person. Maybe I was becoming more than a human. More like the lost boys.

A lost girl.

Finally, I shook my head in an attempt to clear it. It didn't work. All I could see now was red. Red on my skin, red all around me. Red like the skirt I was wearing at Exile. Red like the glowing bellies of the Skull Rock dragons. Then green as I focused again on Peter's eyes. Green like Marty's ninja turtle shirt. Green like the trees in Cannibal Cove. Green and red like Christmas. I wondered if they celebrated Christmas there in Neverland.

"How about a trade then, Pan," Hook said. "Miss Harper's life...for yours."

"I'm fine," I slurred blinking hard.

I looked again to Peter, pleading with my unfocused eyes for him to refuse the offer. A life without him was no life I wanted to live. He had to understand that. He had to.

Peter's lip twitched and he gritted his teeth. "Fine," he seethed.

My lungs collapsed and a whimper left my throat. "No."

Each of the lost boys tried to move. The pirates were quicker though. Jonas and Eddie stilled the twins with blade tips in their bellies and both Kai and Pal had knives to their throats. Scylla retracted her tentacles and let out a helpless moan from below, knowing she couldn't do anything without someone getting hurt.

Again, Hook chuckled against the knife. "I applaud your bravery, Pan," he said then in a flash, flicked his hand up to catch my fist before I could move it. I tried, muscles straining to keep it up but he overpowered me and I dropped the knife. Then he whipped around to face me. My wound was throbbing now, sending a tearing pain up my arm with every pulse of my heart and sweat coated my forehead but I kept my face expressionless, my eyes smoldering, set on Hook. I wished I could make him burst into flames right there. "This will only hurt a bit," he purred then touched his hooked hand to the bloody gash on my free arm. I broke eye contact only so I could watch the broken skin knit itself back together leaving a thin, silvery scar behind. A small gasp escaped my throat before I had a chance to stop it. "Pan isn't the only one with a magic touch, deary," he breathed and gave me a small wink. My energy returned and I lunged at him, my teeth bared. But Russ was on me then, his arms locking around my waist from behind in an iron grip so I couldn't move.

Hook tsked in mock disappointment then turned back around to face Peter. He waved a hand and two pirates I'd never learned the names of, went over to take a hold of Peter's shoulders. He didn't even fight as they pushed him down to his knees. As he fell, my heart did too, and I wanted to look away but his eyes locked on me. My own eyes skimmed over his face as I tried to memorize every detail. His pointed ears that peeked out just barely from under his auburn hair and the two little hoops in his earlobe that glinted in the sun. The way his skin shimmered in the right light and the little dimple that made an appearance whenever he lifted the one side of his mouth in that devilish smirk.

My concentration shattered when the air filled with the awful grinding sounds of something mechanical and my blood turned to ice water in my veins. Peter's expression fell and his eyes darted behind me as four other pirates, each grasping a piece of rope, came up the stairs from the lower deck dragging the black, formless mass that was Peter's shadow behind them. For the first time since I'd gotten to Neverland, I saw terror flash across his face.

Something clicked inside me and suddenly I wasn't in control of my body. I let out a feral scream as I thrashed in Russ's grip. His arms loosened for just a second before he squeezed hard, crushing my ribs against my lungs and forcing me down to my knees. I watched through a curtain of sweaty hair as the four pirates tied the shadow's restraints to the anchor.

The creature tugged hard against the ropes but they held and it reared back and roared. The sound of a foghorn blasted through the air, bouncing off the water shield and shaking the ship. When it finally settled back down, two white orbs appeared on its featureless face and the pirates all turned their eyes to the ground.

I couldn't though. I couldn't bring myself to look away from Peter.

And he looked back, his nostrils flaring, the muscles tight in his jaw as he tried to keep control. "I love you, Wynn," he croaked.

My heart swelled and shriveled at the same time

and I brought my fingers up to cover my mouth and keep the sob in. My throat tightened and my vocal chords cinched causing my words to come out as nothing more than a strained whisper. "I love you too, Peter."

Russ threw me aside and I let him, my body no longer able to fight. When I hit the ground, I stayed there, keeping my blurred vision set on the wood grains of the deck. This was it. This was the end.

The grinding hiss of rope rubbing against wood had me lifting my head quickly just in time to see the loops around the shadow's ankles, wrists and neck tighten. Then it was ripped off its feet and dragged over the edge of the ship after the anchor it was tied to.

Chapter Fifteen

"No!" Hook screamed flinging himself to the railing to look down after it. I rolled over so I was on my back to find Russ standing beside the mast behind me. His hand gripped the hilt of a blade that bit deeply into the pole; just above a pulley that had been holding the anchor's ropes. His eyes glinted with a cold, metallic fire that seared into my own eyes and the corner of his mouth twitched up into a smirk just for a second before it disappeared again.

Then, before I could react, two more pirates were on him, wrenching his arms behind his back until his teeth gritted together. One held a blade to his throat so the skin puckered around it. Everyone stood in shocked silence. I looked to Peter and we locked eyes for a second.

Music filled the air, beautiful and sad. Melodies and

harmonies intertwined, weaving a tapestry that wrapped around each of us, freezing us where we stood.

What was the one thing that could tame a rabid shadow?

My voice quivered as I answered my own question. "A mermaid's song."

They all must have been waiting down below. The music faded slowly until the only sound was that of the waves lapping against the ship and the beat of the dragons' wings from outside the dome surrounding us. I'd almost forgotten about them.

Finally, Hook stirred. He turned slowly, his blue eyes glowing so intensely, I had to look away.

"How…dare you," he snarled taking slow, deliberate steps forward. I started backing away as he drew closer to me and I watched with a hammering heart as he passed by without so much as a glance, his attention set on Russ. Finally, he stopped when the two were standing only feet apart. Russ's nostrils flared as he struggled to breathe against the knife pressed to his throat. "I should gut you like the codfish you are."

Russ let out a coughing, humorless bark. "Right, Hook, you blame Pan for taking your girl away when you know she didn't want to stay here. You were too selfish, too scared to go with her back to her world where you would have to grow up," he said. "You can't think things are going to stay the same here, Hook. Things change whether you want them to or not." Then his eyes darted to mine and I saw something flash across them. Something like gratitude. "Just because you stop getting older doesn't mean you're done growing up." My heart faltered as he spoke my words. Then he set his stare on Hook again. "It seems to me like you're the one who is the codfish."

"You can't blame anyone else for your decisions, James," Peter added as he shrugged his restrainers off of him and got to his feet. Hook turned around to look at him, his face pale. "Just like I can't blame Wynn for wanting to return to her life." Then Peter turned to me. "It's not fair to make someone choose between the people they love. I get that now." My cheeks grew hot as every eye fell on me. Luckily, Peter continued. "And Russ is right. I can't keep myself from growing up. Neverland can't either." His face broke out in that grin of his and I felt the pieces of my heart begin to solder themselves back together. "And that's why I'm going back with her."

My breath caught in my throat. "What?" I whispered.

The confused and protesting voices of the other lost boys rose over my own and increased in volume until the air was filled with shouting and arguing. "Hey!" Peter barked and the noise ceased. "I've made my decision and it's final." The boys lowered their heads like scolded puppies and Peter turned back to Hook. "*You* made your decision" Then he turned to Russ. "And you can't blame Russ for doing something noble for once." Russ's eyes fell to the floor for a second. "It's about time he grew a pair anyway." Then Peter leaned into him. "And it was with impeccable timing, mate."

Russ's eyes sharpened and he straightened up again, his newfound bravery radiating like sunlight from his face. At last he acknowledged the two pirates holding him and yanked free of their grip. They didn't seem too bent on keeping him still. Both were looking to their captain, waiting for orders. For anything.

Instead, Hook was silent, his face white as a ghost's, his blue eyes the color of the sky, bright but no longer burning with anger. Finally, he waved his hooked hand and the dome of water enshrouding the ship started to lower. No one moved as it descended back into the ocean. The dragons still hovered on the other side huffing impatiently as they waited for orders. Peter let out a shrill whistle and they took off back toward Skull Rock. I watched until they were just dark shadows against the cloudless blue sky.

Kai was the first to stir. "Weren't they our ride back home?" he asked wiping a drip of blood from his lip.

In unison, we turned to Hook again. He leaned back against the wall and – to my surprise – trained his eyes on me. Peter walked up beside me and I felt him grab my hand. "At least you don't have to worry about hoisting the anchor."

I elbowed him hard in the ribs, throwing a glare his way.

Hook narrowed his own eyes. "We're not going anywhere," he said with disgust.

I took a tentative step forward, letting Peter's fingers slip out of my grasp. Anger smoldered like coals in the pit of my stomach and it took all I had not to lunge at him and claw his throat out. "Hook," I started slowly. "Great Gran loved this place and for some reason I can't quite comprehend, she loved you too. I'm hoping you were a completely different person back then. She would have wanted you to be happy."

"Well, I'm not"

Peter coughed from behind me. "Obviously."

"Peter, you're not helping," I scolded. "Look, I know things are probably ruined between the two of you but you do have something in common whether you like it or not. You both loved Wendy." I looked to Hook again, "She would have wanted you to go on. She used to tell me that life is a grand adventure but only if you actually live it."

The captain looked down at his metal claw, poking the tip with his thumb. "I told her that," he said sadly.

"Then practice what you preach," I growled. "Be the man she fell in love with. No one deserves to be unhappy, not even you."

"I couldn't go back with her," he said looking up at me with glassy eyes. "I wanted to so badly but…"

"But your life is here," I finished for him. The fire in me slowly died and my anger went with it. He nodded and I let out a sigh. "And that's okay. Wendy would have hated it if she'd taken you away from what you loved."

Peter stepped forward so he was beside me again. "Now, I'm sure you want to just sulk in peace for all of eternity but that's only going to happen if you take me and my boys back to land."

My eyes shifted again to Hook as he stared back. He gnawed at the inside of his cheek in thought, probably trying to come up with some new plan to hurt Peter, then finally, he stepped past both of us and made his way toward the stairs leading down below the deck.

"Smee," he said and his first mate looked down at him from where he stood by the wheel. "Take her to land." Then Hook disappeared down the stairs without so much as a glance back.

Smee stood in a silent stupor for a second as he processed what he'd just heard but then snapped out of it and stood at attention. "You heard the Cap'n," he called out to the rest of the crew. "Put her out!"

The lost boys watched bewildered as their captors left each of them where they stood to get to work on taking the ship inland.

Peter stirred beside me but I couldn't look away from the stairwell; even as he wrapped his arms around my waist and pulled me close. But then his warm breath on my cheek thawed me and I threw my arms around his neck in a tight embrace. Our feet lifted off the ground for a second as he squeezed me tighter and then his hands went up to my face and his lips found mine. I felt like I was clinging to life itself. Like I was dying of thirst and his lips were the stream that could quench it. And as I pressed my mouth to his, I felt his lips curl into a smile and I drank him in.

I didn't care that as we kissed, I could hear the exaggerated retching sounds of the boys behind him. All I cared about was this boy in my arms, whose hair curled between my fingers, whose rigid chest pressed against mine, whose lips tasted the way Christmas trees smelled and like sugar and salt and the ocean and the sky.

When we pulled apart at long last, Peter kept his hands on either side of my face and stared deep into my eyes. "I can't believe you saw me," I whispered to him, not as much to keep the boys from hearing but more so because the kiss had left me breathless. The smile on Peter's face widened as if he knew exactly what I was talking about.

"You're a hard one to miss, Wynn Harper," he replied before leaning in for another kiss.

"Okay, you two," Kai said as he walked up to us. "I think you're about to make Russ completely lose his lunch."

I'd already forgotten about Russ. I twisted my neck around, trying to keep Peter in my arms while also searching for the fox boy. Finally, I found him standing alone at the railing, staring out at the water. Carefully, I slipped out of Peter's arms and made my way toward him. Russ leaned on his elbows and studied the fox mask in his hands. His chin twitched my way as if to let me know he knew I was there but didn't want to say anything. Maybe he still felt bitterness toward me even after everything. Maybe he blamed me for this whole mess, which I guess was justified.

His long fingers traced the eyeholes of his mask, going with the direction of the muddy orange colored hair. Finally, I broke the silence. "You saved Peter." Russ froze for just a second before running the side of his finger down the bridge of the snout. "Thank you for that, I guess."

The wind picked up ruffling the hair that framed his face. "I didn't do it for you," he said in a low voice. Though his words were blunt, the bitterness wasn't there. Like he was stating a fact rather than trying to hurt me. Even if he was, it didn't work. I remembered the way he looked at me when he cut the ropes. That glimmer in his eye, that quick smile. I could have brought either of those up but I didn't. Instead, I gave a quick nod and turned back to Peter. He stood waiting for me, the smile on his face warmer than the sun beating down overhead. I sank back into his arms the way I would sink exhausted into bed after a long day. My cheek rested against his skin and I closed my eyes, relishing in the sound of his steadily beating heart.

"You're really coming home with me?" I asked as I lifted my head back off his chest.

"Well, there isn't much for me here."

Kai let out a dramatic scoff before throwing me a facetious grin.

"Neverland ahead!" Wayland called from back up in the crow's nest.

The lost boys cheered – all except for Russ who was still sulking against the railing – as the island came into view. Colorful flashes painted the water in front of us and I managed to catch a glimpse of a shimmery red tail. It looked like the mermaids would be meeting us on shore.

Even as happiness flowed warmly through my veins, I couldn't ignore the icy pang of sadness in my heart for the miserable captain below deck. "We need to talk to Hook," I said stepping away from Peter.

Fire flashed in his green eyes but quickly faded when he saw the concern in mine. "There's no reasoning with him, Wynn," he said trying to pull me back as I turned to go down the stairs. "He dug himself into a hole. Let him fester in it."

I waved his hand off. "Just let me try," I said. "Obviously Great Gran saw something in him. Whatever it was, it has to still be in there." Then I turned again and headed down the stairs. Peter's footsteps echoed mine as he followed me down the hall and though I didn't say anything, I was grateful to have him with me.

Hook's quarters looked empty at first until I caught movement out of my peripheral vision. He was there with his back to us, standing by the bookcase. The shelves were still askew, most of the books and trinkets littering the ground from his manic search for the little bag of Tink's dust. His crocodile mask rested on the shelf level with his head, eyes gleaming reminding me of the one on the button on Peter's jacket.

Cautiously, I stepped into the room. "Hook?"

He flinched at the sound of my voice then slowly turned around. A different mask rested over the hook on his wrist and his fingers stroked the pale, gray feathers as his sorrowful eyes met mine. They were no longer the bright blue of a cloudless sky but the pale color of the ocean on an overcast morning. Finally, he let out a sigh and looked back down at the mask. "I used to call her my Wendy bird. Even before Tiger Lily presented her with her animal."

"A dove," Peter said flatly from behind me.

Hook let out a chuckle and nodded. "An animal of grace and purity. It suited her well."

The room was filled with silence after that, tension so thick I could feel it pulsing like electricity in the air, raising the hairs on my arms. At last Peter stepped forward and lifted the cord that carried the small leather pouch over his head. "Here," he said, a sharp edge to his voice as he held it out to Hook.

"Tink's magic," Hook muttered taking a step toward us. "I wondered where it went."

"I had to take it to heal Russ all those years ago. He

almost didn't make it."

So Peter had the power to fly and Hook had the power to heal.

Hook shook his head. "It's whatever," he said waving his hand at the pouch and went to go slump into the chair behind his desk. "It doesn't matter now anyway. Not with Wendy gone."

I moved up beside Peter and rested my fists on the edge of the desk. "You can still use it to visit her grave. Maybe it would help."

"No, nothing can help now. It's better if I stay here." His mouth lifted into a sad smile. "Anyway, I have a crew to keep in line."

Peter rolled his eyes "Just take it," he said and dropped the pouch on top of the desk in front of Hook. Then I watched as he turned on his heel and stomped out of the room. I don't know why, but I held back, biting my lip as I tried to come up with something to say. Nothing came to mind. Just earlier I had been ready to cut his throat, but now I felt sympathy for him. The conflict made my stomach churn and finally I just pivoted and followed after Peter, leaving Hook in silence.

Chapter Sixteen

It was weird stepping back onto land after having spent the last few days on the ship. Since they couldn't bring us all the way back to shore, the lost boys – surprisingly including Russ – piled into a small dingy and Morgan rowed them back to land while Peter and I flew. When we landed, I immediately stumbled and almost face planted into the shallow water; luckily, Peter still had a grip on my hand.

"Don't feel bad, Wynn. Not everyone can have impeccable balance like me," he joked and I felt my face get hot.

Before he could do anything, I lunged, wrapping my arms around his neck and he fell backward into the wet sand. I landed on his chest knocking the air out of his lungs. *That'll teach him*, I thought grinning down at him.

"What was that again about impeccable balance?" I asked lifting an eyebrow.

Instead of responding, Peter wrapped his own arms around me and crushed me against his chest as a wave came and soaked us to the bone. The cold water was a shock and I let out a girlish squeal and gripped the lapels of his coat as Peter laughed. His laughter was so bright and loud, I imagined it rolling out over the horizon, reaching all the way back to Los Angeles.

The distant hollers of the lost boys from further down the beach had us getting up and trudging out of the water to meet them. While Russ headed for the tree line, Kai and the twins sprinted toward us arms extended. I managed to jump out of the way just before they crashed into Peter, taking him down to the ground in a dog pile. Their joy was contagious and I found laughter bubbling up and out of me like a spring. And then they were on me, their arms overlapping as we became a Wynn sandwich and I felt like I could cry with relief and happiness. Since coming to Neverland, these boys had become my brothers. It didn't take long for me to notice that one was missing.

I squeezed my way out of the bear hug and looked back up the beach to find Pal sitting at the edge of the water by himself. Before the urge to go join him made me move, a copper colored head came up out of the water to meet him. More heads popped up above the surface as the other mermaids looked at the rest of the boys expectantly. While they all ran past me, I watched Pal and Calliope in the distance. The way his head dipped and his hands fumbled nervously, I guess he was saying something to her. She nodded and watched biting her lip as he hesitantly brought one of his hands up to grasp the nose of his deer mask. My own heart thudded harder when he lifted it slowly revealing the pale skin of his face underneath. The string tied around his head mussed up the hair around his ears and he shook his head to settle it again. Now the mask rested on top of his lowered head. His eyes seemed to be glued to the sand in front of him.

Peter came up beside me and his hand brushed mine. "Looks like he found a reason to finally take that thing off," he said and I could hear the smile in his voice.

Calliope lifted one of her glistening hands to Pal's chin and tilted his head up so he looked at her. I remembered Peter mentioning his scar and I squeezed his hand nervously as I watched the mermaid study Pal's face. She touched her fingers to his cheek and I imagined her tracing the scars etched in his skin. Then a smile broke out on her face and she leaned in, hesitating for just a second before pressing her mouth to his.

My heart fluttered and I suddenly felt my eyes glass over when Pal brought his own hand up to rest on the back of her head to return the kiss. I shook my head and pulled Peter away so they could have their moment in privacy. Kai and the twins were coming back to shore then, water dripping from their tanned torsos and pants. "Hey Pan!" Mika and Finn yelled in unison. "Race you back to camp!"

Peter chuckled and we rose up slowly into the air. When we reached above the tree line, he pumped my hand once. "You're on," he called back then we shot forward like a bullet over the trees.

The fairies were there to greet us when Peter and I touched down in the clearing. They all swarmed me at once apologizing profusely for not being there the other night. I tried telling them that I forgave them but I couldn't get a word in edge-wise. Finally, when the others emerged from the woods, the fairies backed off and I could breathe again. A proud smile appeared on Peter's face when he saw the lost boys' shoulders heaving.

"Just wait, Pan," Kai said between gasping breaths. "One of these days we'll beat you." I turned to look at Peter then and saw his smile falter. Kai must have remembered what had happened back on the ship at the same time. "Oh right." My throat started to tighten as an awkward silence passed between us. Then Kai clapped his hands together loudly. "Well then," he said with a small smile. "I do believe this calls for some kind of going away party, right?"

That evening we sat around the fire and ate our last meal together. The flames danced, reaching toward the sky, smoke curling and writhing like a seductive dancer in a sheer, gray dress. Warmth wrapped its arms around my legs, covering my knees in hot kisses while the cool night air cloaked my back.

Around us, the forest came alive. Even as Peter plucked at the worn strings on his guitar, I could hear the soft buzzing of insects and the rustling footsteps of nocturnal creatures as they woke from their daylight slumber.

Pal had finally come to join us just before sunset and now I looked across the flames at him. His deer mask still rested on top of his head. It was weird seeing him like this, almost like I was looking at a different person. His brown eyes were larger than I'd thought, still giving him a deer-like look without the mask and his dark lashes were thick and long. A spattering of freckles dusted his nose. Then there was the scar. It dragged one corner of his mouth up a bit then continued on up diagonally across the bridge of his nose and ended just above his right eyebrow. It must have looked terrible back when it had first healed and I couldn't blame Pal for feeling like he needed to hide it behind his mask but now it was barely visible. Especially, with how big and bright his eyes were. They overshadowed the rest of his face completely.

He caught me staring and gave me a shy smirk before I had the chance to look away. I returned the smile, noting the way the flames reflected in his eyes. Like two little ballerinas in fiery costumes.

Wind from a pair of tiny wings brushed over my cheek and I turned my head as Nyk landed on my shoulder. Her armor glistened like glowing coals in the firelight. "Are you really leaving tonight?" she asked in a sad, tinkling voice.

More little feet landed on my other shoulder and I turned again, this time to see Lyssa. She ran her hands along the edge of one of her rainbow wings. "We'll sure miss you, Wynn," she said. I wanted to say I'd miss them too but the words stuck in my throat. I just nodded. My eyes started to burn and I blinked hard.

"I should probably go change then," I said brushing the fairies off my shoulders. Then, I left the circle as the tears threatened to fall and managed to make it into the safety of the tree fort before one broke free and slid down my cheek. This was it. I was finally going home. I should have been excited to see Marty again. To hug my mom, to go back to my life but after spending time with all these lovely creatures, I found I didn't want to go.

The room was dark save for the moonlight filtering in through the window. Even in the darkness, though, I could see my pile of clothes lying folded where I'd left them on the table by the couch. My red skirt peeked out from underneath my leather jacket. Trying not to think too much about it, I ripped my tunic off over my head and kicked off my boots.

It was weird wearing my old clothes. Like nothing fit me right. It was all too tight and stiff and manmade. I picked up the tunic off the ground and pressed it against my face so I could inhale its smell. There was the faint scent of sea salt and beneath that, trees and earth. I was going to miss the smells almost as much as I was going to miss the people. I felt so different now. I wondered if I looked any different. As I picked up a piece of my hair, I wondered if Marty would notice.

"Wynn?"

I turned around to find Peter standing in the doorway. The moon lit only a part of his face. "Are you ready to go?"

"I can't go back to Exile looking like this," I said dropping the tangled piece of my hair.

Peter cocked his head to the side. "I think you look great."

I shook my head. "It doesn't matter." It occurred to me I sounded a bit like a crazy person but I couldn't seem to stop talking. "I need to look the same as I did before I left. We need to stop by my house so I can wash my hair or take a shower or something. But then

I'd be going back to the club with wet hair but I didn't have wet hair before so Marty will get suspicious."

In just a few strides, Peter was in front of me, his hands on either side of my face. "Hey," he said softly and I clamped my mouth shut to keep any more word vomit from escaping. "You don't need to worry about anything, Wynn. It'll be alright."

I could only nod as he drew me to his chest for a hug. Of course everything was going to be alright. Peter was coming home with me. I didn't have to say goodbye to him. That made everything more than alright.

Peter still had to change into his human clothes so I sat down on the couch with my back to him so he could have some privacy. As I sat there, a glint caught my eye. The pale moonlight filtering in through the window reflected off the black feathers of my crow mask where it sat on the table in front of me. Carefully, I picked it up and turned it toward the window so I could see the whole thing. I'm surprised I hadn't lost it yet. It always seemed to turn up even when I forgot about it. Though, maybe that was the point. Being a physical representation of my character, maybe it was somehow linked to me in a way that made it impossible to lose. Who knows? Neverland would always be a mystery to me.

"Alright," Peter said startling me. I jumped up and turned to face him again still clutching the mask in my hands. A smirk lifted the corner of his mouth when he saw the spooked expression on my face. "How do I look?" he asked shrugging the army green jacket on over his faded orange t-shirt. Even though I couldn't see the words, I could remember what they said. *Big*

"Great," I croaked causing his grin to widen. "Like you've lived in LA all your life." He held his hand out to me and I took it.

A hint of sadness flashed through his eyes for a millisecond. But just as quickly as it appeared, it was gone and the smile was back. "Let's go home, then," he said, "It's almost time to get back on stage."

The two of us stepped out of the tree fort hand in hand to join the lost boys back by the fire. They all stood at attention as we neared them but when they noticed our clothes, their shoulders sagged in unison.

"Alright, there will be none of that." Peter frowned. "Anyone that cries is out of the running to be my replacement."

Kai immediately straightened back up. "Have any particular person in mind?" he asked not even trying to hide the excitement in his voice.

Peter let go of my hand and crossed his arms over his chest. "I do, actually," he said with mock formality. "But first I must consult my council." Then he let out a short whistle. The fairies floated down from their place in the canopy to huddle with Peter. I couldn't help but giggle. It looked like he was whispering to a string of Christmas lights. They only deliberated for a few seconds before he turned back around to face his audience.

It was obvious who of the lost boys was most determined. Pal still stood back by the fire as more of an observer than a candidate and Mika and Finn held back as well. Only Kai looked straight at his leader, his eyebrows knitted together as if he was trying to telepathically sway Peter's decision in his favor. Peter stared back, eyes narrowed reflecting the fire. Then he relaxed and a grin spread across his face. "How about it, mate?" he asked sticking out his hand. "Do you think you could keep these miscreants in line?"

Kai's own face broke out into a gleaming smile and he gripped Peter's hand tightly. "I'll whip 'em into shape," he said shaking his hand vigorously.

Peter nodded back then pulled him in for a hug. The twins and Pal came over to join, piling on top of their old leader and new leader. This wasn't a place of handshakes or polite head nods. No, this was a place of dog piles and bear hugs and slaps on the back. There was no room for subtle goodbyes in Neverland.

I sat back and watched with glassy eyes until everything smudged together like a watercolor painting. A dark haired, pale-faced blur unhooked from the mass and came at me. Pal's face came into focus just before he wrapped his arms around my shoulders and hugged me tightly. I hugged back, trying not to get his shirt wet and failing miserably. More arms wrapped around me and I again found myself at the center of a lost boy huddle.

By the time we all pulled apart, my face was damp with tears. "It's been fun," I cracked causing them all to laugh. Peter took my hand again and pulled me back away from everyone.

"Don't cause too much trouble," he said.

"Oh we won't," Mika assured him and pulled his badger mask down over his face.

Finn nodded in agreement. "We'll cause just the right amount," he said covering his face with his hare mask.

Kai and Pal followed suit so I was looking at a pack

of animals. The only one missing was the fox.

Russ still hadn't shown up yet and it shouldn't have bothered me after the way he treated me but I still found myself glancing anxiously at the trees. Maybe he was hurt or lost. Could lost boys even get lost? A lost lost boy?

"Ready to go, Wynn?" Peter asked making me tear my eyes away from the tree line.

I gripped my crow mask and tunic tighter in my other hand and squeezed his fingers. "I guess as ready as I'll ever be," I said with an anxious sigh.

Pale shadows flashed in the spaces between the trees below as Kai, Pal and the twins trailed after us, falling behind quickly as we gained speed. The wind pulled the laughter out of me, wrapped it around my neck and threw it over my shoulder like a scarf while Peter's flew by in a tinkling of bells. Shooting stars with shimmering tails streaked across the space below us, weaving in and out of the canopy. Fairies.

The wind whipped my tangled hair back away from my face and my breath caught in my lungs. But I didn't feel like I couldn't breathe. My chest didn't ache, my head wasn't swimming. It was like all of me was suspended in time. And part of me wished I really was. Peter tugged me close, wrapped his arms around me, entangling our bodies and suddenly I didn't feel like I was flying but like I was floating. I closed my eyes letting the wind push its way into my nose, filling my head with the strong smells of evergreen and sugar spruce and the ocean. The heat from Peter's body soaked through the material of my shirt and into my skin, warming my heart. I wanted to stay like this forever.

The aromas of Neverland soon faded away and were replaced with the familiar smells of rain and rubber and exhaust. Smells of Los Angeles. Smells of home. A tugging feeling in my gut made me realize just how much I really had missed it. I must have been so wrapped up in the wonders of Neverland, I'd forgotten what was waiting for me back on the other side of the stars. Not just Marty and my mom but the city I'd grown up in.

We touched down in front of my house. The windows were all dark so my mom must have already been asleep. She'd been going to bed pretty early for the past month.

Taking Peter's hand, I pulled him around to the backyard. Mom always kept the sliding door unlocked when Marty and I went out on Fridays. That way, in case I forgot my key – which I did a lot – we'd still be able to get in without waking her up. Sure enough, it opened soundlessly.

"Try not to make any noise," I whispered to Peter as we crept through the kitchen and toward the stairs.

"Isn't your mom expecting you?"

"Sure," I said, "but not with some strange boy I just met."

Peter scoffed in mock disgust as we started up the stairs. "Some strange boy," he uttered. "I wonder what she would think if she knew what you've been up to with *some strange boy* for the past few days." Then I felt his fingers dig into my sides and a squeal escaped as I fell back into him.

"Wynn?"

We froze.

Light shined out from the crack under my mom's door down the hall. "Wynn, is that you?" she called.

"Yeah, mom," I called back praying silently that she wouldn't come out into the hall where Peter and I stood. "Marty's outside. I just had to grab something really quick from my room."

"Alright, honey. Have fun and be safe."

"I will," I said then grabbed Peter's hand and tugged him quickly into my room and closed the door. I let out the breath I'd apparently been holding. "Thanks for that," I hissed throwing a glare his way.

Peter didn't seem to hear me. He stood in the middle of my room staring at my wall covered in posters of my favorite rock and punk bands. Then he turned slowly, his green eyes skimming over all of my stuff. My bookcase filled with all my fiction and fantasy novels, my dresser covered in framed pictures of Marty and I and Great Gran and my mom. I watched in silence as Peter took careful steps toward my dresser. He reached out a hand and ran a finger along the edge of a more recent picture of me that Marty had taken.

It was not long after Great Gran's funeral and Marty had pleaded for me to go with her to try out her new camera. We'd found a foot alley with walls only about four feet apart.

My hair was down and wild, my make-up edgy and dark and I wore a red and black striped sweater that hung off one of my shoulders and a black tutu with fishnets. I hadn't been back to ballet class in a while so my legs had gotten pretty wobbly and I'd had to use the walls on either side of me to help balance en pointe, but in the picture my legs were pin straight and my hands were out, hovering just off the walls of the alley. Marty had said my somber attitude really added to the feel of the photo; still I had turned my eyes to the ground so I wouldn't have to see them any time I looked at the picture.

I held my breath as Peter picked up the photo and studied it. What did he think? Did having a picture of myself in my room make me seem narcissistic? Did he think it was weird? I finally opened my mouth to make some excuse but then Peter looked up at me. "This is amazing," he said, a spark flashing through his eyes.

"You like it?" I stammered as I felt blood rush to my cheeks. "I think it's kind of depressing."

Peter smiled as he set the picture back down on my dresser, his hand resting on it for a couple extra seconds. "I think it's beautiful." Then he turned to me. "You're beautiful, Wynn," he said and a hurricane churned in my stomach as he formed his hands to the sides of my face. They still smelled like Neverland and my heart sank a bit at the thought of the lost boys and the mermaids and the fairies. "I'm so happy I finally get to be here with you," Peter said pulling me back to reality. "I've spent a long time waiting."

Even though I missed the creatures of his homeland, I was happy too. Truly happy for the first time since Great Gran had died. Really since we found out she was sick. It seemed like everything had changed the first time our eyes had met. When he'd looked down from the stage at Exile and sang to me.

I put a hand on one of his, holding it against my

cheek. "Let's not keep your audience waiting," I said breathlessly.

Peter gave me a serious nod. "Right," he said then turned away and marched into the bathroom off my room leaving me to stand there in a silent stupor.

The faucet turned on and I unfroze, hurrying to go in after him. There was a lot to do before I could show my face again in Exile and we didn't have much time. On my way in, I glanced at the clock on my nightstand. We'd been gone for all of five minutes.

When I got into the bathroom, Peter was standing over the sink with a towel scrubbing at the dried blood that had dripped down the side of his face. I looked at myself in the mirror. What a mess.

The make-up that hadn't been completely smeared away clung to my skin for dear life, speckling my eyelids with black. Wow, I really did look different. Tanner, older even.

No time.

I pulled my leather jacket off and kneeled down in front of the tub. Peter didn't say anything as I turned the faucet on and plunged my head into the stream of water.

No time, no time, no time.

I fumbled for the shampoo bottle blindly and squeezed a bunch of it into my palm until I felt it overflow and start to drip. Then I lathered. Lather, lather, lather. Until my hair was a big foamy mess. I could almost feel Peter's eyes on me as he surely found this amusing. When the soap was all out of my hair again, I reached up and turned the water off. The bathroom was silent other than the sound of the water dripping off the ends of my hair and onto the floor of the tub. I reached an arm out behind me. "Towel?"

A few seconds later Peter pressed a towel into my hand and I draped it over my hair and began squeezing the water out. Hurry, hurry, hurry.

When I wasn't able to get any more out, I dropped the towel and flipped my head up to meet my reflection in the mirror.

"This isn't going to work," I muttered glumly.

Peter dropped the dirty towel he'd used to wash his face into the sink and met my eyes in the mirror. The dirt and blood was gone leaving his skin looking tan and flawless. "You really think Marty will notice if your hair is wet?"

I chuckled. "It's Marty. She'd notice if I shrunk a millimeter."

A warm, assuring smile lifted a corner of his mouth. "Then maybe we spent a few minutes together in the rain." Then his eyes flitted past my shoulder to my alarm clock on the nightstand and his smile fell. "We need to go."

"Give me five seconds," I said yanking the top drawer open and pulling my makeup bag out.

Peter left me alone in the bathroom to finish getting ready. It would have been the perfect chance to just stop and take a breath, clear my head but there was no time.

No time, no time, no time.

After scrubbing the dirt off my face with a towel, I swiped a new layer of eyeliner across my lash line, added mascara and dabbed lip gloss on my lips. *There*, I thought as I studied my reflection in the mirror. Hopefully, this would be enough. I ruffled my hair then grabbed my jacket off the ground and rushed out of the bathroom to find Peter pushing the bottom half of my window up.

"What are you doing?"

The window stuck for a second and he had to jerk it to get it to go all the way up. "It'll be much faster if we fly back." Then he held his hand out to me. "Shall we?"

With Peter's hand grasped firmly in mine, the two of us made our way back into Exile. Luckily, the bouncer recognized Peter from the band so we got back in with no trouble. It felt weird standing in the midst of the crowd, the music still blaring, the lights still pulsing, the air still thick with energy, just like it was when we left. Yet, so much had happened. Peter pulled me close and wrapped his arms around my waist and I buried my face into his neck taking a deep breath. Even though he had just changed and washed the dirt off of him, there was the underlying scent of spruce trees and ocean air. I already longed to be back in Neverland, running with the lost boys, swimming with the mermaids and eating suavas. But more than that, I was with Peter and he felt more like home to me than Neverland or LA ever could. So much had happened in a week and a half. So much had happened since a beautiful stranger asked to dance ten minutes before.

"Well, aren't you two cozy?" she said over the music.

I picked my head up off Peter's shoulder just as Marty shoved her way into the space right in front of me. Her eyebrow arched high when she saw the way I was holding onto the boy I was supposed to have just met. I quickly pulled away, creating a less suspicious space between us. Peter frowned in silent protest. Luckily, he was facing me and not Marty.

"Marty!" I squealed and threw my arms around her. I hadn't realized I'd missed her so much but now I had to fight back the tears that threatened to come.

She laughed in my ear. "I bet you're glad I dragged you here now, huh, Wynn?"

"Very!" Peter yelled and pulled me back in. I tried and failed to hide a smile as he squeezed me tightly then glanced up at the stage. He buried his face in my damp hair. "My band mates are waving me back up to the stage."

"I suppose I owe Marty a dance," I replied with a dramatic sigh.

Peter smiled at me and I saw the wild spark of a lost boy in him. Then with a short but sweet kiss on the lips, he disappeared into the crowd leaving me to smile guiltily as Marty stared slack-jawed. Before she could say anything, the DJ cut the music and the crowd began to cheer as Peter took to the stage.

"Did you all miss me?" he asked with his devilish smirk. My heart, along with the hearts of many other people in the crowd, melted. "This next song is one that I love." Then his eyes fell on mine. "And I'm dedicating it to the girl I love."

If Marty's jaw was gaping before, it wasn't even attached now. I peered at her out of the corner of my vision as she gawked at me. Peter's bassist started in with a funky riff, going for a measure before the guitarist, keyboardist and drummer leaned into their mics and whistled a catchy bit in unison. Peter bobbed his head, counting in his mind before starting in along with the drums. On beat he opened his mouth and started in on the verse, rocking from side to side with the upbeat tempo.

This song had such a different feel from the rock song he'd first sang. While that one had been heavy and dark, this one was happy and reminded me of warm, tropical things, ocean and suavas and bonfires with flames that reached up into the night like the arms of dancers.

When Peter broke into the chorus, he began bouncing on the balls of his feet, getting the crowd to join in. Everyone jumped with him, the blue lights scanning over us, transforming the audience into a living, breathing ocean. I grabbed Marty's hand and raised both arms into the air, moving my head as I danced with the beat. My hair fell over my face and sweat beaded on my forehead and soon I found myself shrugging off my jacket.

The bassist and the whistling led us into the second verse and Peter started clapping as he sang. This kid knew how to give stage presence; confidence radiated out of him like sunlight. His voice was so pure like honey, so full of joy that it was hard not to dance along. The music was infectious, his energy contagious. No one in the club was immune.

Then we were back in the chorus, all jumping to the beat, arms stretching to the ceiling. Fingers grabbing for the music that filled the room as if it were something tangible that we could cling to. Peter stepped right up to the front of the stage, the toes of his gray converse hanging off the edge and he leaned forward. The drums stopped and the keyboardist started into the chorus again and he was singing directly to me. His voice reaching into my chest to hold my heart. Sweaty bangs hung down in front of his eyes but I could still see how beautiful and green they were. Green like his faded pirate coat, green like Brucie's skin, green like Calliope's tail, green like Neverland.

Then he bounced back on his heels and the drums joined in again for one more go at the chorus. The other band members joined to whistle in the background until it was a loud blending of melodic noise. All at once, it stopped, leaving Peter to sing the last few words in silence. Only a beat passed after he was done before the crowd erupted in chaotic applause. He managed a breathless thanks into the mic and then the room was filled again with techno music. Marty clung to me as I fought the current of people heading away from the stage.

Then she watched in silence as Peter hopped off the stage and made his way over to us. He wrapped his arms around my waist and twirled me in a circle. Laughter bubbled up my throat and out my mouth and I felt again like I was flying with him over Neverland, racing the lost boys to Mermaid Lagoon.

When he let me down again, Marty's eyes narrowed "I missed something here," she said as her gaze shifted between the two of us.

There was no hiding this from her any longer. I grabbed her hand and laced her green-gloved fingers in mine. "I have so much to tell you."

Chapter Seventeen

"So, you're saying your great grandmother really did go to Neverland," Marty said as she inspected my crow mask. She sat on my bed while Peter stood awkwardly in the corner by the window. If my mom came in here at that moment, she would have freaked out. I had never brought a boy home, and now I'd basically lived with one for a week. It was probably best not to mention any of this to her. Marty, on the other hand, needed to know.

"Right," I confirmed.

"And you're Peter Pan." Peter nodded. "And my Nana was Tinker Bell." She didn't sound very convinced. "So what, I'm like some human, fairy crossbreed?"

"Not exactly," Peter said getting up off the windowsill to come stand by me. "If anything or anyone from Neverland is away from there for longer than an earth day, it loses its powers."

Marty narrowed her eyes. "Oh, okay, that makes more sense," she said sarcastically.

I shot a glance at Peter and furrowed my brow. "So you won't be able to fly anymore?"

He shook his head, his bright green eyes hinting at sadness. But one corner of his mouth lifted into a reassuring smile. "I'll be fully human like you. It's alright, though," he said locking my fingers in his. "You're very much worth it."

I felt my cheeks get warm and I looked down at my feet shyly. Marty cleared her throat and my eyes met hers again. "Alright," she finally sighed, "this is all just lovely and adorable and all but I'm still confused."

With a loud huff and a roll of his eyes, Peter snatched my mask out of Marty's hands and clasped onto her wrist. She started to protest but didn't have a chance to say anything before all three of us were suddenly floating outside my bedroom window, two stories above the ground. I had to try not to laugh as I watched her cling onto Peter's arm for dear life like a cat being dangled over a bathtub with her eyes squeezed shut.

"Marty."

She shook her head erratically, refusing to look at me.

"Marty, it's alright," I said. "Peter won't let you fall."

"I believe you," she blurted, her eyelids still locked up tight. "I believe you, I promise I do. Just get me down!"

With a chuckle, Peter brought us back in through

the window and we touched down gently on my carpeted floor. Marty immediately fell back onto the bed, breathing hard as if she'd just climbed a mountain. "I can't believe it," she murmured breathlessly. "It's too bizarre. It's too ridiculous."

Peter glanced at me out of the corner of his eye. "Want me to take you out again?"

Marty shot upright. "No!"

It took some convincing but eventually the confused lines in her forehead smoothed out and the suspicion left her eyes. When I started talking about the lost boys, my voice cracked and I went silent. Luckily, Peter picked it up where I left off, his fingers still gripping mine. When he was finished, the two of us waited in silence for Marty's reaction. Her eyes darted between the two of us and she bit her fuchsia bottom lip. Finally, she opened her mouth with a smack. "Well, Wyndy," she said then crossed one leg over the other and drew her lips up into a mock, sultry smile. "Looks like you have a date for homecoming."

I heard the music before we even reached the entrance to the school. Annabel had really gone all out with this ridiculous "Masquerade Under The Stars" theme. The short hallway had been transformed into a tunnel of crepe paper and cardboard trees, limbs hanging down overhead like a forest canopy. Through the spaces between the paper leaves, light from a hidden disco ball speckled the ceiling. It felt oddly reminiscent of Neverland and I found myself wondering what the lost boys were up to. Time there was different from here so years had probably already passed since I was there last. I wondered if they still thought about me.

"Wynn?"

I looked over at my date and gave him a sad smile. Peter looked amazing in his homecoming ensemble. A black bar vest hugged his slim torso and contrasted nicely against the gray shirt underneath. Just the top buttons were undone, exposing his tan throat. His auburn hair was gelled into a purposefully unkempt shag partly to keep his ears hidden until they rounded out, and a leather mask, with a subtle resemblance to a hawk covered the top half of his face. Luckily, his vibrant green eyes were still completely visible, and right then they were filled with concern as he studied me.

I looked down at my own outfit. Marty and I had spent hours earlier that day up in the attic searching for Great Gran's black swan costume. I was worried it was gone when Marty opened a box and squealed in delight, holding up the outfit in all its lacy, feathery glory.

I'd originally planned to wear my Neverland mask even though Marty said it was too realistic and might gross people out. I guess it would be weird to wear a big crow head to an elegant masquerade. Luckily, after digging a little deeper into the box, I found the one Great Gran had worn during her performance. It was magnificent.

The whole thing was made of sturdy plastic and covered in satin. Black sequins created swirling patterns around the eyeholes and up the bridge of the nose. Foil filigree shaped like lace protruded from just one of the top corners while more of it edged the whole other side and swooped out like a delicate, ornate wing.

Now I looked back up at Peter, peering through the eyeholes of my mask and into his. "I'm okay," I said with a small smile and a squeeze of my silk-gloved hand.

Peter smiled back, bringing my hand up to kiss my knuckles. "You look gorgeous," he said against my fingers.

The sadness in me vanished, leaving me feeling light as a black bird's feather. "Thanks," I said, "You don't look so bad yourself."

He bowed at the waist and a giggle bubbled out of me. Then without another word, he pushed open the doors to the cafeteria, washing the hallway out in blue and white light, and gestured for me to go first. I gave him a mock curtsy before waltzing in and smacked right into the back of Annabel.

She spun around, her curled, blonde hair fanning out around her like a dancer's skirt. "Well, well, well," she sneered, glaring daggers through the eyeholes of her silvery mask. "If it isn't Elvira. I didn't think you'd show up."

"Well, here I am," I sighed.

"I figured you'd be cooped up in your room sacrificing cats or whatever it is you freaks do." Then her focus shifted over my shoulder. "And you brought a date. A fellow cult member no dou–"

"Hi," Peter interrupted from behind me.

Annabel's pink glossy mouth dropped open as she stared at him. The hairs on my arms stood up and I gazed back at Peter with pride. "Annabel, this is my boyfriend, Peter," I said then grabbed his hand. "And while I'm sure he'd love to be stared at all night, we're going to go dance."

Peter dipped his head. "Nice meeting you…Agatha was it?"

"Annabel," she murmured as she turned to follow us onto the dance floor with her eyes.

Students swayed to the slow song that drifted from the speakers on the makeshift stage by the DJ booth. The two of us wove our way through the crowd, my eyes searching for Marty. Finally, I found her near the middle with her arms around a boy from our English class. Instead of going up to her, we stopped a few feet away and I wrapped my arms around Peter's neck.

Breathing in deep, the smells of Neverland filled my head. I hoped he'd smell this way forever. I hoped that even though in just a couple hours he will have been here for a full Earth day, there would always be something to remind us of where he came from. With that thought, I held him close and my heart swelled when his own arms tightened around my waist. He rested his cheek against mine and I felt his warm breath on my ear.

"I love you, Wynn," he whispered and I closed my eyes with a smile, letting the feel of his heart beating against mine become the music we danced to.

All too soon, the song ended and a new one, faster and louder, began. Before I had the chance to pull away from Peter, I heard a squeal and Marty jumped me from behind.

"Wynn! You look fabulous!" she yelled over the

music and grabbed my hands. She looked pretty amazing herself. Her dress was a deep teal, the corseted top cinched tight around her small waist while the bottom poofed out like a ballerina tutu. Bright green and purple tulle peeked out underneath and flowed down to the floor in the back making her look like a psychedelic peacock. "Dance with me!"

"Well, what do I do?" Peter shouted back as a couple of girls bumped into him. One started to apologize then froze when he turned around to face her. I couldn't hide my amused smile. I guess no one had ever seen a boy as attractive as him in our school. There wasn't another like him in existence; at least not in this world. Again, I found myself missing the other lost boys. My brothers.

"Why don't you take your beautiful self and go get us some drinks. I'll take good care of our Wyndy," Marty answered then grabbed my hand and spun me around. By the time I'd made a full rotation, Peter had disappeared into the crowd. Marty threw her arms around me and pulled me close. "Everyone has their eyes set on you tonight, Wynn," she yelled in my ear as we spun again.

I smiled and shook my head. "No, everyone has their eyes set on Peter."

Marty froze mid-spin and gaped over my shoulder. I twisted my neck around to see what she was looking at and came face to face with a dark scaly mask. Two bright blue eyes sparkled back at me. "What are you doing here?" I asked over the music.

Hook's mouth curled up into a smile. "Mind if I cut in?"

Marty leaned into me so the peacock feathers on

274

her own mask tickled my face. "Who's he?"

"A friend," he answered.

Not exactly. My eyes didn't leave his.

"So how about it?" he asked and held out his hand; the hooked one was well hidden, tucked into the pocket of his suit jacket.

"She's all yours," Marty purred and put my hand in his before bouncing off to find herself a new dance partner. I rested a black-gloved hand on his shoulder and the other cupped his good hand and we swayed in silence to the music. Soon, his hook found its way out of his pocket and tangled itself into the feathers of my skirt.

Whenever I glanced at him, his eyes were set on me. I squirmed, uncomfortably against the metal hook on my side. "Peter won't like that you're here," I finally said to break the silence.

"You can't really blame him, I guess," Hook sighed. "After all, I did try to kill him."

"So, you didn't answer me." I said. He waited like he wanted me to repeat the question. "What are you doing here?"

A smile spread across his face making him look like a grinning crocodile. "Well, deary, I thought I'd follow up on your suggestion to go see Wendy."

"Oh." Now I felt bad. He wasn't here to cause trouble, just wanted to say goodbye. To finally have some closure after however many Neverland years of thinking she'd never loved him. I stepped back so we were no longer dancing. "I can take you there," I said dropping my hands. "I know where the cemetery is. Marty came here in her parents' car. She can drive us."

Hook smiled again, this one much warmer than the

other. "I'd like that," he said gratefully.

"What's he doing here?"

I turned again this time to find Peter standing there. Though the plastic cup in his hand was held out toward me, his narrowed eyes were focused on Hook.

"I thought I'd drop by and see how things are going here on...Earth." He spit out the last word as if it left a bad taste in his mouth.

I frowned and turned back to Peter. "He came to see Great Gran," I explained and took the cup from his hand. He gripped it so tight, I thought it would shoot out of his hand and peg somebody. "I told him we'd take him."

The neon lights bounced off Peter's face, highlighting the lines in his jaw as he ground his teeth together. "And that's it?" he asked. "You won't cause any trouble?"

Hook held up his hand. "You have my word."

"Right, because what could be more reliable than the steadfast word of a pirate?" Peter grumbled as he took my hand and pulled me toward the exit. Hook followed on my heels as we made our way through the maze of bodies. On the way out, I snagged Marty's arm and pulled her with us.

"We're going for a drive," I said in her ear and she threw me a bewildered look.

Chapter Eighteen

It was a long, awkward ride to the cemetery. Marty's parents' had loaned her their car for the night so we were all crammed inside the little two door Honda. Peter and Hook sat as far apart as they possibly could in the back which still meant their shoulders were touching. It would have been comical if not for the nagging feeling growing in my gut as we neared the cemetery.

When we got there, Marty pulled off onto the gravel shoulder just before the gate and put it in park. "I'll stay in here," she said giving me small smile. "My parents would kill me if anything happened to Rhonda."

"Rhonda?" Hook grunted from the back as he wrestled with the seatbelt.

Marty turned around to face him. "You name your

ship, I name my parents' car. This is Rhonda the Honda," she said patting the steering wheel proudly.

"Well, isn't that bloody brilliant," he muttered then let out a frustrated growl and gave up trying to unhook himself. "Would somebody get this wretched thing off of me?"

"Here Hook," Peter said with a chuckle. "Let me give you *a hand.*"

The backseat erupted in a scuffle of flailing limbs and curses. "Hey, cut it out!" I yelled and the boys stopped to stare at me. "Could we just get through this without you two trying to tear each other's throats out?"

"He started it," Hook grumbled readjusting the mask over his eyes.

"Are you sure they aren't really teenagers?" Marty asked me. "They sure act like it."

With a roll of my eyes, I got out of the car and pulled the seat forward so they could climb out. Peter came out first, giving me an apologetic smile as he smoothed his rumpled clothes. Then came Hook grumbling behind him.

I had to pick up my dress so the feathers didn't get dirty as we made our way through the cemetery gates and down the dirt path. Most people would have been creeped out walking among the headstones, especially at night but I'd always found it peaceful. I didn't believe in ghosts anyway. Of course, I hadn't believed in Peter Pan and Neverland until very recently either and look where that got me.

Only the sounds of our shoes crunching on the gravel filled the silence. That and the sound of Hook's metal hook as he tapped it against a button on his coat, nervously. "Which one is it?" he finally asked from behind Peter.

The path veered off toward a small grove of trees and I followed it, turning sharply on my heel. "It's just through here."

We entered the grove and I stopped, standing now in front of two trees in particular. Great Gran had planted the birch tree here next to her husband's grave when he had died. I'd never met my great grandfather but she used to go on about what a wonderful man he was. Then, when she died, my mother had paid someone to take the oak tree from her backyard and plant it on the other side of her grave. Just in the last month, the two trees had somehow tangled their branches together. As if they were two souls that had been reunited after so many years apart. Maybe that was the case.

Hook made his way past me slowly, reaching into his jacket. When he pulled his hand back out, it was clutching the gray dove mask. Great Gran's mask. Moonlight reached down through the branches above us to dust it with pale light. Peter and I stood back and watched silently as Hook got down onto his knees before the headstone. "Was it quick?" he asked, his voice quivering.

I felt a chill run up my spine and I hugged my bare arms against my ribcage. "Uh..." I stammered. "I don't think she was in any pain." Peter stepped closer and hunched his shoulders to shield me from the wind. His body heat on my back helped a bit.

"That's good, I guess," Hook muttered then leaned forward to clear a few wilted, soggy bouquets away that must have still been there from the funeral. He sucked in a sharp breath. "What's this?"

I stepped forward, leaning to the side to look at the headstone. "What's what?"

"This," he said pointing down near the bottom of the stone. "There's something written there." Then he began digging at the dirt, scraping it away with his hooked hand.

Throwing a confused look back at Peter, I went and got down with him, parting the feathers so my bare knees rested in the dirt. He was right. Faint lines like letters were etched into the part of the stone just above the ground. As he scraped the mud away, they became more visible. When he was done, I used my glove to wipe the grime away. Hook sat back on his legs, gaping at the words etched into the stone.

Always, your Wendy Bird.

"She did love me," he whispered.

I squinted at the cursive writing. Surely, this was something Great Gran had mentioned in private to whoever was in charge of making her headstone. Perhaps, in a moment of lucidity. Maybe even before she got sick.

I got up carefully, blinking back tears. "Hook, I–"

"Could I have a moment alone?" he asked steadily, his head down so his face was hidden in shadow.

Again, I looked back at Peter and he gave me a small shrug. "Sure," I said. "We'll be back at the car. Do you think you can make it back okay?"

"Yes. Thank you."

And that was that. Peter held a hand out to me and I stepped carefully back to him, being extra cautious to keep the heels of my shoes from sinking into the soft ground. As the two of us made our way back out of the trees, I stole a glance back over my shoulder, the moon outlining Hook's silhouette in silver.

"Where's Hook?" Marty asked as we climbed back into her car. Then her eyes grew wide and she shot a look back at Peter. "You didn't kill him, did you?"

Peter laughed once. A short bark with no humor in it.

"He's fine," I assured her. "We'll just…give him a few minutes." Marty must have picked up on my tone because she nodded solemnly and sank back in her seat.

So, all this time Great Gran had been keeping her feelings a secret. I didn't remember ever even catching a hint of it. Everything was about her and Peter and Hook as a team, never about just the two of them. Could it be possible that she regretted leaving Neverland? If that were the case, she probably thought her family would feel bad. Maybe even unloved. If there was anything I'd learned about Great Gran over the past week it was that she very much loved her family. Without even knowing what the future held for her, she'd left Neverland, left Hook and came back to Earth. And though she'd grown up and loved her husband, her children, her grandchildren and great grandchildren, her feelings for her first love never changed. I could only hope my love for Peter would grow into the kind she'd had for Hook.

A sharp rap on the window made me jump and when I looked out, Hook's shadowy face looked back at me. Quickly, I fumbled for the handle, tangling my fingers in my feathery skirt in the process and yanked the door open. "Are you okay?" I asked him as he climbed into the backseat. I noticed he was no longer holding Great Gran's dove mask. He must have left it back at her grave.

"Yeah, I'm fine," he grumbled in reply and settled down into the seat behind me.

"Want help with your seatbelt, mate?" Peter asked.

"Shut up."

Marty revved the engine to silence them, then pulled back onto the road and we headed for the school.

We were able to talk Hook into staying at the dance with us for a bit longer. Actually, it was more Marty than anyone else. Her convincing argument was that "while you have a terrible attitude, you make for some great arm candy." I couldn't disagree. At any other dance he would have stuck out like a sore thumb in his elaborately brocaded coat but here he fit right in.

Peter pulled me close as another slower song started and I rested my head on his chest. I could tell he was still a bit tense, what with his nemesis dancing with my best friend only a few feet away, but after a while, his body relaxed and my stomach settled. This was turning into a perfect night. I felt the familiar tug of sadness in my heart as I thought again of the lost boys. Well, almost perfect.

"Mind if I steal your girl for a bit?" Hook asked from behind me.

I craned my neck around to face the pirate and felt Peter tense under my hand. "Alright, but if you try anything –"

Hook rolled his eyes. "You'll what, mate? Cut off my other hand?" Peter didn't look amused. "I won't try anything," the captain assured him.

"I'm fine, Peter," I said laying a hand on his heart. He met my eyes. "Dance with Marty for a minute." With a small nod, he slipped out of my arms and went to Marty.

Hook stepped in and I rested my hands on his shoulders. We danced in silence at first, the tension feeling like a thick comforter wedged into the space between us. I figured he'd wanted a chance to talk to me but now I wasn't so sure. Maybe he wanted me to start.

Both of us opened our mouths at the same time to speak.

"How did–"

"So I–"

I pressed my lips together and waited for him to continue. Hook took a deep breath. "I...just wanted to...thank you, I guess. For taking me to see Wendy."

This caught me a bit off guard. "Oh," I stammered. "Yeah. You're welcome. No, I'm glad you could get some kind of closure."

"Yeah. Me too." He bit his lip nervously. Where was the headstrong captain I'd known in Neverland? Then he took in a sharp breath. "What were you going to say?"

I was confused for a second until I realized what he meant. "Oh. How did you get here? I mean, not to be rude, but you don't really seem like the flying type."

Hook let out a chuckle. "A good pirate never travels anywhere without his ship."

My eyes widened. "You flew your ship? Where is it?

Where's your crew?"

"They're all waiting with her in the harbor."

They were all here. Morgan and Jonas and Wayland and the big football player looking one, Eddie. All just a few miles away off shore. Was it weird that I missed them? I mean at least Morgan and Jonas. The others hadn't said much more than a word to me while I was aboard the ship.

Hook's focus darted past my shoulder for a second. "Oh yeah," he sighed with a roll of his eyes. "Your woodland creatures pestered me into bringing them along too."

"Woodland creatures?" I turned around just as a pair of arms scooped me up into a tight hug.

"How's it going, Wynnie?"

"Kai!" I squealed throwing my own arms out to return the hug. When he finally let me down again, I was able to step back and look at him. Pal flanked the squirrel boy on one side and the twins on the other. All four of them looked like they'd stepped out of an Armani catalogue in their tailored slacks and shirts and the masks over their eyes were elegant versions of their Neverland ones. "I can't believe you guys came!" I yelled over the music as I hugged the rest of them.

"Of course we came," Mika said in my ear when I got to him.

"Do you have any idea how boring it's been in Neverland without a girl around?" Finn asked as he squeezed me extra hard. When he let me go, he furrowed his bushy eyebrows. "Brucie and Lyssa have been bugging us like crazy to bring another one back."

I chuckled, feeling a tug in my chest at the mention of the fairies. Pal met me with a soft smile and pulled me in for a hug as gentle and sweet as his heart. "How are things with Calliope?" I asked praying to God they were still together.

When I pulled away from him, his grin spread wider across his face and his brown eyes sparkled behind his mask, reflecting the white Christmas lights overhead. "Never better," he chimed.

Girls jostled us left and right as they tried to get the attention of these mysterious, masked heartthrobs. Surely, Annabel was somewhere close by wondering if I'd made some sort of deal with the devil.

"Seriously, Wynn," Marty said as she slipped in between Mika and Finn. "Where do you find these guys?"

Peter followed after her, clapping each of the twins on the shoulder. "They're with me," he said with a smile. "Care to stay for a bit, boys?"

Pal, Mika and Finn turned to look at their newly appointed leader. Kai smirked, pride gleaming in his dark eyes as he threw an arm around my shoulders. "I call dibs on the next dance with Wynnie."

"Do you guys really have to go?" I asked fighting back tears. Peter and I stood on the dock with the lost boys to say our goodbyes. It was late – almost eleven – and the cold wind coming off the water made me shiver in my strapless dress. I didn't care about the cold though. All I could think about was the fact that this was the last time I'd ever see the lost boys again.

Kai pressed his mouth into a thin, solemn line and looked down at his feet. The rest of the boys didn't seem to want to make eye contact with me either. Kai cleared his throat hard. "I wish we could stay, Wynnie," he said, his voice hoarse. When he met my eyes again, they shined silvery like onyx. "But this isn't our home."

I nodded and bit my bottom lip to keep it from quivering. Peter wrapped his fingers around my own and squeezed. "We're glad you guys could come," he said with a nod. "Maybe some day we'll find a way to come visit."

Kai nodded back. "I'm holding you to it."

The clang of a bell cut through the night and the air in front of us shuttered as if it were a wall of water. Then in a spray of mist, the Jolly Roger came into view at the end of the dock, rocking back and forth on the tide. We all watched as Hook appeared behind the railing. "Come on, boys!" he called down to us. "I'm not waiting forever!"

With that, I rushed forward, throwing my arms around Kai's middle, sending him stumbling back. "I'll miss you so much," I said squeezing my eyes shut and breathing in deep. He smelled so much like Neverland and images of the Neverwood Forest and Mermaid Lagoon and Cannibal Cove flashed through my mind. Finally, I pulled away and looked at the rest of the boys. "I'll miss all of you." And I hugged the twins and then Pal, holding onto each of them for as long as I could.

"We won't ever forget you, lost girl," Pal said giving me an extra squeeze before releasing me.

There was no use fighting against the tears any longer. I just let them fall, watching with blurred vision as the lost boys grabbed onto a rope ladder hanging off the side of the ship and started climbing. Peter came up behind me and slipped his arms around my waist. His chin rested on top of my head and his heart pounded against my back and the two of us just watched in silence as they went.

A little raccoon head popped up over the railing above and I blinked rapidly to clear the tears away so I could see. A hand came up and pushed the mask back revealing Morgan's childish face and he gave me a wave and goofy grin. I couldn't help but smile and wave back. He must have convinced Hook to let him go with the lost boys. Finally, he'd be able to be the child he was.

Movement caught my attention farther up and my eyes darted to the crow's nest. Standing on the crossbeam next to it was a dark figure. He stepped out of the shadows and held my gaze, looking at me through the eyeholes of his fox mask. My breath caught in my lungs. I wanted to do something. Call up to him or wave. Anything. But I found myself frozen in shock, my mind completely blank.

Then the ship was moving, gaining speed, cutting through the water, carrying everyone away from me. Still, I couldn't take my eyes off Russ. I wished I could yell up to him. Ask him where he'd been, if he was happy. But even if I could muster the breath, he was too far away now to hear me. I wondered if he still hated me. The ship arched up then, pointing toward the moon. And just when it began to lift out of the water, Russ dipped his head to me in a nod, as if to say everything was alright. I regained control of my body and returned the nod. Then the Jolly Roger sailed into the air silently, riding the wind as if it were filled with helium.

The tiny figures of the lost boys waved at us wildly from the railing and Peter and I waved back, my heart climbing higher in my throat as the ship climbed higher into the sky. We didn't look away until it was gone and even then neither of us moved for a long while.

Finally, Peter broke the silence, stumbling back away from me and I spun around to see what he was doing. His eyes ignited bright green like a couple of fireflies and whatever skin was visible glowed as if the sun were shining on it.

"Peter, what's going on?" I stammered as fear churned inside of me.

He looked down at himself, clutching at his chest and his stomach. "I don't know," he gasped and fell to his knees with a cry of pain.

"Peter!" I raced forward and sank to the ground not caring if Great Gran's dress got dirty. "Are you hurt? What's wrong?" I put a hand on his shoulder then immediately pulled it back. His skin radiated an intense heat that penetrated both his shirt and my glove.

"I don't know," he yelled and ripped his hands through his hair. "I think...I think..."

"What?"

Another roar of pain escaped his throat, piercing the air and echoing out over the water. The light coming off his skin faded slowly and he crumpled to the ground motionless.

My breath came out in quick bursts, fogging in front of my face as I waited for him to move. "Peter?" I whimpered. I touched a hand again to his shoulder.

It was cold. "Peter?" I shook him. "Wake up." He let out a moan and rolled over onto his back and I fell onto his chest, too relieved to care if I was hurting him or not. "Oh, thank God," I sighed heavily. "Are you okay, Peter?"

"Yeah," he wheezed putting his hands on my shoulders. "Yeah, I'm okay. Just let me up."

I sat back again, grabbing his hands and helped him to his feet. His eyes weren't glowing anymore and his skin didn't shimmer the way it had before. He looked perfectly fine. My eyes swept up from his feet, checking for anything that could have caused that strange occurrence. When I settled on his head, I froze. "Peter," I whispered. "Your ears."

He brought a cautious hand up to touch the side of his head. His fingers brushed his ear lobe, skimmed over the two silver hoops, then trailed up along the ridge, following it as it rounded out and connected back to his skull. "They're human," he said gaping at me. "I'm human."

"I guess this was around the time we came back yesterday, huh?" I said with a small smile. When he didn't smile back, mine fell. "What's wrong?"

Peter turned away from me and went a few paces up the dock, his fingers still feeling his ear. He turned around again, worry in his green eyes. "I'm not magic anymore."

I nodded. "Right. You're human now…like me." Still the concern didn't leave his face. Suddenly, worry coursed through my own veins, turning my blood to ice. "That's okay, right?" Did he regret coming here? Was he going to blame me? Hate me?

"Is it?"

I narrowed my eyes. "What are you hinting at, Peter?"

He closed the gap between us in just a couple strides and grasped my hands as if he were clinging to life. "I can't fly anymore, Wynn," he said, "I'm just...normal now."

A hysterical laugh bubbled out of my mouth. "What exactly is the problem here?"

Peter bit his lip and looked down at our hands. "I just...you still want me, right?"

I stared in disbelief for a second, my mouth hanging open. "That's it?" I cracked. "You think I wouldn't love you anymore because you're *just normal?*"

"Wynn, I—"

"First off," I interrupted and smacked him in the arm. When he protested, I held a finger up to silence him. "There's nothing wrong with being normal." The corner of his mouth twitched. "Second...I didn't fall in love with you because you were some magical being from Neverland. I felt something the minute I saw you at Exile. And then you looked at me." I bit my lip as his smile widened. "You saw me, Peter. When no one else did."

He rested his forehead against mine and closed his eyes. "What can I say," he whispered. "You're a hard one to miss, Wynn Harper." Then he touched his soft lips to mine.

I knew that, come Monday, everything would still be the same. I still had classes to go to, and tests to take, still faced another eight months of not having a car. I was going to have to get back into the routine of going to work and ballet class. And before that day I would have dreaded it. I would have clung to the sadness that had latched onto me when Great Gran died. I would have gone through life trying to stay invisible, just trying to survive in this world of pain and loss. But no longer did I have to go through it alone. Sure, I still felt the ache of losing one of the most important people in my life but now I had someone to help me through it. To ease the pain.

The future was bright and scary and unknown but with Peter by my side, it was an adventure I was ready to take.

❧

THANKS:

First and foremost to my Creator for giving me life and my love for writing. None of this would matter if not for Him.

Second, thank you to my loving and supportive husband, Mike. You are the most amazing, selfless person I've ever known. I couldn't possibly ever thank you enough for the support you've given me.

To my fellow author and beta-reader, Marisa: You rock! Thank you for helping me whip this novel into shape. I couldn't have done it without you.

Thank you also to my other beta-readers, Melissa J., Melissa C. and Stephanie, for taking time out of your day to help me out.

Finally, thank you to all my fans. You guys make writing fun! Your support and excitement for my work seriously means the world to me. Thank you.

ABOUT THE AUTHOR

Shay Lynam is author of *The Tree House*, *The Trial*, *Places I Never Meant To Go* and *Never*. When not at work, you can find her at home or at her favorite coffee shop, typing away on her newest novel.

Shay lives in Kent, Washington with her husband and beloved dog.

You can keep up on what Shay is doing by visiting her online at facebook.com/shaylynam.

PLAYLIST FOR NEVER

- ➤ Paper Thin Hymn – *Anberlin*
- ➤ Runaways - *Anberlin*
- ➤ The Feel Good Drag – *Anberlin*
- ➤ Stay the Night *ft. Hayley Williams* – *Zedd*
- ➤ Young Blood (Renholdër Remix) – *The Naked and Famous*
- ➤ Start of Time – *Gabrielle Aplin*
- ➤ Moonlight – *Yiruma*
- ➤ A Sky Full of Stars – *Coldplay*
- ➤ Shatter Me *ft. Lzzy Hale* – *Lindsey Stirling*
- ➤ Cosmic Love – *Florence and The Machine*
- ➤ Lost Boy – *Relient K*
- ➤ Traveler's Song (The Piano & String Sessions Version) – *Future of Forestry*

Printed in Poland
by Amazon Fulfillment
Poland Sp. z o.o., Wrocław

56308890R00170